ACCLAIM FOR DANIEL SWENSEN'S
ORISON!

"This is sword-and-sorcery done right…not only is the writing and editing almost flawless, the plotting, the character development and the world-building are all at a very high standard. I seldom see a book this good."
– Mike Reeves McMillan, author of *Hope and the Patient Man*

"I could hardly put it down until I finished (if I had a choice, I never would have put it down)."
– Brooke Johnson, author of *The Clockwork Giant*

"This book immersed me in a new world, gave dragons a fresh spin, and introduced me to characters I know I'll want to go back to."
– Emmie Mears, author of *The Masked Songbird*

"Orison [is] an example of a book where there are characters with intelligence, nuance, integrity and strength weaving a compelling page-turner of a tale."
–Lex Larson

"As wonderfully deft and balanced as the setting and pacing are, it is its main character where this tale really, really shines."
– Ethan Nichols

"Orison presents a fantasy world and cosmology not quite like any other I've read."
– Eric Honaker

ORISON

DANIEL SWENSEN

ORISON

Cover and map design by Tracy McCusker

First Printing: August 2014
Nine Muse Press

10 9 8 7 6 5 4 3 2 1

ISBN-978-0692025444

Find out more about the author and upcoming books online at www.ninemusepress.com.

Enjoy a zoomable, full-scale map of Calushain at orison.ninemusepress.com/map/.

NINE MUSE PRESS®

ACKNOWLEDGMENTS

The list of people I'd like to thank could go on forever. In particular, I would like to thank: Gina Swensen, for always being my #1 fan;

Angela Goff, Ruth Long, and Eric Martell for being valuable beta readers and supporters;

Anna Meade, for being a patient editor and friend;

Tracy McCusker, for revisions, suggestions, a marvelous cover and support too diverse and amazing to recount here;

Khairul Hisham, for awesome character art;

Lisa Tomecek-Bias, for a helping hand in dark days;

Aaron Engler, Matt Kessen, and the rest of the "Saturday Group" for coming on the initial journey of imagination that inspired this book.

Thank you all.

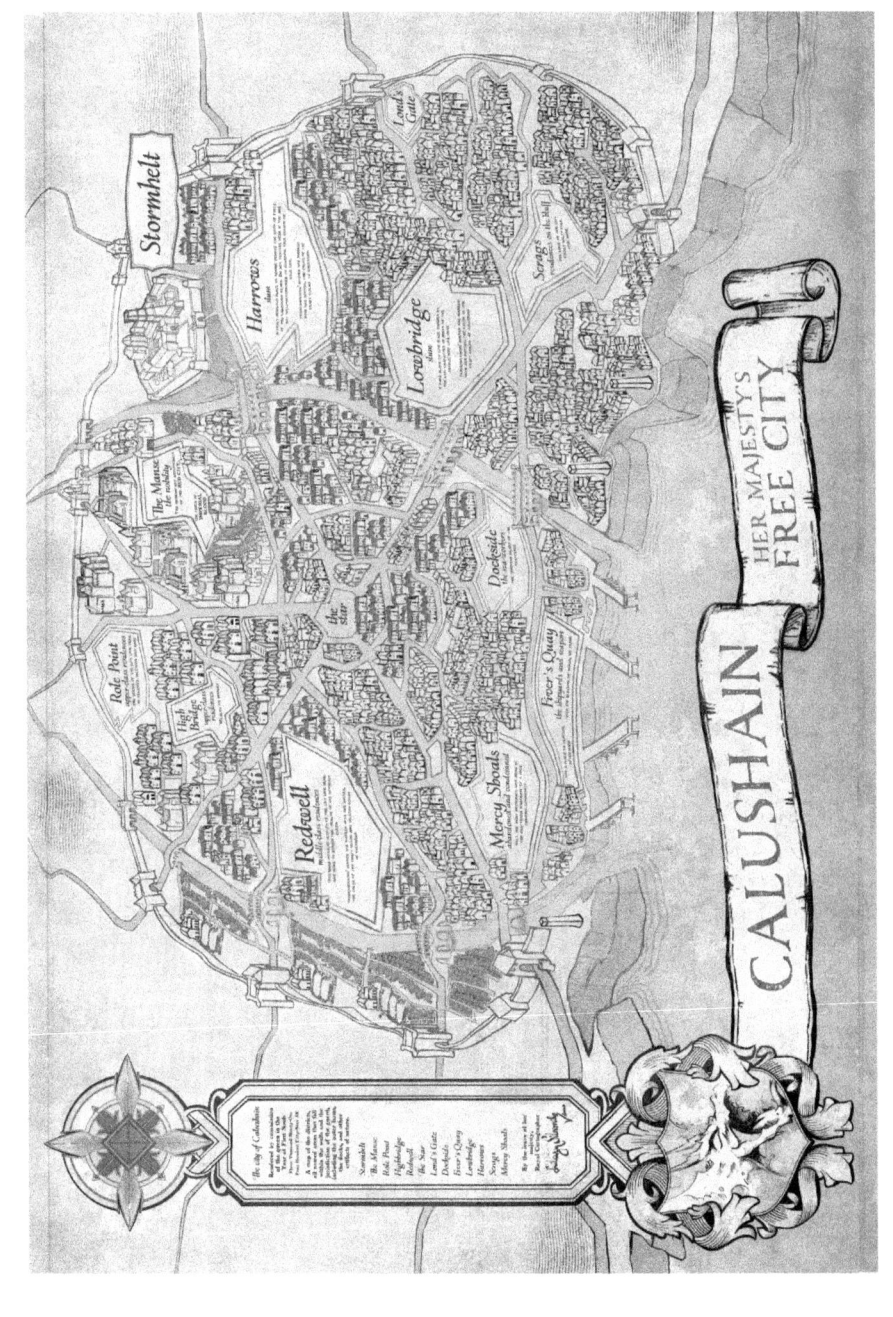

CALUSHAIN

HER MAJESTY'S
FREE CITY

Stormhelt

Harrows

Lord's Gate

Lowbridge

Scrip (or the Jail)

The Mercats

Rale Point

High Bridge

the Shire

Dovedale

Redwell

Mercy Shoals

Freor's Quay

CHAPTER ONE

NEVER STEAL FROM A SORCERER, her brother had told her.

It's only dangerous if they find out, she'd replied, with all the confidence of a thief who had yet to really screw up.

Crux had rolled his eyes. *Sooner or later, they always find out.*

Even Galon had warned his crew never to rob a sorcerer — or at least make sure Galon never heard about it.

But sorcerers had such *nice things.* One good night raiding a sorcerer's home could put her ahead on her quota for weeks. Tonight's haul would bring her closer to getting out of Calushain and away from Galon Luster, forever.

But now, as Story Khai Tann raced across darkened rooftops with a slavering demonic predator five paces behind her, she remembered something else Crux liked to say.

You can't spend it if you're dead.

She jumped over a narrow alley, the guardian demon loping after her. The demon was a raizhi, a four-legged canine knot of muscle and bone, puckered flesh the color of uncooked poultry. Tufts of ebony fur sprouted from its back like spines.

This shouldn't be happening, she thought to herself. Sorcerers summoned raizhi to guard the towers and libraries of upscale neighborhoods, not cut-rate houses in the Calushain slums. Story had underestimated her mark.

She could hear Crux mocking her already. Life was simpler for him — as a leg-breaker and thug for the Barrens, he rarely had to worry about the finer details of burglary. Most of all, he didn't have to justify his membership in Galon's crew with a quota. Story

1

did. All the thieves did — and sometimes, when Counting Day approached and pickings grew thin, risky choices had to be made.

Like now.

She sprinted across the low stucco roof, a leather bag of loot tucked under one arm. It was all she'd had time to grab from the sorcerer's house before the raizhi had lunged from the darkness. Raizhi were clumsy but fast, and the first snap of its narrow jaws had nearly taken her head off.

Story was not a fighter. She was a burglar, and, when circumstances called for it, a runner. So she ran. She knew the broken-down tenements of Harrows better than anyone else in Calushain.

At the end of the roof, she cut north, toward the towering cluster of crimson-roofed shops and tenements that were Redwell. Behind her, she heard a yelp and scuttle as the thing slid across the surface of the rooftop.

She leaped across another alley to land on a second-floor balcony, then dove through an open window. The interior was dark and long-abandoned, like much of Harrows. Story had spent months learning all the empty places of the slums, cataloging bolt-holes, hiding places, and shortcuts. She'd been through this building a half-dozen times in the course of her work, and picked her way through the darkness by instinct.

A demonic snort sounded behind her, then a meaty thud. The raizhi was still right on her tail, claws scrabbling on the edge of the balcony as it pulled itself up. Heart pounding, Story took the narrow stairs that wound to the third floor. There, she could cross to the wealthier neighborhood of Redwell. Most guardian demons, by the laws of Calushain, could only travel so far from their point of summoning. She only needed to reach that threshold. If she could just slow it down somehow —

Stupid! Of course she could.

At the top of the stairs, she knelt quickly in the darkness, dropping her bag to search inside her cloak pockets for the package Wrynn had given her.

As quickly as she dared, she unwound the waxed paper that held in the acrid scent of lochweed, an herb from the Mudfoot swamps. According to Wrynn, guardians hated the scent.

Just use it sparingly, he had said between coughs.

Weeks in her cloak had battered the dried herbs to powder. Story pinched a bit between thumb and forefinger. An instant later, she heard the rapid click of talons on the stairs and barely rolled out of the raizhi's path as it dove at her, ropes of saliva dangling from its maw. A claw shredded her right sleeve, drawing bloody lines across her forearm. Story tried to flick the herb in the demon's direction, but missed. A puff of dry leaves floated in the moonlight for an instant before vanishing.

The raizhi skittered across the trash-strewn floor, recovered, then lunged, jaws clacking. She kicked at it, seeing in her mind a vision of the raizhi biting off her foot at the ankle. Instead, she hit it squarely in the eye. It recoiled with a yelp.

Great, now you've just made it mad.

She still held the crumpled bundle of lochweed in her now-bloody fist. The raizhi lunged again, and she flung the whole package into its face.

The demon gagged and thrashed, pawing at its own face with a gnarled claw as it stumbled backward. A moment later, Story understood why, as her nose began to sting like someone had stuffed burning pine needles up both nostrils.

Her eyes swam with tears. Blinking frantically, she ran past the convulsing raizhi and snatched her loot bag. She stumbled across the room, groped for the rooftop ladder – finding it more from memory than vision — and scrambled up. Enraged howls of pain echoed behind her.

She reached the hatch that led to the roof and pushed. The hatch was bolted. She pawed at the bolt, her bloody fingers too slippery to draw it back.

"Come on, dammit!"

Story threw her shoulder against the hatch in burgeoning panic, still blind in the dark. Below her, she could hear the ragged coughs of the raizhi growing closer. Even through its pain, it was coming for her.

Story braced her feet on the ladder and threw herself against the hatch with all her strength. Pain blossomed in her shoulder, but the hatch banged open. She scrambled through.

3

A quick breath of arid night air swept away the burning scent, but her eyes still streamed tears. She stood on the threshold between boroughs: the grimy tumble of Harrows tenements behind her, the clean red-brick lines of Redwell just across the narrow alley. Some stairs and a second-floor landing lay just across the gap.

She'd made this leap a few times before. Maybe even enough to make it half-blind, like she was about to.

Story's heart thudded in her chest. She stood paralyzed for a moment, before the scuttle of the raizhi's claws on the ladder terrified her into action.

Two steps right from the trap door, five to the edge, then jump.

She ran forward and threw herself into the open air, free arm pinwheeling. If she hit the landing, it was a short drop to street level. If she missed, it was a thirty-foot fall to hard stone. With her eyes swimming, at least she wouldn't see it coming.

For a moment, there was nothing but the whistle of the wind and the sound of her heart. Then she landed, the edge of her foot clipping the rail. She tumbled, struck the wall, and skidded to a stop an inch short of tumbling down the stairs. The bag slipped from her hands.

Grimacing with pain, Story pushed herself up. Her impact had left a smear of blood on the wall from her injured arm. She peered across the street to see if the raizhi was following, no longer certain she had the strength to run or fight.

She saw no sign of the demon — but then, she could barely see at all.

Seconds crept by. The demon did not appear. Either it had lost interest in pursuing her, or it couldn't travel beyond Harrows.

Or it's finding another way to get to you.

She cringed and glanced at her arm. The scratches were painful, but not too deep. The bleeding would probably stop in a few moments.

Either way, it's time to go. Story rubbed her sore, puffy eyes and fumbled for her bag. Securing it under her left arm, she stuffed her right arm under her cloak, limped down the stairs to the street and made her way into the tidy, affluent labyrinth of Redwell.

At this hour, the Scarlets would not be out in force, but she stuck to the back alleys and side streets out of habit. She knew the Scarlet patrol patterns well enough to make her way home without being bothered.

As she walked, she listened closely for signs of the raizhi's pursuit. She heard none. Thunder murmured overhead, and she caught the sharp scent of oncoming rain.

That was a close one, Story. Crux's phantom voice again, sardonic, never quite satisfied. *One day you're going to make a mistake you can't run from.*

She pushed his voice from her mind. She'd outrun the demon and gotten away with a bundle of good loot. Come Counting Day, she would be that much closer to leaving this city.

Six blocks from Harrows, the fear began to fade, yielding to the thrill of escape and a job done, if not necessarily done well. A slow grin crept across her face.

Just another night in Calushain.

Sometime after midnight, Wrynn Sendir concluded he was lost.

He was disappointed, if not surprised. Even in daylight, the neighborhood of Dockside was a snarl of side streets and back alleys, built on paths beaten by madmen and sailors. The neighborhood sprawled with dirty tenements, clustered shanties, streets dank with old urine and gray autumn rain.

No gaslights illuminated the streets here. Wrynn had been navigating by Pale, but the white moon had set, and now only the dark moon Skyshadow remained. In this light, the unlit facades of Dockside all looked equally forbidding. The empty eye sockets of windows gaped in the dark.

Wrynn was also quite drunk, which didn't help.

"Never again," he swore to a fencepost as he stumbled along the empty Dockside streets. He'd begun the evening with every intent of staying sober. A man needed his wits to win at the card table. Of course, a man also needed a good glass of Gundulan whiskey to take the edge off. He'd found that delicate balance, ever so briefly, but then the whiskey kept coming. Now whiskey, money and wits were gone, and he was lost. Even the pale moon had abandoned him.

Wrynn gave up and chose an arbitrary direction in the hopes that it would lead him to the Doorstop, the dilapidated hostel where he made his home. With his pockets empty, even a room would be beyond his means tonight, but perhaps he could find a crate and stay out of the rain.

"Oh, one more hand of cards will turn everything around," he muttered to himself. "Fool."

Once, he had been a landed sorcerer. Pride of the Praxis school, poised for a comfortable position in the Empire's court. He could have been an adviser to kings, with servants and money. Instead, he'd chosen to throw it all aside for his principles — principles now long vanished with whiskey, money and moon.

"But at least I'm free," he confided to the sky, offering an obscene gesture to the luminous spray of draconic constellations around the black-red smudge of Skyshadow.

The stars did not answer. That suited him. It had been a long time since Wrynn had looked for omens.

He rounded a corner, drawing up the hood of his smudged gray cloak as the rain intensified. The drink was beginning to wear off, and the cold Calushain night was closing in. With a sigh, he looked for a landmark of some kind, something to orient himself. A pale shape loomed ahead. As he approached, his disappointment turned to annoyance.

"Oh, it's you," he said.

Like the stars, the statue did not answer. Streaked with rain, the stone monument to the semblance of the dragon Thesis looked sky-ward with a resolute expression. The statue wore a billowing great-coat, long hair flowing, its androgynous face beautiful but stern.

The thing looked almost benevolent. The lie of it offended Wrynn. Unlike the Empire and most of the world, the Red Cities worshiped the dragons directly, rather than the human demigods created by them. They believed that the dragon semblances, cre-ators of humanity and custodians of the world, bestowed favors and good fortune.

6

Wrynn knew differently, from first-hand experience. He had met Thesis, face-to-face, known the terrifying coldness of its gaze, on the day of his exile from the Praxis school.

This is the dragon's principle, the dragon had told him, even as Wrynn's masters had written his fate in the school's black book. *Every instrument is the instrument of another.* Then its lips had curled into a grin, brass draconic eyes blazing, and he had seen the true emptiness of its human mask.

The memory brought the bitter taste of failure to Wrynn's mouth. He scratched his head as if he could claw out the memories of the Praxis school, of his shame and exile, of years lost to drink and regret. On the day of his exile, Wrynn had vowed never to become a dragon's instrument. So far, he thought he'd done a damn fine job of it. Down here in Dockside, he was just another drunk spiraling into the sewer of Calushain, soon to be flushed out to sea.

At least Wrynn knew where he was now. The statue faced north, toward home. To show his appreciation, Wrynn stooped, picked up a round stone, and hurled it at the statue.

"All thanks to you," he said as the rock bounced loudly off the dragon's brow.

Wrynn heard a stir of motion. His casual blasphemy had drawn attention. Four figures emerged from the shadows behind the base of the statue with a chorus of mutters.

Fear clawed away Wrynn's romantic notions of splendid ruin. Lost in drunken thought, he had forgotten he was still in Dockside after dark. This was not a good place to be.

The men swaggered from the gloom in a semicircle, sinewy and sleek. Their lank hair was tied into topknots, warrior's arms ringed with tattoos of draconic totems. The leader's bald head gleamed with livid battle-scars.

Wrynn peered at the totems. Silandra, Semblance of Dreams. These men were Fireborn, mage hunters from far Halak. In his time at the Praxis School, they had raided supply ships, burned villages, and assassinated lone sorcerers on the empty roads of the East. They believed sorcery corroded reality, that each spell gnawed at the veil that held back madness and death. Ironically, Wrynn agreed with them. But he doubted they'd believe that.

He offered the statue a sardonic look. The dragon had bested him again.

"You shouldn't taunt the dragons, friend," the leader said, spitting casually into the mud. "It's bad luck."

"You're more right than you know," Wrynn said. "Did you gentlemen lose at cards tonight? Because I certainly did."

"You're lost," the leader said.

"I should say the same of you," Wrynn replied, swaying slightly on his feet. His mind, fumed with drink, sorted through escape plans, none of them practical. "You're far from home, mage hunters. Don't you know this city's run by a sorceress queen?"

"How did you know we're mage hunters?" the leader snapped. The others stepped forward.

Damn it, Wrynn, you idiot. "I happen to be a supporter of your cause," he slurred, pointing at their tattoos. "Sorcerers are the worst sort of people. Worthless, the lot of them."

"Don't we know it," the leader said in a heavy accent. "Sorcery seeps through this city like a stench."

The four men spread out to surround him, footsteps shuffling in the dark. Wrynn felt a pang of regret. It would be a shame to get knifed to death only a few blocks from his nice warm crate. He sniffed theatrically.

"A stench. Yes, there it is. Quite right." He moved to slip past them. "I won't keep you, then-"

The leader grabbed his wrist in a grip tight enough to grind bones. Wrynn grunted and tried to pull away. The Halak yanked Wrynn's sleeve up to the elbow, revealing dark braids of purple ink encircling his forearm.

Wrynn's gut clenched in sudden terror.

"Imperial strands," the Halak said with a smug grin. "Fancy man's a sorcerer himself. Broke the rules and got himself outcast. Still stinks, though."

With a whisper of steel on leather, the Halak drew a long-bladed knife with his free hand.

You're a fool, Wrynn, he thought to himself. *You can't be what you are, but you certainly can't hide it either.* He took quick stock of the situation. Outnumbered four-to-one, not a Scarlet in sight. Not that they'd stop to help the likes of him. He was alone, drunk, and a fool.

So be a fool, then.

Wrynn unleashed a barrier spell at his wrist. A blue-white parabola of light broke the Halak's grip, sending the man's own hand flying into his face, even as the backlash from the strands seized Wrynn's arm with agony. Wrynn bit back a scream and clutched at his numbing arm.

The Halak reeled. Wrynn stumbled into a clumsy run, making almost five steps before tripping and sliding into the muck again.

They caught up to him quickly. A foot lashed into his stomach, pushing the air from his ribs. Wrynn curled into a ball. The leader's bald head loomed over him, face twisted with rage.

"Lawbreaker can still use sorcery, even through the strands," the man said with a wry grin. "Tough sort, aren't you?"

"Not really," Wrynn managed between coughs. The Halak punched him in the head, and the world began to shudder and dim.

"Maybe I take that hand, lawbreaker. Make sure you never use magic again."

The Halak brandished his knife, going on to say something Wrynn could no longer make out. Something about making the world a better place by removing him from it. Wrynn tried to say it seemed like a worthwhile plan, but then fists and feet hammered into him, driven by shouts of hatred. He raised his hands to the deepening gloom, as if offering them up for the taking, and then the world faded away.

The sting of a slap brought Wrynn back to wakefulness. He first felt cold, then the disappointment of sobriety, then pain — in his face, his stomach, his legs.

"Ow," he muttered, and opened his eyes. He lay sprawled with his back to a cold stone wall. The orange glow of gaslights threw a feeble radiance across the mouth of the alley. He could smell the salt air of the ocean.

He was not in the same place he had fallen. Someone had moved him.

"Are you all right?" a voice asked.

Wrynn looked up. A tall Halak stood over him, dressed in a shirt and trousers of midnight blue. A gray cloak was draped over one shoulder, broadsword strapped across his back. Shoulder-length hair, black streaked with gray, framed a gaunt face with blunt cheekbones and a short beard of slate-gray stubble.

"Well enough," Wrynn said cautiously. This was not one of the men who had attacked him. He rubbed at his arm, which still ached from the backlash of the strands. "I seem to not be dead, which is pleasant."

"Are you sure?" the man asked in a soft, gravelly voice. "You seemed rather eager for death at the time."

The truth of the barb stung. Wrynn chose to ignore it. "Where are we? I was on my way home."

The man glanced over one shoulder, as if just now considering his environs. "Mercy Shoals. Where is home?"

"North of Dockside."

"You were going in the wrong direction, then."

Wrynn knotted his brow in confusion. "I was? But the dragon..."

"What dragon?"

"Nothing." He checked his extremities for any missing bits. There seemed to be none, although a wet red smear of blood stained the front of his robe.

"Is this mine?" he asked hesitantly. His whole body ached with cold, and he could feel the burgeoning bruises where the men had struck him.

"No," the other man said.

"Then what happened?"

"Those men wanted to kill you." The man's lips tightened into the shadow of a smile. "I discouraged them."

Wrynn braced his back against the wall and slid to his feet, still feeling shaky. "And why exactly would you do that?"

"Because they were waiting for me, not you. You merely annoyed them."

"I have that effect on people." Wrynn struggled to his feet warily. "Why would they be after you? You're no sorcerer."

"No." The man looked over his shoulder again, eager to be gone. "I'm something much worse to them. You should leave before they gather their courage again."

"You didn't kill them?"

That thin smile again. "Not all of them."

Wrynn coughed. "I'm in your debt," he said at last, the sentiment seeming inadequate.

The man nodded once and turned to leave.

"I don't even know your name," Wrynn called after him.

"Go home," the man said, and walked silently into the night.

Wrynn blew on his hands. The rain had stopped, but the sun was not yet up. The city was bitter cold, and he still had far to walk. He stretched painfully, drew his tattered robe around him, and shuffled toward the gas-lit streets.

At the crossroads, he ran across a squad of Scarlets out on their nightly duties. He hugged the shadows, afraid they might catch sight of his bloodied robes and question him. But they merely glanced in his direction and turned away, uninterested. As if he were nothing.

Just like you wanted it, Wrynn thought, and started walking.

Just after sunrise, Story finally returned home.

From Redwell, she cut through the Star, the hub of the city where the five main streets of Calushain met in a cluster of stalls and shop fronts. The merchants and vendors had just begun to emerge, sleepy-eyed and stern, to gird themselves for the day's business. This was Story's favorite time of day: the quiet inhale before the city's first breath of life and commerce.

At a fruit stand, she traded the vendor a grubby half-talon for two tangerines. She thanked him politely, and on her way past the stall, surreptitiously rolled two more tangerines off the pile into her bag.

No one saw. All the same, her heart thudded softly in her chest until she had safely turned the corner, out of the vendor's sight. She picked up her pace as she headed for home.

Every theft one-third honest, every lie two-thirds truth. Galon had taught her that. A good thief paid when she needed to — but no more often than that.

Story didn't particularly like stealing. She just happened to be suited to it, and little else. She was short, slender, and inconspicuous. She dressed in the dun tunic and trousers common to a ditchdigger or mason, though it had been a long time since she'd done any honest labor. The bristly ponytail of her black hair and the freckles across her cheeks lent her an innocent demeanor, perfect for talking herself out of trouble. She was strong enough to discourage some attackers, and quick enough to outrun the rest.

To the city, she was just another grubby, impoverished girl of nineteen. Just the way she wanted it.

Story's home was the Doorstop, a four-story wayhouse of charred red brick north of Dockside. As trade with the Ladris Empire dwindled, the neighborhoods furthest from the docks had suffered most. The Doorstop had deteriorated at roughly the same rate as Calushain's relations with the Lotus Throne.

Bront, an ex-assassin from the Face of Night, ran the Doorstop by a sort of barter system. The tenants traded food, talent or any coin they could scrape up in exchange for a room. Notions of personal space came loosely interpreted. Quarrels and fistfights were common, but stopped short of lethal. Anyone who drew a blade in the Doorstop got a visit from Bront. The rules were simple: thieves would be hobbled with hatchets, and stabbers would, in turn, be stabbed.

Bront took his duties seriously, and the Doorstop was one of the safest places in Calushain for a thief like her. It was quiet, secure, and kept her daily affairs away from prying eyes.

Story turned down the garbage-choked alley next to the wayhouse. She had one last stop before she bedded down for the morning. Kicking aside a damp knot of trash, she squatted in front of a battered crate to peer at the sleeping figure inside.

Wrynn was taller than Story, but not by much. Tufts of unruly copper hair, matted with straw, sprang from his head. He wore tattered robes, once bright blue, now a canvas of gray smudges.

"Spare some coin?" the man grunted, half-awake.

"Wrynn, it's me."

He blinked at her. "Oh. I thought it might have been an honest citizen."

"An honest citizen? Behind the Doorstop?"

"Is that where I am?" Wrynn squinted around the inside of his crate. "Oh, yes."

Story's shoulder and legs throbbed, and her body ached for sleep, but she sat on the cold stones next to Wrynn. He was one of the few people Story could call friend, and she suspected that Wrynn had even fewer.

She frowned at him. "Why didn't you just go up to your room? Nice and warm and dry. Well, dry anyway." Wrynn rented the room beside Story's, when he wasn't wandering the streets or gambling.

Wrynn yawned. "All those stairs seemed like so much work. Also, Bront wanted me to pay rent."

She lifted an eyebrow. "Lose all your money playing cards again?"

"No. All right, yes, but there's a very good reason."

"I doubt that." Story began to rifle through her bag, but Wrynn coughed in disapproval.

"I won't take your money, so don't bother," he said. "This is a very luxurious crate."

"Bront's rent is a talon a night. I can spare it."

"No. I don't need you to save me."

"I'm not saving you. I'm just giving you a hand."

He smiled stubbornly. Story sighed and pulled two of the tangerines from her bag. "Fine. Here. Don't trade them for drink like last time, all right?"

Wrynn leaned forward. As his face emerged from the shadow, Story saw a livid smear of bruises across his eye and cheek.

Story's breath hissed between her teeth. "Wrynn, what did you do?"

Wrynn poked at the bruises self-consciously, as if hoping to coax them out of sight. "Oh. Bit of a disagreement with some fellows. I wanted to go home without a beating. They disagreed."

"They look like they hurt," Story said softly, reaching out to touch his face.

Wrynn accepted her touch for a moment, then gently drew away. "It looks worse than it is."

"Where did this happen? I'll send the crew after them."

"No," Wrynn said. "I don't want you getting involved. Or your brother. Especially your brother."

"We can help."

"Thank you, no." His tone told her he was finished discussing the matter.

Story handed him the tangerines without further argument. As he reached for them, she caught sight of the intricate braided swirls of purple ink decorating his wrists.

Wrynn cradled the fruit to his chest. "You're very kind."

"Are you ever going to tell me where to get tattoos like yours?"

Wrynn began slowly peeling one of the tangerines. "You don't want tattoos like mine."

"Why not?"

"They're a poor decision."

She narrowed her eyes. "You're awfully straitlaced for an avowed drunkard. How do you know I don't have any tattoos?"

"I watch you while you sleep," he said drily.

She snorted laughter. "You're disgusting."

"Don't forget charming with the ladies."

"I wasn't."

She smiled and watched him quietly. For as long as she'd known Wrynn, he had been terrible at taking care of himself. It felt good to do something nice for him, even something very small.

They sat in silence while Wrynn finished peeling. After a moment, Wrynn caught on. "You're waiting to see if I actually eat them. Don't you trust me?"

"Nope," she said brightly.

Wrynn mock-scowled and shoved a bright slice of tangerine into his mouth. "How's that?" he mumbled around the mouthful.

"There's all that charm I was waiting for."

He chewed, swallowed, and pointed at her bag. "How did your evening's work go?"

"Not bad. Some good stuff off a summoner in Harrows. He was pretty well-equipped for a hedge wizard."

Wrynn nodded toward the scratches on her hands. "You run into any trouble?"

"He had a raizhi."

Wrynn scowled. "Those things are trouble. Are you all right?"

She shrugged with a confidence she didn't feel. Once the thrill of outmaneuvering it had worn off, the realization of how close she'd come to being wounded or killed had settled into her bones like a chilly fog.

"Nothing I couldn't handle," she said.

He looked like he didn't quite believe her, but didn't press the matter. "I'll never understand why sorcerers keep pets from Kulraizhan. Once you bring something like that across the threshold, you never really control it."

"Is that your opinion as an expert drunk and herbalist?"

He narrowed his eyes at her and ignored the question. "You should be more careful. You could have been killed, you tiny fool."

"Actually, I should thank you. I used that vile herb you gave me. Which, by the way, almost killed me too. Thanks for warning me about that."

"I *did* warn you about that. What did you do, throw the whole thing?"

Story opened her mouth, then shut it again. Wrynn wheezed laughter.

"I couldn't help it," Story said, ducking her head in embarrassment. "I was in a rush."

"You always are," he said with a grin.

"Wrynn," she said, changing the subject abruptly, "you really should join Galon's crew. We could use someone like you. That lochweed saved my — it kept me out of trouble last night. Galon would pay you for your services. I've even mentioned it to him. He said—"

"Thank you again, but no," Wrynn said, his good humor fading away. Story bristled with frustration. She'd made the offer a dozen times, only to meet with Wrynn's stone-faced refusal each time. Wrynn never elaborated on his reasons for refusing, or judged her for working for Galon. But he always said no.

Story wished she could convince him. It would be nice to have a friend in Bladesbarrow. Someone besides her brother. Someone she could trust.

"Fine," she said, as if his refusal didn't sting a little. "I should get some rest. Can I buy some more lochweed from you? It's pretty handy to have around."

"I'll see what I can do," Wrynn said with a tiny grimace. "I don't exactly keep the stuff on me."

She grinned and rose to her feet. "What would I do without you, old man?"

"You'd have more tangerines for yourself. And don't call me old man."

"Filthy hobo?"

"Better." Wrynn drew up his hood and leaned back to enjoy his breakfast.

Story ran up the switchback stairs along the outside wall of the Doorstop, hopped the rail of the third-floor balcony, then climbed through the window to her room. She'd kept her door locked and double-barred since her first night there. She never used the door if she had a choice, instead using the window to come and go. Crux accused her of doing everything the hard way. He was probably right.

There wasn't much to Story's home. The room was just big enough to contain a wooden cot, a set of empty drawers she'd glued shut to annoy potential burglars, and a pile of blankets and hides for getting through the biting Calushain winters. The pale blue paint had long since peeled off the walls, so she hung dyed burlap sheets of orange and gold to keep it dark and warm during the day. Despite her attempts to keep the place clean, dust and debris flew in through the shutters whenever the wind picked up.

All she had in the world was in this room, and there was little she couldn't walk away from at a moment's notice. It was another lesson Galon pressed upon his crew. Possessions and friendships were weight, best kept to a few necessities. Galon even had a chant he made his people recite:

How does a thief steal?
She moves without sound. She walks unseen.
What does a thief take?
No more than she can carry.
What does she leave behind?
Shadows and silence.

Story fastened the shutters, blocking out the bright morning light. Stretching to relieve the pain in her shoulder, she sat cross-legged and dumped the contents of her bag onto the floor to take stock of the night's haul. A nice silver goblet, twelve Imperial talons, a silver-and-moonstone necklace in the shape of a dragon, three small bolts of silk, some silver rings, and a few sticks of incense Wrynn claimed were both expensive and common among sorcerers.

She made a mental note to slip some coin into Wrynn's robes when he wasn't looking. Whether he wanted to admit it or not, she owed him, and she always paid her debts.

Meticulously, she sorted the goods out by size and value, arranging them in front of her. Knowing the street value of something relative to its portability was a key skill in her line of work, and Story knew her job well. Not a bad haul, despite the raizhi cutting her night short. If she weren't under orders to deliver her spoils straight to Galon, she could fence these for a hundred talons or so.

But that was not the plan.

Story drew her knife, took a tangerine from the pile, and held it between her teeth as she rose. She lifted the corner of the chest of drawers, dragged it several inches, and gently set it down again. Beneath the rear leg lay a loose plank, which she pried up with the edge of her knife.

Inside lay a fat pouch tied with leather strings. She dropped the twelve talons and the moonstone necklace into the bag, then replaced the plank and the chest of drawers. Then she flopped on her blankets and began cutting the tangerine into wedges, gazing at the water-spotted ceiling.

This was her long game. She knew the count of her secret wealth down to the last half-talon. With last night's take, she was up to two hundred and sixty-six. Nearly enough to buy herself passage on a ship out of Calushain. A real ship, not some black-sailed Mudfoot galleon where she'd end up lashed to the sweeps or sold as a slave. She would leave on her terms, not as a servant, but a free woman.

Another two weeks and she could leave Calushain — as long as Galon didn't find out she'd been skimming. Coin was about the only thing she dared keep to herself. Trying to fence stolen goods without Galon noticing was too high a risk.

It was a dangerous game to be playing. As far as Galon was concerned, she belonged to him. Ten years ago, the boss had purchased Story and her brother from an orphanage on Fiver's Quay. He'd put her to work as a thief and burglar, him as a pickpocket and later an enforcer. Galon had named her his "second-story girl," a moniker he'd eventually truncated to Story. If she had another name besides that, it no longer meant anything to her.

She should have been grateful — at least, so Galon reminded her on a regular basis. Galon had given her a life and a profession. The privilege of paying for her own room, out from under Galon's watchful eye, had been hard-won with years of faithful service. She had risen in the ranks, but to Galon, she was less a daughter than an asset, useful only as long as she brought in talons.

Stealing for herself, aside from food or clothing, was strictly forbidden. Everything went to Galon, and he distributed a portion back to his crew as he saw fit. That was the rule. Anyone who broke it risked exile or death, and Galon was rarely forgiving enough for exile.

And so she carefully hid her hopes beneath her feet, a few coins at a time, waiting for the day she could be free of Galon, Bladesbarrow, and Calushain itself.

Exhaustion outfought hunger, and Story curled up to sleep, the tangerine uneaten in her hand.

CHAPTER TWO

Every nine days, Camana, Queen of Calushain, left Stormhelt's gray keep and took a carriage to Shadowcourt to honor the dragon Amaraxis. There, Ashen One-Howl, her general and bodyguard, waited a respectful step behind her as she attended the ceremonies of the dragon temples.

The temple of Amaraxis, like all the dragon temples in Calushain, featured the vast stone likeness of a winged dragon coiled around the interior of the temple apse. Its tail embraced the altar, its fanged maw rearing above the pews in a silent roar. Dwarfed by the image of his god, the dragon-priest lifted his arms and retold the story of Sorolaine, First of the Folk.

Ashen waited next to Queen Camana, who stood with her retinue in an alcove to the left of the nave. He paid little attention to the parable, which he had heard many times, and which always seemed to carry themes of obeisance to temporal power whenever the queen attended.

The queen's face was hidden beneath a veil of pale gold, hands folded demurely as she listened to the sermon. By tradition, when the queen wore the veil, she was not to be spoken to, or even acknowledged, until she addressed someone first. Camana, who disliked flattery and obsequiousness, almost always wore the veil when she left Stormhelt.

The retinue still drew stares, likely because of Ashen himself. Every few minutes, someone in the congregation would glance his way, give him a look of fear or disdain, then quickly look away again.

It had been this way since the day he had been given to the queen as a gift.

Ashen did not mind. He understood how he looked to them. Ashen was warborn, a being created by Imperial sorcerers. His appearance was deliberately inhuman: a long face, simian and sleek, with deep-set predator's eyes and pointed, furry ears. Fangs gleamed between his lips. Hackles of dark gray fur sprang in points from his jowls above the iron collar and chain fragment he wore.

The people's dislike went beyond his appearance. Ashen was a creature built for battle, created by the Ladris Empire. He was a symbol of Imperial might and power, in the court of Calushain, and he had no place in the holy houses of the Red Cities.

That, too, suited him. Ashen shared few sentiments with the Empire, but like them, he did not believe in the benevolence of dragons. As gods, he considered them terrors, notable only for their cruelty and caprice. Their chosen ascendants, the etherics, were revered by the Empire as demigods and agents of draconic divinity. Camana was such an etheric, and while Ashen did not worship her as a divine being, he revered her nonetheless. And so he endured these sermons out of duty.

Even the queen did not choose a patron semblance. Her worship, though punctual, varied by season. In times of harvest or famine, she paid homage to the dragon Mithetis; in times of war, Silindel or Merathu. When she fell into occasional melancholy, she would visit the temple of Aporos and listen to the dragon-priests expound on the circular nature of time and the fecund primal chaos to which all creation returned.

Today, the queen was to meet with the other rulers of the Red Cities, and so she came before the altar of Amaraxis, Semblance of Power, seeking the dragon's favor in the negotiations to come. The dragon-priest, sensing a chance to flatter the queen, wrestled his parable of Sorolaine into a lecture on the importance of independence and freedom, of the courage to defy the threat of Imperial rule and the grasping hand of the Lotus Throne.

Camana shifted restlessly. *Do you think he knows?* Her voice whispered in his mind. As far as Ashen knew, her ability to converse without speaking applied only to him: partially her magic, partially their bond as Born and Sworn. Ashen had found, to his puzzlement, that only Camana could initiate these conversations, and she did so rarely.

Ashen inclined his head, formal even in their shared thoughts. *Majesty?*

The dragon-priest. About the meeting. He's talking an awful lot about courage and fortitude.

Are these not worthy themes for a sermon, Majesty?

The corners of her eyes crinkled as she smiled behind the veil. *I think he wants to seem portentous so I'll donate generously.*

Ashen grunted his amusement. From Camana's left side, Ravano, the queen's seer and adviser, glared briefly in his direction. Ravano was gaunt, bent with age, unruly gray hair sprouting in a cloud above the burgundy folds of his robe. Though he could not hear their thoughts, he knew what they were doing and clearly disapproved.

The warborn returned his attention to the sermon. Certainly, the people could use a positive omen. The Ladris Empire longed to call the southern city-states its own, and Calushain was the jewel in the crown of the Red Cities. While the other rulers had balked at a formal military alliance with Camana, they had gathered together instinctively against the rising Imperial threat. Only the promise of a hard-fought war and economic ruin kept the Empire from launching an outright attack on the Red Cities.

So far, Camana had kept that promise through appearances and diplomacy. The queen had wound herself in a skein of fiction, written herself into a figure of legend: the queen who had sipped from the veins of Amaraxis and become an etheric. The queen who defied the Lotus Throne and protected the Red Cities from the Empire's jaws. Even her true name was rarely spoken outside the brooding stone walls of Stormhelt. To her city, she was known as the Queen of Storms.

Humans said she was beautiful. Ashen had trouble grasping human notions of beauty. His warborn instincts saw the queen's body as frail and unimposing. Attributes like her hair, lips and eyes, praised by minstrels and an unending series of frustrated suitors, meant nothing to him — nor to her, it seemed. She sported weaknesses deliberately bred out of his own species, yet possessed the tenacity and power to lead Calushain and the Red Cities. If anything was beautiful about her, it was that.

Ashen cared little for legends or diplomacy. His only loyalty was to her, his Sworn, and he would lay down his life for her. That was the one commandment of his people he had not forsaken.

The sermon ended on a note of hope, leavened by the need for loyalty and obedience and a final veneration to Amaraxis. The queen bowed her head with the rest of the congregation, placing two fingers at her throat in a gesture of worship to the semblances.

The worshipers rose and began to file from the temple. Gray-robed almoners swung brass cannikins from their stations at the temple doors, while others collected coins and gave blessings.

A few brave souls from the court passed before the queen in the hopes of being addressed. Ashen stepped in front of her, arms folded, teeth bared, and none dared speak to her directly.

"You enjoy that far too much," Camana remarked behind him as the last of the worshipers retreated in disappointment.

"One must relish the small pleasures, Majesty."

As the temple emptied, the dragon-priest approached, bald head gleaming with sweat. He bowed silently.

"Thank you for the sermon, Exalted," the queen said, giving the priest permission to speak.

"My Queen. Your presence honors us."

"I come to pay honor to the semblances, not to bestow it."

The priest bowed his head. "Of course. May the strong eye of Amaraxis pass over you." He placed two fingers gently on his throat. His gaze swung to Ashen. "What did you think of the service, Master One-Howl?"

Before Ashen could answer, a voice broke in.

"The warborn don't revere the semblances, Exalted," Ravano said. "They were born in Imperial vats, not from dragons' clay. They worship the sword and the arrow."

Ravano's discourtesy did not surprise Ashen. The seer had never bothered to hide his contempt for the warborn race and their terrible purpose. Like many citizens of Calushain, the seer was an

Imperial expatriate himself, and deeply conflicted about the Lotus Throne's history. Ravano took pleasure in characterizing the warborn as a mindless killer, though they both knew better.

Ashen bared his teeth in a pantomime of a human smile. "'From clay to clay, sculpted by semblance's claw, all works upon their table,'" he quoted.

The priest's eyes widened. "You know the Tome of Shadows."

"One must know one's enemy," Ashen said. Centuries before, the warborn had been created by the Empire to destroy the mad etheric, Drog Ungru. "Should not the slayers of demigods know their scripture? Must we not know the weight of what we do?"

"Yes," the dragon-priest said, uncomfortable. "I suppose so."

Ravano looked displeased.

Ashen inclined his head. "May I ask a question, Exalted?"

"Of course."

"The semblance Librus created humans as a curiosity, never expecting them to survive. Amaraxis preserved them and protected them, also out of curiosity. But the other semblances see humanity as parasites or toys. Is this not true?"

"In a sense," the dragon-priest said.

"So the Prayer of Semblance calls upon the dragons to ignore humanity, to spare humanity their wrath," Ashen said. "Much as the free warborn hope our creators will forget us."

"Wasn't there to be a question?" Ravano sneered. Camana glanced in the seer's direction, and his mouth snapped shut.

"Only this," Ashen said. "If to court the attention of dragons is to invite despair and death, why do we gather here? How long will the strong eye of Amaraxis pass over these pews?"

The dragon-priest coughed as he tried to form a reply. After a moment, Camana smiled gently and nudged Ashen.

"A fascinating question, but I fear the business of running Calushain calls us. Thank you again, Exalted. My seer will attend to your donation."

The priest bowed, and Ashen saw the relief in his eyes, tempered with anticipation for the generous flow of gold.

Come along, Ashen, the queen said silently, and he saw the combined amusement and reproach in her eyes as they departed the temple.

They emerged into the light of the morning sun, the air already warm with the promise of afternoon heat. Shadowcourt lay at the base of the hill beneath the keep of Stormhelt, a circular plaza fed by four city roads. Ten dragon temples had been built in a circle around the court, one for each of the ten semblances worshiped by Calushain. Above the edifice of each temple, two draconic statues loomed: below, the human form of each semblance, facing its brothers and sisters across the central fountain of the court; above, their draconic form, the barbed shadows of their wings embracing Shadowcourt.

Carriages and wagons crowded the street around the temple of Amaraxis. The queen's carriage waited at the base of the red marble steps, the footman already standing at attention. Ashen escorted Camana into the carriage, giving the temple behind them one last glance. He doubted Amaraxis would remember today.

"I know you get bored at the temples, Ashen, but you shouldn't bait Ravano like that," the Queen said as he sat across from her. "Nor taunt the clergy."

Ashen tilted his head in a submissive gesture. "It was not my intent, Majesty. I sought only to ask the dragon-priest about matters of theology."

The queen lifted her veil, revealing a pale oval face and eyes flecked with gold. Her face was etched scarlet with the intricate tattooed sigils of her office, arranged around her eyes and cheekbones in thorny patterns.

"You're smarter than that," she said. "You let Ravano manipulate you into showing off so the priest wouldn't think you were a thug. I thought the warborn were supposed to be imperturbable."

"I am not perturbed, Majesty."

She laughed softly and relaxed into her seat, her stern public demeanor gone. "I know he was trying to goad you. But for my sake, do not make Ravano angry. His visions suffer when he loses his temper."

"Then perhaps you need a new seer, unmoved by anger." Ashen tapped the ceiling twice with a mailed hand, and the carriage lurched gently into motion.

Camana's smile faded. "Ravano's position precedes my own. He has powerful connections in the Red Cities and beyond. I need him, especially now."

Ashen understood. The leaders of the Red Cities — Irongate, Scarl, and Kintas — waited for the queen's return to Stormhelt to discuss matters of a formal military alliance against the Lotus Throne. The Red Cities held three major ports on the sea between the heart of the Empire and its eastern outposts. The whispers of spies carried word that the Emperor had tired of tariffs and trade agreements. It was only a matter of time before the Emperor sought to make those ports his own. If the Red Cities failed to cooperate with each other, the hand of the Empire would pluck them, one by one, like bloody flowers.

The queen gazed out the window as the carriage tilted and slowed as they left Shadowcourt and wound their way up the grass-lined road to the gray spires of Stormhelt. Camana's fear did not show on her face, but Ashen read it in her scent, in the tension of her muscles and the tight orange glow of her magesight aura. It was not panic he saw, but a burning trepidation, a certainty that hardship lay in wait.

"Has Ravano foreseen the outcome of the negotiations?" Ashen ventured.

"Nothing," she said. "I would not be seeking the favor of Amaraxis otherwise."

"In the Tome of Shadows, Amaraxis favors the strongest, and abandons the weak," Ashen said. "You are strong."

"The Empire is stronger. Will she not side with them? That was the point of your question to the dragon-priest, wasn't it?"

The gentle reproach stung him with shame. "Majesty, I beg your forgiveness. That is not what I meant."

Though Ashen had adapted far beyond most of his warborn brethren, the finer points of human interaction still eluded him. In Camana's veins flowed the blood of Amaraxis herself. The queen already had the semblance's favor, and enough power to face the

Empire without trusting to the fickle gods. Even the legacy of her blood offered her no bond with Amaraxis. The dragons cared nothing for humanity. Why could the queen not see that?

He longed to try to explain, but feared he would only make things worse. Or that he understood less than he imagined.

The queen said nothing. Through the window, Ashen watched the lush trees and gardens of the Manse drift by, the buildings beautiful yet somehow gloomy in the cloud-dappled light of morning. Red Cities architecture always seemed somewhat somber to Ashen, lacking the grandiosity of Imperial construction.

"Whatever happens, the people are behind you," Ashen said at last. "The Empire wants the Red Cities for a bauble. The people want freedom from Imperial rule. Lust for freedom is stronger than lust for coin."

She glanced at him. "Do you truly believe that?"

"It is what I have heard."

"From where?"

"One of your speeches."

Camana narrowed her eyes. He had displeased her. "You didn't answer the question."

"No, I do not believe it. The people crow about freedom while their bellies are full. Hungry or frightened, they will sell whatever they have, freedom quickest of all."

"So I must promise prosperity and freedom both," Camana said. "Not an easy thing, if the Empire cuts off trade with us."

"And war will soon follow."

"With war comes hunger and fright," she said. "Freedom will go cheaply. Will I not need the dragon's favor then, more than ever?"

Ashen could no longer meet her gaze. "A dragon's favor is the worst slavery of all, Majesty."

Upon their return to Stormhelt, Camana dismissed Ashen from her side. She retreated to her throne room to meet with the seer Ravano and the other lords of the Red Cities.

Though he was loath to leave her, he understood her reasons. No matter how loyal his actions, his presence would undermine the confidence of the other rulers. He instructed Mathes, captain of the Scarlets, to take his place and ordered a double guard around the queen during the negotiations.

With no further duty facing him, the warborn passed the time with exercises in Stormhelt's south barracks, sparring enthusiastically with Scarlet recruits. The heat of the afternoon grew oppressive, and soon he found himself alone in the practice yard, swinging at combat dummies with fists and feet.

The queen's reproachful look in the carriage haunted Ashen. Though the warborn were bred to be devoid of ego, the offense he had given gnawed at him. He knew the queen was stronger than his words, stronger than anything he might think of her. But he had showed disrespect by flaunting his knowledge in front of Ravano and the dragon-priest.

Ravano's presence galled him. Not because of any slight to Ashen himself, but because the seer's visions had not yet provided a solution to the dilemma facing Calushain. If Ravano's prophecies brought no wisdom of the coming war with the Empire, then what use was the seer, or the semblances themselves? Calushain had placed reckless hope in the hands of uncaring gods. Ravano's divinations were noise. Ashen knew the Empire better than any in that throne room.

But they would not trust Ashen. He had been an Imperial gift, a piece of property from the Medeccia family to help woo Camana into an agreement with the Empire. The queen had taken him in as her own, broken his bond with the Lotus Throne, accepted his undying oath of fealty. Yet many in the court still thought him to be a spy, even an assassin.

And so he squandered his time on the practice grounds, exile within exile, while the Empire sharpened its claws.

The warborn lashed out at a dummy with a savage kick, splintering its base and knocking it into the dust. His anger drained away, leaving him empty.

This was absurd. He was an instrument of battle. When battle came, he would serve. It was not his place to question his queen's wisdom. Trying to be more than that would only bring him pain.

Closing his eyes, he breathed in the hot dust of the practice grounds, waiting for the poison of his ego to drift away. When it had gone, he retrieved his sword and went inside.

Bitterness still lingered in Ashen's belly as he traveled the cool darkness of Stormhelt's lower halls. The light and heat did not reach here, and Ashen was grateful for the solitude.

He retreated to his sparse quarters, closed the door, and sat cross-legged on the cold floor without shedding his armor. Still troubled by the events of the morning, he closed his eyes. His body, tensed into readiness by his sparring, still quivered with the desire for action, for battle. He pulled back his emotions, peeling away the layers of aggression, but his ego still taunted him. He needed calm and comfort.

With a deep breath, Ashen invoked his magic and opened the Door of Shadows. Sorcerous currents flowed over him, numbing his body and caressing his mind into bliss.

Ashen's magical talent was known only to a few within the court of Calushain, and the irony of the gift was not lost on him. Sorcery was born of dragons. All sorcerers drew their power from the dragon-world Kulraizhan through the omnipresent, invisible Door of Shadows. Every spell was an echo of a dragon's power. For this reason, sorcery was taught to few and forbidden to most; uncontrolled confluence — the clash between the dragon-world and this one — could tear reality itself apart.

Magic was a river, to be sipped from carefully, and to drink too deep was poison to the world.

Yet there was a harmony to the confluence, when taken in small sips, and Ashen let the power flow through him, unraveling his ego and loosening his muscles. Such comfort was an abomination to his people. Warborn lived for the battle and the blade. To indulge like this made Ashen a blasphemer twice over. In another life, his talents would have meant a death sentence. But he had hidden them from his warborn Imperial brothers, kept his secret until entering the service of his queen.

He drew upon a miniscule amount of power, just enough to lull his predator's senses into rest. Sorcery drew a languid whirlpool of colors around him: incandescent strands of green, blue and violet. Beyond that, his perception receded to smoke and shadow, and the walls of Stormhelt melted away.

The warborn knew how to use such power on the battlefield as well. The sorcerers of the Iron School used magic to increase their strength and quickness, to ignore pain and the limits of their own bodies. Though Ashen had never been allowed in the Imperial Academy, he had studied their books, learned from other exiles, and mastered their disciplines. After years of practice, he could kill as well as any Imperial mage, and the day was coming when he would prove that to the Lotus Throne itself.

Something stirred in the dark. He was not alone.

Ashen nearly dropped out of his vision. Souls had been known to meet in the shadow gap between the two worlds, but it had never happened to him. He steadied himself in the radiant gloom, giving his consciousness form and solidity — a courtesy between travelers. Though he could choose any form he wished, he chose his own. A façade would be pointless — there would be no hiding his true nature from observers in the shadow gap.

The mists around him gelled into the curves and planes of architecture. Ashen waited, letting the shapes coalesce until he stood on a phantom of Calushain itself, a city of light and fog.

A humanoid figure approached from the ghost-light. The figure's skin gleamed, pale and veined like polished marble, an angular face beneath black hair merged with the shadowy currents. Black eyes swirled with gray motes, each pupil a twist of stars. On each hand, six fingers ended in pale talons. Her body smeared creation like paint as she moved.

A dragon semblance.

Fear turned in Ashen's stomach: a novelty for him. His remarks at the temple suddenly seemed like folly. The semblances were the shapers of the world, the authors of mythology and civilization. Reality was their reflection in the still waters of the cosmos — in this place, Ashen was less real than she, a shadow of a word.

The woman approached. Ashen did not know whether to kneel and scrape, as a dragon-priest would, or bow as he would before a visiting prince from Snowcastle. So he stood his ground, ears pulled back in puzzlement. He was warborn, after all, and this was not his god. If she wanted to hurt him here, she could annihilate him with a thought.

Do you know who I am?

Her lips did not move, but her voice rang in his head like an unruly choir of hundreds.

Ashen tried to piece together the scraps of mythology he'd learned, the sermons he'd listened to on temple days. His gaze drifted to the iron amulet around her neck: an eye ringed with a broken circle, radiating spikes like a black sun.

There was a reason he did not know her from Shadowcourt. This was the tenth semblance, the one few in Calushain worshiped, the one the Empire dreaded, the one whose children he had been created to slay.

"Penumbra," he said. "Sister of Amaraxis."

I've something to show you, she said.

"I will not bargain with you, Semblance of Shadow," Ashen said through his fear. He knew enough to understand that dealing with a dragon was a doomed gamble, more so for a capricious and scheming god like Penumbra.

I offer no bargains, Penumbra said, her tone one of gentle reproach. *Only knowledge.*

Ashen felt a surge of sympathy, then realized it was magically imposed. Penumbra was twisting his will with her own. He squared his shoulders and clamped down on his emotions.

"At what price?"

I ask none.

"I find that unlikely."

The woman flicked her wrist. With a snap of light, a gleaming red stone appeared in her palm, shot through with ragged swirls of black. The color drifted over its surface like liquid beneath glass.

Penumbra stepped forward and held it toward him, its crimson light illuminating her face from beneath.

Ashen made no move to take it.

Is it not beautiful? Are you not curious?

"It is beautiful, and no."

What if I told you it has the power to bring all Calushain to ruin? Her tone seemed designed to entice, as if offering such power to him.

"In the hands of a semblance, such power is common. I have heard the sermons. The dragons lay waste to civilizations on a whim."

She tilted her head. *And what would you do with such power?*

"Refuse it."

Do this for me, warborn. Ask your Queen of Storms what she knows of this stone. Then you will care. My gift is on its way. The only question is who will receive it.

"A dragon's prophecy is poison," Ashen said.

For a moment, Penumbra's mask broke apart. He saw the razor fangs behind those lips, the gnarled horror beneath the delicate human face.

You're interesting, warborn. I like you.

Then she was gone. Ashen's vision smeared to gray, then black, and the weight of his body returned to him. He opened his eyes, breathing spasmodically, surprised to feel his own heart pounding fast.

He sat up and smoothed back the fur along his jowls. Leaning over, he dipped his hand in the water bowl beside his mat, and slapped water on his face.

If Penumbra had offered this mysterious bauble only to him, he would have forgotten this had ever happened. But she mentioned the Queen of Storms, his Sworn. He could not conceal this from her.

A few moments with a semblance, and already choices lay beyond his grasp. Such was the way of gods.

The sun had set while Ashen lingered in the shadow gap. He left his quarters — a tiny room with the decor of a dungeon cell — and returned to the dim, arched corridors of Stormhelt. It was a lonely walk from the east wing of the castle, through silent arcades and halls hung with tapestries. The moon Pale threw colorless slats of light across his path, and his footsteps echoed in the quiet dark.

Climbing the broad marble steps to the queen's chambers, he ordered the chamberlain to announce his arrival. A pair of Scarlets stood before the door, the blades of their pikes giving off the faintly hissing red smoke of runic enchantments.

The chamberlain waved him in, and the guards let him pass without a word. Ashen stepped into the room, feeling a pang of trepidation at disturbing her so late.

The queen had not been sleeping. She sat at her desk, writing in a heavy book with a silver quill. She wore no veil, nor the ritual red sigils she wore in public. Her pale hair did not shine with unnatural luster, but lay fine and unruly around her shoulders, shades darker than it appeared at court. Even the magical glamer of her immaculate skin had lapsed — Ashen could see the uneven green of her eyes, the lines at the corners of her mouth, and the light spray of freckles across her nose.

Her true appearance was a vulnerability she afforded few others, Ashen knew, and it honored him to see it. He wondered if men would still find her beautiful like this, or if it was only the artifice they could love.

"Majesty, I apologize for intruding at this hour."

She continued writing, not looking up from her book. "What is it?"

Now that the moment had come, Ashen was less confident. "I had a vision," he blurted.

Without a word, the queen put down her pen and propped her chin on her hand, waiting. Though the queen knew of his magical talents, he could only imagine how this must look to her after his criticism of Ravano's visions in the carriage.

"As I was traversing the shadow gap, I saw something."

"That's not unusual, Ashen." The use of his informal name pleased him in ways he couldn't quite grasp.

"It is for me." Ashen described the phantom Calushain and the appearance of woman he knew to be Penumbra. When he described the red stone, the queen rose to her feet. Ashen's ears flicked to attention.

"Describe it again," she said, her gaze intent. Ashen tried to read her emotions — fear? anger? — but realized that her glamer had returned, her skin and hair turned radiant, her eyes vivid green. Whatever she was feeling laid behind her artifice now.

"A round red stone, a hand's breadth in size, polished. Black strands like liquid swimming within. She said you would know its importance."

"She said it was coming here?"

"'My gift is already on its way. The only question is who will receive it,'" Ashen quoted.

The queen turned away from him, biting down on one finely manicured fingernail.

"Majesty," he said after what he hoped was a courteous pause. "What is this gift?"

"Yes," she said in a small voice. She turned to face him again. This time, he saw the dark worry in her eyes. "Orison."

"I do not understand."

"Chaos. Ruin. The oldest magic. Old when the first humans first crept out of Eiler into the heat of the sun. You must get it for me, One-Howl. If it's in the city, the other lords must not learn of its existence. It would tear these negotiations apart."

"Why?" Ashen realized that the queen was afraid and, for the second time that day, felt fear himself.

The queen stood silent for a long time before replying. "Because of what it represents. The favor of dragons. The most powerful favor they have. Ashen, you must speak to Penumbra again."

A dragon's favor is the worst slavery of all, Ashen thought. Loyalty and dread churned in his stomach. Surely the queen could not trust the Semblance of Shadows. There must be some greater game he did not understand, and dared not ask about.

"But I refused her," he said.

"Then find her again!" she snapped, rounding on him. Ashen stepped back involuntarily.

I don't know how, Ashen began to say, then snapped his jaws shut. He understood at last that his atonement was upon him. He would find this orison for his queen, and if it brought all Calushain to ruin, as Penumbra promised, then so be it.

She was his Sworn. If she asked for the sun, he would climb the sky until he burned.

"It will be done, Majesty."

CHAPTER THREE

THE PRESTIGIOUS BASTARD CATERED TO a specific clientele: sorcerers and cheaters.

Mages from every part of the world brushed elbows in the Bastard without coming to blows. Waxy-skinned shamans played cards with geomancers; the shamans chanted quiet illusions to change their hands, while the geomancers magically stacked the deck with every shuffle. Battle-scarred Iron School mercenaries threw darts with the bearded Isoren from the Court of Stars. The mercenaries wound their reflexes spring-tight to take perfect shots, and the Isoren warped the dart mid-flight to strike false. Then everyone would drink and laugh.

Cheating at the Prestigious Bastard was both allowed and encouraged. The proprietor, a disillusioned Praxis mage from Snowcastle, had only one immutable rule: no blowing up the house or one another. Everything else was fair game.

On good nights, the bar sang with confluence, magical energies keening a crystalline madrigal within its walls. Fortunately for all, the power to cheat at cards was not enough to create much trouble, even in aggregate. Winning at cards at the Bastard was easy for everyone.

Unless they bore Imperial strands. Then it became much more difficult.

Wrynn tried to ignore the throbbing pain in his head and concentrate on the game in front of him instead of the whorls of purple ink encircling both forearms. There was no use in hiding the strands here. Even if he managed to cover them, the simplest magesight would reveal them, and reading auras was standard practice in the Bastard.

His opponent was a smug-looking, round-faced Theoris mage named Faunt. The Theoria were scholars and mathematicians. They dealt in abstracts and symbols. The man spread his cards between fat, ring-studded fingers and smiled. For all Wrynn knew, the other man wasn't even using his power to cheat. If Wrynn used his magesight with the strands on, he would send daggers of pain into his own temples.

Imperial strands were a punishment for refusing service to the Ladris Empire. He could still cast a few minor spells, for the price of considerable pain — but a major spell, the kind that could earn a living, would blow both his hands off at the wrist. The Praxis School did not take well to apostates.

The strands could be removed, and in Calushain any number of practitioners would be happy to do the job. But none worked for free, and Wrynn had stepped off a Merrekanis galleon with nothing but threadbare robes and enough coin to put a roof over his head. That coin was long since gone, and what little he had left, he was about to wager.

Faunt dealt, flicking cards across the table with practiced motions. Wrynn had his first good hand of the night, good enough to take home some real money. But the Theoris had been stingy with his bets all night, quietly collecting a pile of talons and folding whenever things looked dodgy.

The other man also seemed pleased with his cards. "Ten talons," he said, pushing a neat stack of coins forward on the table.

Wrynn shifted a bit in his seat, then tapped his power. A whisper of confluence crossed between them. The spell was a nudge, an emotional tweak to make the recipient feel insecure. Mental magic was Wrynn's specialty. He overpowered the spell by a touch, made it ostentatious, so the man would know what was happening. If the Theoris bought it, he'd think Wrynn was trying to get him to fold.

"See you and raise," Wrynn said. "Twenty." He stacked his coins, trying to look confident. If this hand went south, he'd be sleeping in the alley again tonight. Sober. But even more than a warm bed, he wanted to buy more lochweed for Story, and the girl had no idea how expensive those herbs actually were.

Faunt smirked. He'd felt the spell, and it bolstered his confidence instead of undermining it. Manipulating emotions magically tended to ruin even the best poker face. "Raise twenty."

Wrynn twisted the arcane flows, trying not to grimace at the lancing pain in his wrists. This time, he drove the man's confidence up further, masking it beneath a shrouding cantrip. The masking spell drove hot iron rods up both arms, making him breathless with pain. He grabbed his mug of beer and polished it off in two swallows.

"Raise another ten," he gasped, banging the mug on the table. He let his shoulders droop, ran nervous fingers through his red hair. *Might as well throw a mundane finesse in there.*

The Theoris nodded. "All in," he said, and shoved his pile of coins onto the table.

Wrynn shrugged, pushed his own meager holdings into the pot, and tossed down his cards. "Jack and seven, lion ascendant."

Faunt stared at the cards for a moment, then spread his own on the table. "King and five, dragon ascendant. You lose."

Crushed, Wrynn sat back and watched the man take the meager scrapings of his life. His gaze drifted to the dragon face card in Faunt's hand. The bronze ouroboros of Thesis stared back at him. The dragon had won again.

"That masking spell was good," the Theoris said. "But you overdid it. With those strands on you? You're trying too hard."

"I live life to the fullest and take no prisoners," Wrynn said sardonically. "Spare a talon to buy a man a drink?"

Faunt gave him a look of pity, flicked a coin onto the table, and left. Wrynn took a moment to soak up the contempt, then reached for the coin. At least there would be one last drink for the night.

A black-gloved hand reached over his shoulder and took the coin. Wrynn felt the point of a blade touch the back of his neck.

"Hello, Wrynn," a voice said.

Wrynn didn't move. "I beg your pardon, have we met?"

The blade left Wrynn's neck, and he turned slowly in his chair. The man before him was tall, with knotted muscles drawn taut by sorcery, a long black braid over one shoulder, and heavy brows over a lean face shadowed with stubble. The left side of the man's face was black with bruises, his lip split in two places, and the sword in his hand crawled with smoldering sigils of faint orange light.

"Jhal," Wrynn said. "Thought I lost you back in Surain."

"Oh, you did," the Iron School mage said. He still held the blade, pointed at Wrynn's throat. Wrynn spread his hands, palms up, fingers flat, in the traditional sign of surrender among mages. "But you were never too skilled at disappearing."

"Don't suppose I can offer you my winnings and we could just forget this whole thing."

Jhal pocketed Wrynn's last coin. "You didn't win."

"You've got me there."

Jhal's cold, lopsided smile didn't reach his eyes. "The Seventh House paid me well to find you, Wrynn. You can't have thought I would just give up."

Wrynn's throat closed. Silence fell around them as players looked up from their cards. Every expatriate in Calushain knew and feared the name of the Seventh House, the Empire's political assassins. Even kings themselves were not beyond their reach.

"Oh, is that who's after me?" Wrynn asked, trying to seem nonchalant.

"It is."

"Surely not," Wrynn said. "Because I burned a few moldy old scrolls back in Praxa, they're going to send the House of Serpents after me?"

"I didn't ask why they want you," Jhal said. "I'm just here to fetch the goods."

The bartender walked over cautiously, hands at his sides.

"We don't want any trouble here, friends," he said to Jhal. "If you have Imperial business, take it outside."

"Wrynn won't be any trouble," Jhal said, his eyes locked with Wrynn's. "He's going to come with me to the gaol, and tomorrow he'll be on a ship bound for Snowcastle. Isn't that right, Wrynn?"

The Bastard took a collective breath and held it, waiting.

Wrynn looked down at the strands on his wrists. He'd never been a fighter by nature. He preferred the subtle magics, the quiet manipulation of energies. If not for the strands, he could lay down a swath of destruction if he wished, perhaps even enough to take down an Iron School disciple like Jhal. He could gather his power for a surprise first strike and send Jhal through a window. Perhaps he could even unravel Jhal's memory, make the bounty hunter forget his quarry.

If not for the strands.

But that had been another life. All he felt now was despair pooling in his belly. His power was crippled. Wrynn could no more defeat Jhal than he could arm-wrestle the wind. He tried to tell himself that now was not the moment, that he would pick a more opportune time to battle. But it only felt like giving up.

Wrynn stood slowly. Jhal put the point of the blade against his throat, a smirk on his face.

"What are we waiting for?" Wrynn asked. "Let's go."

Every Counting Day, before she presented her stolen goods to Galon Luster at Bladesbarrow, Story liked to take her sack of goods to a rooftop above the quays and watch the ships.

This was her tradition. The narrow alleys of Harrows and Fiver's Quay formed a second road high above the city streets, and the Scarlets rarely looked up. Here, she was as safe from scrutiny as it was possible to be. On the streets, in the back alleys and dark corners where Story made her living, focusing on the next moment was the key to survival.

Down there, it was easy to forget why she stole, why she struggled, why she lived every day with secrets that could mean her death. Up here, the bright sky and salt air put her mind at ease, and she felt the person she wanted to be linger close, almost within her grasp.

Most of all, the sight of the ships fired her imagination. Story had never lived anywhere but Calushain, or even traveled beyond its walls. Even places in the city like the Manse and the Stormhelt were forbidden to the likes of her. The ships represented a vast and unknown world. As one of the biggest trade ports between the Empire and Esterlund, Calushain attracted ships from across Lastris.

She sat and drew her knees up under her chin, looking down at the distant ships and their crew. Today alone, she saw bone-oared longboats from Ivlein, fat trade galleys from Merrekan, a privateer from Karsh, and an ivory-sailed galleon from Castariel. Story would imagine their journeys, weave stories about their crews, and assess each one as a potential means of escape from the city.

The Ivlein crew looked too rough and grim for her taste, with their black cloaks and close-cropped hair and dour expressions. The Karsh sailors were nothing more than pirates — or so the other thieves at Bladesbarrow had told her. The Castari looked fastidious enough, with their shining armor and white tabards, but Story had heard that the Castari were mostly religious zealots, likely to ship her to Tyr Challerain and put her in a convent.

The Merrekani, though, looked like prosperous merchants, dressed in functional silks and fine hats. Story imagined signing on as one of the crew, seeing the serpent cities in Sethwas, the brass towers of Praxa. She could go anywhere she wanted. Be anyone she wanted.

That was fantasy, of course, and she knew it. A Merrekani ship was just as likely to take a dull route between Mudfoot and the West, carrying spices or Imperial prisoners. Choosing her destination was a luxury she could never afford.

But she could choose to leave. And anywhere was better than here.

Crux dropped his sack with a thump and sat down beside her, starting her out of her reverie.

"Drooling over the sailors again, little sister?" He grinned.

Like Story, Crux was slight, dark-haired, and nimble in dark gray pants and a battered black coat. As he sat, she spied the outline of the sheathed longknife inside his coat. Like Story, he traveled well-armed.

She nudged her brother with her shoulder in a perfunctory show of affection.

"Yes, they're all so handsome," she said, pointing to a cluster of black-cloaked drokai merchant marines, their hair greased into bright clan colors, stony gray skin lined with ritual scars. "I'm thinking of marrying the big one with half a jaw."

"I heard the drokai have two or three wives apiece. Think of all the company you'd have. And the festive nights—"

Story grimaced. "You're disgusting."

"Just looking out for you."

"I'm sure."

"How'd you do for Counting Day?" Crux asked.

"Not bad. A nice cup, some jewels. A couple smell-sticks."

"Oh, that's what that stench was. I thought you'd fallen into a privy."

She punched him on the shoulder. His hand grabbed her wrist, so fast her eye barely followed it. He examined the deep scratches along her arm.

"You run into some trouble?"

"Nothing serious." She pulled her arm away. "I fell through some flimsy roofing."

The lie came easily, as did the guilt at the silently growing divide between them. Ever since she'd started holding back loot for herself, she'd tried to make every job sound as boring as possible. She didn't want Crux knowing about the raizhi just yet. At best, he'd have questions, which made her nervous. At worst, he'd tell Galon, who'd assign her a partner, and that would be the end of her plans.

Over the past few months, their relationship had begun to change. Much of it had to do with Crux's rise in the ranks at Bladesbarrow. Just as Galon had used Story's small frame and unremarkable face to shape her into a good burglar, he'd used Crux's short stature and plain demeanor to make Crux into a thief and killer. No one expected slim, mild Crux to be good with a knife. Most of them never saw it coming until too late.

Crux had always made a show of being the reluctant fighter, doing only what was necessary to keep himself and his sister alive. But Story saw the look in his eyes when he worked. He enjoyed killing. Working so closely with Galon had changed him, and as much as Story loved him, she could no longer trust him.

His eyes searched her face for a moment, all trace of good humor gone.

"You should be more careful," he said, and let her go.

"I will," she said, trying to sound sincere. "Thanks."

"Sky's turning orange," Crux said as he stood. His coat billowed behind him in the evening breeze. "We should get to Bladesbarrow before dark."

"I'm ready," she said. She'd wrapped the coins and jewelry tightly in oilcloth. The sack barely made a sound as she hefted it over her shoulder.

As Crux leaped across the rooftops toward Harrows, Story took a final look at the quay, where the Merrekani merchant ship hoisted sail for more promising waters.

"I'm so ready," she said.

To outsiders, Bladesbarrow was just another dilapidated Harrows edifice. Once, it had been a temple to the etheric Castar, and missionaries from across the sea had brought the sardonic wisdom of that demigod to the Red Cities. But fading relations with the Lotus Throne had eroded sympathy for foreign religions and the missionaries had abandoned their temple. Now nothing of its glory remained but chipped stone and peeling murals of silver and blue. Galon had made it his own. The Scarlets knew nothing of the underground tunnels that led from Bladesbarrow to every part of the city, nor of the labyrinthine snarl of ledges and rooftops above.

As the sky darkened over Calushain, Story followed Crux across the Harrows rooftops and onto the second-floor balcony of Bladesbarrow. They slipped through a window into the attic, stepping along a predetermined path to avoid the many traps disguised as debris. They moved down the spiral stairs, past the hidden guards at the rear of the nave, and into the cloister, where they took the cellar door behind the altar to the catacombs.

Beneath the rotting exterior lay the truth of Bladesbarrow — a series of roomy catacombs, the heart of Galon's underground empire. The monks of Castar had built these catacombs to house the dead, but Galon's men had transformed it into a refuge for the living. Bladesbarrow featured rows of stiff but serviceable bunks, an armory, a kitchen, and a squalid and largely self-defeating public bath.

Galon's crew had no name, no symbol. Few even knew who he was. Galon's ambition was not to infamy, but to amassing quiet fortune in Calushain's shadows.

On Counting Day, as it was called, all the cutpurses and second-stories dumped their goods on the great round table in the main chamber, making as great a noise as possible, while onlookers drank and cheered. Galon picked what he liked from the pile and dispensed bonuses to whomever he favored that week. The loot remained on the table all night while everyone drank themselves blind. Then Galon's reckoners hauled it away to the treasury to count, appraise, and redistribute accordingly: the lion's share for Galon, and a fair wage for his crew.

Every so often, someone had a little too much to drink, and tried to slip something off the table. They received one warning. Those thieves who persisted, or who otherwise crossed Galon, now guarded the proceedings as a row of severed heads, kept in pickling jars above Galon's velvet throne. Galon never reminded anyone of his disapproval when it came to stealing from their own. He let the grisly display speak of loyalty for him. Story avoided looking at the heads whenever she entered Galon's sanctum.

Counting Day was already in full swing when Story and Crux arrived. A dozen lanterns lit the vast round chamber, the center table heaped with coins, jewels, fur and spices.

Brother and sister emptied their sacks onto the table, adding to the noise of the room. Thieves, brawlers and burglars applauded as they added to the week's haul.

Galon shouted at Crux from across the room. He lounged on his velvet chair, a blonde woman on his lap. He was tall and pale, a mane of white hair framing his gaunt cheeks and thin red lips. His brown eyes were nearly black under heavy brows. Galon had the look of a man who had made a conscious decision to stay hungry.

"That's my Crux!" Galon bellowed. "The boy who can open anything!"

Crux lifted his arms to the crowd, who whooped as if he were a champion gladiator in the Snowcastle arena.

Story tried to be happy for her brother. After completing their training years ago, Galon had never so much as nodded at Story again. Even though everything she knew of Galon told her it was best to stay out of his eye, being in her brother's shadow galled her. But then she would remember the row of heads over his throne, and remind herself what Galon's attention could cost.

She jostled her way through the crowd to the kegs to get herself a drink, ignoring the steady stream of leers, catcalls and grunting propositions. One of Galon's retinue, Nibs, a burly legbreaker with a wiry crown of black hair, shambled over to her, drunk. His breath was sickly-sweet with Karsh rum.

"Hallo, girlie," he said with a lecherous grin as he groped at her. "Give us a kiss—"

Story sidestepped, hooking her foot around his ankle, using his own momentum against him. He toppled onto his back with a bellow, and she delivered a good stomp to his midsection.

"Good seeing you again, Nibs," she said as Nibs vomited noisily.

A roar of jeers and laughter went up. No one came to Nibs' defense. Galon's thieves were rough and crude, and as one of the few females on the crew, Story got more than her share of unwelcome attention. But the crew did have a certain sense of fair play. A man who laid hands on her against her will was breaking the rules, and she was free to put him on the ground for it.

She poured herself a pint of warm bitters, downing it quickly so that she could get a little drunk without having to taste it too much. The cluster of men around the kegs seemed to take this as a sign of comradeship, and applauded wildly, as if a girl doing a little hard drinking were somehow novel in Bladesbarrow.

Story saluted with her mug, then filled it up again.

"Easy, sister," Crux said from behind her. "You might get sallied enough to make some bad decisions."

Again, she felt that momentary flicker of annoyance. Crux had his adoring crowd. Why was he sneaking up behind her, as if she couldn't take care of herself?

"Already made them," Story said, and belched lightly.

"I think he's sweet on you," Crux said, pointing to Nibs, who had picked himself up off the floor. Nibs nodded blearily, as if to acknowledge he'd had that coming. He fetched a mug, started drinking again, and appeared to forget all about it.

Crux smiled. "Maybe you should ask him to dance."

"No thanks." Her brother's teasing usually amused her, but lately it had turned sour. Too often, his jabs seemed pointed and accompanied by suspicious glances, as if he hoped his joke would irritate her into revealing some secret.

"So it looks like you did pretty well sacking that sorcerer's place," Crux said.

"It could've gone better," Story said, her tongue loosened a little by drink. "He had a raizhi—"

Too late, she remembered she wasn't going to tell him that.

"Nothing too vicious," she added quickly, "but I had to use all my lochweed to shake it."

Crux's mouth gave a moue of disapproval. "You're careless. Always rushing in. How about a little reconnoitering first?"

"I don't tell you how to pick locks, Crux."

He drew himself up smugly. "Because there's nothing you can teach me."

"And you've got something to teach *me?*"

Crux reached inside his vest for a small brown bag, tied tight with leather strips. He held it up for Story to smell. The odor was thick and pungent, like flowers gone to rot. One sniff made her light-headed.

"Nightburn," Crux said. "A nose full of this stuff will put anyone under for hours."

"Do you use it on your girlfriends to keep them from running away?"

"Very funny. You don't even have to drug their food. Just put it somewhere where they'll take a deep breath of it and you can do your work in peace."

"Sure, assuming they don't notice the horrible smell and splitting headache."

"That's why you wait until they're asleep," Crux said. "Are you learning yet?"

"Fine. So give me some."

"The lesson is free. The herb is expensive. Get your own."

Story swung her arm underhand as if to slap the bag into his face. Crux flinched, putting the bag away with a glare. "Harpy."

"Jackass."

They laughed and returned to the kegs for more beer. The Counting Day atmosphere grew more convivial as the loot piled high on the table and the drink flowed freely. Crux and Story sat together off to one side, watching the raucous display.

As Crux finished his third pint, his expression softened suddenly, and Story felt his hand close around her arm. "Listen, can I talk to you in private for a moment?"

She glanced at him, instantly worried. "Sure."

Crux led her through two short tunnels to an empty chamber. This had once been the temple's library — now strewn garbage and the wreckage of the temple's bookshelves were the only decoration. They sat on a pair of crates in the far corner.

"What is it?" Story asked. Her brother had that face he always made when he was about to confess something awful or troublesome.

Crux chewed on a thumbnail. "Story, I've been thinking. I want us to do a job together again."

She blinked at him. "What? Why?"

"I want to get you in Galon's eye. I know he doesn't pay attention to your work. And I think it's because your scores tend to be... a little on the safe side."

"Excuse me?"

"Don't take it personally. I just mean your jobs lack a certain flair. You need something big that will get you noticed."

She rolled her eyes. "Crux, my jobs bring in money for the crew. I don't get caught, I don't blab to the Scarlets, I don't steal from the red list." The red list was Galon's list of forbidden targets, mostly relatives or valued contacts.

"Yeah, but that's dull," Crux said.

"No, it's *smart*. You got Galon's attention because you're fast and strong and like hitting people. And because you're a boy."

"That's not true."

"Yes it is. I'm sorry, Crux, but I'm not going to endanger myself just because you think it will get me a promotion."

Crux opened his mouth to argue, then slumped with hurt and disappointment. Story felt a pang of regret — but Crux had played

48

on her emotions before. She could never be sure when his emotions weren't an act.

"I miss the old jobs, Story. I'd open the locks, you'd get in the small spaces no one else could go."

She stared at him incredulously. "What's to miss? The bruises and splinters?"

"The excitement."

"Getting nicked and eating gaol food?"

"The adventure!"

She laughed softly. "You're insane."

Still, she understood. Their early days with Galon *had* seemed more like an adventure, the two of them against the rich and powerful of Calushain, and less like a dangerous job. In those days, Crux had been someone she could trust. She missed it. Perhaps he did too.

He touched her hand hesitantly. "I want to work together again, Story. Like we did before we..." He shrugged.

"Grew up?" Story said.

"I suppose."

Story looked at the dirty floor of Bladesbarrow, listening to the sounds of music and celebration from the next room. There was little she would miss about her life in Calushain, but the thought that this might be her last Counting Day filled her with a sudden, inexplicable regret.

Think this over, Story—

She took a deep breath. "All right, Crux. I'll do it."

He sat up straight. "You will?"

"You already have something in mind, don't you?"

"You *do* know me."

Chapter Four

In the interest of efficiency, the founders of Calushain had built their gaol as a six-story tower just north of Fiver's Quay. The lowest and busiest level was reserved for minor offenders: pick-pockets, burglars and drunkards, who moved in and out on a daily basis as their crimes were judged and fines sentenced. As offenses grew more severe, the prisoners ascended to cells on the higher floors, with the upper floors reserved for murderers and traitors.

Wrynn had been in and out of the gaol many times, but never ascended higher than the first floor. This time, he counted the risers as the Scarlets escorted him up the winding stairwell. Six floors, all the way to the top.

Once there, they shoved him into a dark, hot cell and slammed the bars shut behind him without a word. Even Jhal didn't drop by to gloat. Still a little drunk from his evening at the Bastard, but not nearly drunk enough to numb the despair in his heart, Wrynn lay on the narrow cot and dozed fitfully until morning.

The rising heat woke him early. Already, the cell stank of sour sweat and hot stone. Wrynn laid on the cot, hands folded on his chest. His cell measured three paces by two, with high narrow windows over each cell the only illumination. On the top floor of the tower, the black stones cooked the cell like an oven. Aside from the heat, there was little way to tell what time of day it was.

Not that it mattered. No help was coming for him. In Surain, he'd had friends. Here, he had no one, except perhaps Story. But he couldn't bear the thought of telling her the truth, even if she knew where he was. He was stuck here, with no idea how long he'd be waiting, or even what judgment he was waiting for.

That was the crowning irony of his life. The Seventh House, one of the most feared organizations in the Empire, wanted him for extradition back to Snowcastle, and he had no idea why. He could only speculate that they didn't yet want him dead.

But that isn't true, is it, Wrynn? You know what they want you for.

He pushed the thought away. The Imperial Academy at Praxa had revoked his rank and fitted him with strands to keep him from ever effectively using magic again. If they, or the Seventh House, expected him to recant or otherwise undo his apostasy, they would get nothing from him. Wrynn was nobody. His public execution would barely draw a crowd.

He heard footsteps and a metallic clatter as a Scarlet slid a tray of food under the bars to his cell. At least that was something. They weren't leaving him to starve.

The guard hobbled off. Wrynn rolled over to pick up the tray.

"Don't eat the stew," a voice said.

Wrynn looked up, startled. Another prisoner sat in the cell across the corridor. Between inebriation and restless slumber, Wrynn hadn't even noticed.

"What?"

"It's tagol," the man said. "They take the dead ones that get disease from the canals, chop them up after they've been rotting in the sun, put it in the stew. Eat it and you'll be sicking up whatever's left in your guts."

Wrynn picked up the chunk of black bread instead. "The bread all right?"

The man shrugged. "It's half wood shavings, but you can keep it down."

Wrynn sat back against the wall. "So what's a Halak doing in a Red Cities prison?"

"Waiting to go back to Rull Halak," the man said quietly. Something in his voice sounded vaguely familiar. "Where are you from?"

"Ladris. Also going back home, apparently for my execution."

"My condolences."

Wrynn chewed on the bread, which did indeed taste like wood shavings. "How'd you land in here?"

"I'm politically unpopular back home," the Halak said. "Bounty hunter picked up my contract."

Wrynn blinked. "It wasn't Jhal Alafein by any chance, was it?"

"Tall fellow, braid, face looks like it's carved out of wood?"

Something in the man's voice seemed familiar. Wrynn looked over at him. In the faint light, he could barely make out the man's dark gray hair and gaunt cheekbones. "Wait. You're the man from Dockside! You saved me from those men!"

"Those men were after me," the man said. "Trust me, saving you from the stew was a greater service."

"Then I suppose I owe you twice over."

"I suppose you do," the man said with quiet amusement.

"My name's Wrynn Sendir."

The Halak nodded. "Mar Dunnac. So what did you do to earn a trip to the top floor, Wrynn Sendir?"

"I'm not really sure," Wrynn said evasively. "I'm not anybody important."

"I doubt that," Dunnac said. "Those Imperial strands on your wrists, the House of Serpents whispering your name. You've got to be important to someone."

Fear clutched the base of Wrynn's skull. "How did you know about that?"

"Saw the strands the other night. Heard the Scarlets whispering about the last bit."

"Oh. The truth is, I really don't know why the Seventh House wants me."

"That must be frightening."

Gnawing at a fingernail, Wrynn changed the subject. "So, you're the one that gave Jhal that black eye and split lip, then?"

"We had a disagreement about my return home," Dunnac said.

"Well, as far as I'm concerned, that makes us friends. He's been chasing me since I left Praxa."

"That's a long way to chase someone, new friend."

Wrynn couldn't tell if the man was being sarcastic or not. "I'm just glad someone could pay him out. With these strands on, I'm no match for Jhal."

"I bloodied his lip well enough, and I've no magic at all."

"I'm not much of a fighter."

"Maybe you should look into that," Dunnac said.

Time passed. The heat rose. Wrynn thought to time his stay with meals, as he often had while languishing on the first floor. But the Scarlets did not return to feed either of them. It soon grew too hot to talk comfortably, and so Wrynn dozed again, his throat dry, his stomach grumbling with hunger.

His cell was dark when he woke to the clang of a key hitting the lock. He had just opened his eyes when a boot smashed into his ribs. He rolled to the greasy floor, clutching his side.

"None of that, please," a delicate male voice said.

"Just discouraging our boy from running," Jhal's voice replied.

The man next to Jhal was short and round, with droopy eyes and a thick mustache, dressed in silk the color of tarnished bronze. Behind them, a bored Scarlet held the cell door open.

"He seems perfectly discouraged already. I don't want him damaged," the man in silk said. "Pick him up, please, and let's get to work."

"With pleasure." Jhal hauled Wrynn to his feet and shoved him through the cell door. Wrynn stumbled and struck the bars of Dunnac's cell.

The man in silk waved with a fishy hand. "The Halak too."

Jhal scowled. "He wasn't part of the arrangement."

"What arrangement?" Wrynn asked.

"Bring him," the man in silk said.

Jhal growled. "Move it," he said, and gave Wrynn another push as the guard moved to release Dunnac from his cell.

They were escorted back down the winding stairs by Jhal, the well-dressed man and three guards, and hustled past the main foyer and through the front doors. Balmy night air greeted them, and

Wrynn had just enough time to draw in a grateful breath before he and Dunnac were shoved into a black carriage of canvas and steel. Two more Scarlets barred the doors from the outside. A moment later, the carriage jerked into motion.

Wrynn examined the interior of the carriage, running his hand along the door. The carriage was solidly made, obviously for transporting prisoners. A thin strip in the steel doors let in a slip of moonlight. Otherwise, the carriage was dark and empty.

Fear began to well up inside Wrynn. This was not what he'd expected. The man in silk dressed like a Red Cities merchant, not a bureaucrat or magistrate. And why was Jhal taking orders from him?

"Don't suppose you have a knife on you," Dunnac said. The Halak sat back, hands folded, apparently relaxed.

Wrynn gave him a skeptical look. "Left my extensive arsenal in the cell, alas."

Dunnac pointed upward. "The roof is canvas. With a knife, we could cut through, get out that way."

"You'd be decapitated."

Dunnac shrugged, resigned. "Have to entertain myself somehow."

Wrynn squinted out the narrow windows, but could see nothing but a dark gray blur. "They must be taking us to the harbor," he said. "Putting us on a ship."

Dunnac shook his head. "We turned right after we left the gaol. That's north. Deeper into the city. I'd guess someone wants to talk to us."

Wrynn scowled. "Why would anyone want to talk to me?"

"I've asked myself that same question," Dunnac said dryly.

Wrynn gave the Halak an annoyed look. "You seem awfully nonchalant about all this. We could be going to our deaths, you know."

"Flailing about in panic isn't as helpful as it might seem."

"I am not *flailing about in panic*."

Dunnac said nothing, only stared placidly until Wrynn sat back with a huff. They rode in silence for a while, the sound of hooves muffled through the steel doors. Wrynn felt the front of the carriage tip upward. Dunnac had been right — they were going north, uphill. Wrynn began to tense again.

"You never told me what you were in for," he said, hoping a conversation would calm his nerves.

"You never asked," Dunnac replied.

Wrynn looked at him expectantly. The Halak stared back in silence.

"Well?" Wrynn finally asked, exasperated.

A smile touched the corner of Dunnac's mouth. "Rull Halak has grown theologically troubled. My political views there are... considered dangerous. I left. They want me back. That's basically the story."

"That doesn't really explain much," Wrynn said.

"Imagine that." Dunnac's steady gaze held a silent challenge. Wrynn decided against further conversation, and they rode the rest of the way in silence.

Wrynn estimated a half-hour's ride before the carriage stopped. The bars slammed back and the Scarlets ushered them out. The carriage was parked in front of a townhouse of sandy brick. The front walk was lined with anemic ferns. A fountain trickled brackish water into a dirty granite basin. This was a nobleman's house that had seen better days.

The man in silk stood nearby, Jhal at his side.

"Please, be welcome," the man in silk said, gesturing to the house as if they were honored guests.

They walked inside, past a narrow foyer and into a parlor lined with bookshelves, with a threadbare carpet the color of old wine.

"Make yourselves comfortable," the man in silk said. Dunnac slouched back into a chair, putting one foot up on the seat. Wrynn sat hesitantly on a divan. Jhal stood against one wall, looking unhappy.

"Are you thirsty?" Without waiting for an answer, the man in silk rang a bell, then sat across from them. A servant arrived with a tray bearing wine and tiny loaves of soft white bread.

"All right," Wrynn said, rubbing his chin as he stared at the food and drink. His stomach rumbled. "I'm guessing this is Highbridge, which means you're a merchant, not a noble. You're not wearing Calushain robes of office, so you don't work for the queen. I haven't worked out the rest yet."

The man in silk took a wine glass and leaned back in his chair. "Let's begin with introductions, then. My name is Shoneg Vulker. You both know Jhal, and of course we know who the two of you are."

"Fine. What is all this?" Wrynn asked, his patience nearing its end. He was tired, hungry, afraid, and still in no small amount of pain from the kick to his ribs.

If Shoneg was offended, he gave no sign. He pulled two envelopes from inside his robes and laid them on the table. One bore the wax seal of the Empire, the other a seal Wrynn didn't recognize.

"Those are your bounties with the Empire and Rull Halak," Shoneg said. "I've paid your bonds. By law, you are now mine to turn over to your respective homelands."

"But you don't want that," Dunnac said, taking a piece of bread. "You want us for something else."

Shoneg smiled. "Quite right. As far as Calushain is concerned, you are now beneath notice. That suits my purpose. I'm looking to make a dangerous acquisition, and I need desperate men."

"What makes you think we're that desperate?" Wrynn asked.

"Your impending executions," Shoneg said. "You're both facing a death sentence back home. Look at your bounties if you don't believe me."

Dunnac stopped chewing. His eyes narrowed. Wrynn looked from the Halak to the merchant, then to the glass of wine in front of him. He was thirsty, but not ready to trust Shoneg just yet.

"As I said, I know who you are, Mar Dunnac," Shoneg said. "I know what pursues you."

Dunnac frowned with displeasure. "What are your terms?"

The merchant looked pleased. "You get me what I want. I pay Jhal handsomely, and he informs Snowcastle and Rull Halak that you're both dead. You'll then be free to live in miserable obscurity for the rest of your days."

Wrynn barely suppressed a groan. This kind of scheming was all too common in the Empire. He hadn't missed it.

"That's the payment," he said to Shoneg. "What's the job?"

"So glad you asked." With a smile, Shoneg produced a small, ornate wooden box from beneath his chair. He opened the lid to reveal a round crimson stone resting on a bed of blue silk. Mottled swirls of black and red decorated its surface.

Wrynn's blood froze. He grabbed a glass of wine and drained it.

Dunnac leaned forward to examine the stone. "What is it?"

Shoneg looked to Wrynn, like a proud parent encouraging a child. "Wrynn knows. Don't you?"

"An orison," Wrynn blurted.

Shoneg looked pleased. "I see I've chosen wisely."

"I don't think you have," Wrynn said. "My answer's no."

"What's an orison?" Dunnac asked, looking warily from Wrynn to Shoneg.

"There's no need to fear," Shoneg said. "This is merely a replica."

"I *know* it's a replica," Wrynn said. "I'm not a fool. Can I go back to prison now, please?"

"One of you tell me why this is important," Dunnac snapped.

Shoneg cleared his throat, then gestured to Wrynn. "If you would?"

Wrynn pushed back his red hair. He was sweating — from the wine, the heat, or fear, he wasn't certain.

"First, you have to understand a bit about magic. Sorcery draws upon the power of Kulraizhan, the world the dragon semblances come from. It transfers power from that world into this one. It allows a sorcerer to shape reality. But it strains reality at the same time, sometimes violently. We call that strain 'confluence.'"

Wrynn had taught this to first-year students in Praxa. He lifted his wine glass, realized it was empty, and put it down. Shoneg gestured for more.

"All sorcery draws on draconic power," he continued. "But some — a very few — can draw upon that power without causing much confluence. They can use magic at will, with almost no limitations. We call them the etherics."

"People like Lond, Castar, Cinder, Drog Ungru, Valakyr," Shoneg said to Dunnac. "Even the queen of this city, or so she claims."

"The Ladrish gods," Dunnac said with contempt in his voice.

"They're not gods," Wrynn said. "They're people with the power of gods, given to them by the dragons themselves."

Jhal sneered. "That's blasphemy, sorcerer."

"Maybe in Ladris," Wrynn said, his gaze fixed on Shoneg. "Out here, people understand where the real power lies."

Shoneg smirked. The servant arrived with more wine. Wrynn sipped this time.

"The jewel's an orison," Wrynn said. "I suppose you'd call it a form of communion with Kulraizhan. They're made by the semblances, as gifts to the ones they favor. That's the legend, anyway. Those who tap the orison's power and survive become etherics."

Shoneg laughed, as if this all delighted him. "But it's deadly. Legends are full of dead heroes who squared off with a semblance. Kulraizhan rushes into them and rewrites the history of their soul. If they can't control the confluence, they're simply torn apart. First mentally, then physically. It's a gift and a test."

"So the orison kills those who touch it?" Dunnac asked, drawing back in his chair.

"Not quite," Shoneg said. "You can touch one and not be harmed. You have to know what the artifact is, know what it can do, and desire the power it contains. The semblances can't judge the ignorant."

"Or so the Tome of Shadows says." Wrynn drank to mask his look of concern. For a merchant, Shoneg knew a lot about the inner workings of sorcery — and for a Halak who was supposed to hate magic, Dunnac suddenly seemed much too interested.

"So why not send ignorant men to do this job?" Dunnac asked.

Shoneg sipped wine. "The ignorant get careless easily. I want people who will show the artifact, and the job, the proper reverence."

"Even possessing one is enough power to frighten sane men," Wrynn said. "Which could mean an awful lot of political influence. What is this really about?"

Shoneg shook his head. "I'm not political, Wrynn. I want the purse this artifact will fetch. Nothing more."

Wrynn frowned and kept his doubt to himself. "The Empire and the Red Cities could easily go to war if they knew an orison was there for the taking."

The merchant smiled indulgently. "I love a risky investment. It's a dangerous job, and that's why I chose you. What if I told you it was in the city, right now?"

"I'd ask when the first ship sailed back to Snowcastle," Wrynn said. "I don't know about the Red Cities, but carrying an orison is punishable by death in the Empire. I'll take my chances with the Serpent's mercy."

"This isn't a thief's work," Shoneg said. "I already have a man holding it for me. I'll tell you where to get it, and you'll retrieve it from him."

"I'll do it," Dunnac said, finally picking up his wine glass.

Wrynn glared at him. "You don't know what you're getting into." He turned back to Shoneg. "How do you know we won't just flee the city with orison in hand?"

Shoneg counted off on his fingers. "You're wanted by the Empire, you were living on the street prior to your imprisonment, and you're reluctant to take the job. Not to be impolite, but you're not the sort of man who'd want such responsibility for long."

Wrynn jerked his head at Dunnac. "And him?"

"The Halakin have no desire to see their beloved Silandra awake." Shoneg spread his hands, as if that settled the matter. "I assure you, Wrynn Sendir, this deal is very simple. You retrieve the package, you give it to Jhal, and you leave the city as free men. But my time is limited, and my patience at an end. Will you take my offer, or not?"

Wrynn grimaced. He was tempted to ask what would happen if he declined, but the bounties on the table had already made that clear. It was this or death.

Fine, then. If this was his choice, then he would negotiate the only way he could. "I'll need my magic. If I'm going to do this, I want the strands off."

Jhal's eyes bulged in anger. For a moment, Wrynn feared Shoneg might laugh in his face. Then the merchant laughed easily and nodded.

"I know a man who will unravel them. I'll even pay the fee."

Wrynn tapped his fingers on the arm of his chair, searching for some kind of certainty. The only certainty that lay before him was the gallows. This merchant's plan was naïve and probably doomed. But with the strands off his wrists, he at least stood a chance when Jhal inevitably betrayed him.

"All right," he said. "You have a deal."

Shoneg smiled broadly. "Excellent. Tonight, you will dine and drink with me, and enjoy a night's sleep in soft beds. Tomorrow, you can begin your work. Congratulations. You're about to become free men."

CHAPTER FIVE

"WHY DID I LET YOU TALK ME INTO THIS?" Story asked.

Crux grinned back. "Because you knew it would be fun."

The two of them ran along the narrow roofs of a row of Highbridge houses, leaping over the narrow gaps with practiced ease. The roofs sloped sharply down over winding stone streets. One wrong step would send either of them tumbling down, to broken bones or worse.

Still, Story felt an old familiar rush, being up above the prying eyes of the Scarlets. The sun warmed their backs as they made their way east toward the center of the city. From here, she could see the colorful lines of Highbridge, sprawled out in painted glory: reds and blues and greens, dormers and balconies illuminated with the orange glow of the sun.

Highbridge was the district for merchants and nobles: those rich enough to live in the north end of the city, but not quite rich enough for the Manse, which belonged to the Queen of Storms and her immediate court. Sacking a Highbridge house was a risky job, but not as risky as some. Story had seen enough of sorcerers' abodes for a while.

It was still too early to do anything but watch, so they climbed to the roof of an abandoned Londic temple after leaping across to the decaying staircase winding along the outer wall. They sat on the stone balustrade, legs dangling over the edge as they looked southeast toward the Star. Side by side, they waited for the sun to go down.

"You didn't have to be in such a rush," Story said.

"It's your fault. You made us late by searching after that drunk."

Story had insisted they go by the Doorstop and look for Wrynn, whom she hadn't seen since the morning of her run-in with the guardian demon. He wasn't in his crate, and Bront hadn't seen him. It wasn't like Wrynn to just disappear for very long.

"Wrynn is not a *drunk*. All right, he is, a little. But he's my friend."

Up here, the air was free of the reek of urine and grime. There was only the cool scent of the salt breeze and the gently rolling clouds. They leaned forward in comfortable silence, shoulders nearly touching. Her heart still pounding a little from the journey, Story watched the insectile flow of shoppers and vendors crowding the Star.

"So what house are we hitting once it's dark enough?" Story asked at last. "I know you have it all picked out."

Crux pointed northeast to the red gambrel roof of a three-story town house. "I've been casing it for a couple of days. There's just one mercenary guard and he's a drunkard who gets soused by mid-afternoon. So, just your type."

She ignored the jab. "How many people?"

"An old man and his mistress. Nobleman from Scarl. I figure he's got an attic full of old junk we can pilfer."

Story peered at the house. The house featured a wide third-floor balcony, but she saw no easy way to reach it from the street. The front and back were too far away from nearby buildings.

"There's a drain pipe on the back side, facing the alley," Crux said. "We can snake up it and make our way along the roof to the balcony."

Story wrinkled her nose. "That roof's pretty steep."

"Criticizing me already?" Crux teased.

"No! But if it rains, those tiles will be slicker than a bag of wet snakes. Why today?"

He nudged her with his shoulder. "Because today is as good as forever. You're the second-story girl, you'll be fine." He looked skyward. "Besides, I prayed to the semblances for clear weather."

Story rolled her eyes. "Oh, *that* ought to do it."

Crux scowled at her sarcasm. "You don't believe in the dragons, do you?"

"I believe in them," Story said, drawing her knees up under her chin. "I just don't think they believe in us. I just don't see how the dragons could care about us, any more than we cared about that bunch of baby spiders that hatched in the molding of our window when we were kids. Remember that?"

Crux smiled. "I remember."

"They were so tiny, and mindless, and crawled everywhere. The only time we noticed them at all was when they bothered us, and then we just squashed them without a second thought. Do you think we cared if the spiders prayed for a clear sky?"

Crux groaned. "Why would they create something just to abandon it?"

"Ask our parents," she said quietly.

"That's not fair. We don't know why they left us."

"We don't know why the semblances do what they do, either."

"I suppose," Crux said, sulking a bit. "I just prayed because I want this to go right, Story. We worked so well together, once upon a time. Didn't we?"

"We did," Story said, nudging him affectionately with her arm. "And I don't mind that you prayed. We've always needed every edge we could get."

Her brother smiled at that. "I'm glad you're here," he said.

Story tried to ignore the sudden pang of melancholy that lanced through her. They watched the Star in silence as the sun went down.

The alchemist's shop in Lowbridge smelled of acid and lavender. The sun painted greasy strokes of orange light along cluttered racks of bottles and jugs as Wrynn entered, Jhal following close behind. Shoneg had ordered Jhal to escort Wrynn to the alchemist's, and it was clear Jhal had not yet worked through his anger at the situation. Wrynn wasn't sure what the deeper game was between Jhal and Shoneg, but he suspected it would end badly for all involved.

Jhal probably thought Wrynn was going to bolt and run the second his strands were off. In truth, Wrynn had considered it. But the prospect of laying eyes on an actual orison was too tempting.

Wrynn had a sorcerer's curiosity. There would always be time to run later.

The alchemist was a thin, elderly drokai, with frail limbs and the taut, glossy face of a man who'd extended his life with potions and poultices. Like most drokai, he was hairless, with pointed ears, dark watery eyes and skin the color and texture of black marble.

"Jhal Alafein," the alchemist said with a razor-toothed grin. He hobbled over and extended a bony hand. "What have you brought me today?"

"Good to see you again, Morlun. This fellow has some Imperial strands he'd like taken off." Jhal pointed a thumb at Wrynn.

"Ah," Morlun said. "Strands. Imperial magic. Very strong. That would make you a fugitive, yes?"

Wrynn spared the drokai a weary glance, but didn't answer, instead inspecting a row of herb bottles. The alchemist had some expensive stock. Apparently, despite his broken-down rowhouse, Shoneg really could pay for the best.

"He prefers not to talk about his past," Jhal said. "Mysterious loner type."

Morlun nodded. "Undoing this sort of magic illegal. Dangerous. It would take—"

Jhal pressed a fat bag of coin into the drokai's claw. "I need you to take special care of him."

The alchemist shook the bag. "Yes, good. I will close up shop. We not be disturbed."

Morlun barred the door, then led Wrynn and Jhal to a cramped back room. The walls were lined with tottering wooden shelves that groaned with jars, boxes, and sheaves of dried plants. A lopsided table and a single wicker chair occupied the center of the room.

Morlun leveled a claw at the chair. "Sit." Wrynn sat. Jhal began cleaning his fingernails with a knife while Morlun picked through the shelves, muttering and humming to himself.

"So what do you think of your new friend, the Halak?" Jhal asked.

Wrynn drummed his fingers on the arm of the chair. "Seems like a good sort."

"He isn't."

"I was being polite." Wrynn had no interest in giving Jhal any useful information if he could help it.

"He's nobility, you know," Jhal said. "A prince. The king exiled him for trying to kill his brothers and stage a coup. He's a traitor. Rull Halak. Bloody savages, all of them."

"You're an idiot," Wrynn said.

Jhal stopped cleaning his nails. "Say again?"

"The Halak have some of the finest libraries in Esterlund. The Praxis School would send ships full of students over to Walastri to study every spring."

"I'm sure they're very cultured," Jhal said, "as long as you stay clear of politics. Then it's a bloodbath."

"So unlike our refined and bloodless Imperial politics."

Morlun chuckled as he collected an armful of jars.

Jhal glared. "Watch yourself around him."

"Because he doesn't care for fratricide?" Wrynn asked. The items Morlun was collecting made him nervous. Goading Jhal kept him centered.

"Because he's a killer."

"I'm touched at your concern. I hope you'll write me after this is all over."

Wrynn decided he would deal with Jhal's information later. Jhal had little reason to share it, other than to drive a wedge between Wrynn and Dunnac. Likely as not, the bounty hunter was anxious for them to fail.

Jhal sneered. "Keep it up, mage. Wouldn't want your mission to go south because you turned your back on your associate at the wrong time."

"I wasn't aware you and I'd become such good friends."

"We're not. Shoneg doesn't pay me until your little task is complete."

Morlun had gathered his reagents and was now mixing a watery, slate-colored paste with a mortar and pestle, humming to himself. A hot, acrid scent rose from it.

"Is this going to hurt?" Wrynn asked, already anticipating the answer. The application of the imperial strands had been some of the worst pain he'd ever felt. Worse was the sickening feeling of his own power turning in on itself, gathering around his heart with no place to go.

"Oh, yes," Morlun said with a wet laugh. "Yes, yes, oh yes. Roll up your sleeves, please. Yes."

Wrynn blanched. "Lovely."

Morlun finished mixing the paste and applied it to Wrynn's arms with a rusty palette knife. It felt cool for a moment, then warm, then hot.

"That's very unpleasant," Wrynn said, his voice tight, and then bit back a scream as pain lanced through both arms. Thousands of tiny needles, hot and diseased, punched into his muscles and twisted.

"Not like removing mundane ink," Morlun said. "The ink binds with the magic, coils it up like a sleeping snake. Dragon devouring its tail. Have to wake it up, make the magic remember."

Wrynn clenched his teeth so hard he feared they were going to crack. Nonchalantly, Morlun pressed a paintbrush handle into Wrynn's mouth and began returning the reagents to the shelves. Jhal smirked with satisfaction.

Wrynn looked down at his arms, expecting to find flesh sloughing off in smoking chunks. Instead, he saw the purple Imperial strands glowing orange, twisting and unfurling like tugged laces. The ink bled hot from his flesh and bonded with the gray paste to form smoking gray chunks of coral. They fell away and crumbled to the floor.

Abruptly, the pain vanished. Wrynn flexed his fingers, feeling for the magic. It was there, faint but smooth, without the ache and dread of the strands.

"Do not use the power again yet," Morlun warned, taking the brush from between Wrynn's teeth. "It will take time to fully return. Could still hurt you."

"How long?" Wrynn asked, standing. He could already feel Kulraizhan flowing through him again, anxious to break free, to reshape the world at his will.

The alchemist shared a glance with Jhal, then shrugged. "A day, perhaps. Maybe more."

"A day!"

Jhal sneered at Wrynn's displeasure. "Don't worry, mage. You have some time before the appointed hour. Time enough for magic tomorrow."

Wrynn stared at his arms, seeing them unadorned for the first time in years, and tried not to think of what he could do now that he had his power back.

He met Jhal's eyes and knew the bounty hunter was thinking the same thing.

Ashen knew he could not find Penumbra without help. So he sought it in the only place he could think of. He requested an audience with Ravano, the queen's seer, asking the chamberlain to arrange a meeting.

If Ashen was the Queen's right hand, Ravano was her left. A former member of the Circle of the Watch and an Imperial expatriate, Ravano was the closest thing in the Red Cities to a true diviner – and, unlike the warborn, Ravano had the trust of the court.

Ashen knew that Ravano would see his request as a sign of weakness and an opportunity to stroke his own ego. He did not care. All that mattered was fulfilling Camana's wish.

They met in the funereal emptiness of the Stormhelt meeting hall, at a table that dwarfed both of them. The old man hobbled in and sat, showing none of his traditional court theatrics.

The seer listened, expressionless, while Ashen related the story of his vision. He deliberately left out any mention of the orison itself, saying only he had met a dragon semblance in the shadow gap.

"It cannot have been Penumbra," Ravano said when Ashen had finished.

"What makes you say that?" Ashen growled. He expected the seer to be surprised, or at least sympathetic. Instead, the seer dismissed him with a wave of bony fingers.

"The semblances do not appear to just anyone, and certainly not at random to warn of some portentous fate. Penumbra is not in the habit of warning humanity of impending threats, when she feeds upon the mayhem we create."

"I am not human," Ashen said, drinking water from a heavy iron cup. "As you take frequent joy in pointing out."

Ravano sniffed. "All the more reason she would not appear to you. A semblance would seek someone with the proper faculties for understanding a vision—"

Ashen narrowed his eyes over the rim of the cup.

Ravano cleared his throat. "That is to say, the proper education and arcane background to interpret... symbolism."

"You believe I cannot interpret symbols."

"I believe you are of the wrong background to receive a visitation from a semblance. You are Iron School, of a sort. Your discipline is martial and your power is used for killing people. No offense intended."

"None taken."

"Your talents are no doubt formidable, but you're little more than a bodyguard. What would the semblances have to say to such a... person?"

The seer's face could not conceal the glee of landing the petty jab. Ashen ignored it. The warborn did not consider words a weapon.

"Valakyr was a beggar. He once sat upon the Lotus Throne," he replied. "Castar was a common man, a criminal, and a wanderer. Lathia was a child. The semblances spoke to them. What were they that I am not?"

Ravano merely shrugged. Ashen saw the answer in the seer's eyes. *They were human.*

"I'm not sure what you expect of me," Ravano said at last.

"Tell me how to find Penumbra in the shadow gap. How do I look for her?"

Ravano sighed. "To teach you to ride the confluence in such a way would take months. I'm surprised you can manage it at all."

"Then teach me."

"I cannot." Ravano ran a gnarled hand through his gray hair. "I mean no insult. A dragon semblance does not come when called. Not even for the demigods they created. Camana herself could not invoke Amaraxis, should she wish it. I cannot teach what cannot be learned. Perhaps if you told me more about what the queen supposedly said—"

Ashen had seen this coming. Ravano smelled intrigue and a whiff of power and he wanted a part of it. Ashen finished his water and stood. "Thank you for your time, seer."

Ravano looked dismayed. "I can help, One-Howl, but I need—"

"No. I will find her myself." Ashen stalked from the hall. He would seek the solace of his room and enter the shadow gap where he had left. It was a slim hope, but all he had.

Night fell. No rain came.

Crux and Story descended to the street and cut across the south edge of the Star toward their target. They stuck to the back alleys, away from the well-known paths of the Scarlet patrols. By the time they reached the red-roofed house, the sky had turned the color of smoldering ash, and the red moon Hunter rose in the east.

As Crux promised, there was a drainpipe on the back end of the house. The street there lay empty. The first floor windows were lit but shuttered. There was no guard in sight.

Story wrapped her hands around the pipe and shook. Solid.

"You first," Crux whispered. "I'll stand watch."

With a nod, Story scrambled up the pipe to the third floor. She had to make a breathless, short leap from the pipe to the overhanging roof beam, but she caught it easily and hauled herself up. She crouched and signaled to Crux, who began his climb.

Once he reached the top, they walked delicately along the roof to the front of the house. Story dropped to her belly and craned past the edge of the roof to peer at the balcony below. The windows were shuttered and dark. Story seized the center beam and swung herself silently onto the balcony.

A moment later, Crux followed. He tried the shutters gently. "They're locked," he whispered.

"Your turn," Story said and sat cross-legged on the balcony floor. Crux flipped open his tools and set to work.

Story watched him, feeling a pang of regret over her remark earlier. Neither she nor Crux could remember their parents. They spent their first decade in a Calushain orphanage, before Galon purchased them for his crew. Their childhood consisted of begging and picking pockets, advancing to burglary when they were old enough to "use their heads", as Galon put it. No one at the orphanage had known why Crux and Story's parents had left them. They were long past the point of ever finding out.

Galon's crew, though close-knit, was ultimately still a band of thieves and mercenaries. Galon liked to talk about family and loyalty, but to him, it was all just business. Crux was the only true family she would ever have.

Watching her brother work — his gaze intent, motions precise, tongue poked between his teeth the way he did when he concentrated intensely — she realized it wasn't going to be so easy to leave him behind when she fled Calushain. The knowledge had always been there, a painful bruise in her plan, easily ignored but never quite going away.

He was right about their differences. Their lives had been going in different directions. Crux was an enforcer, a sword-arm, delivering beatings or worse to Galon's debtors and enemies. She was just another second-story girl, putting in her share, with no designs on joining Galon's inner sanctum or taking a place at his side. This was a job, the only one she'd ever known, and yet she yearned to do almost anything else.

She had pushed away these thoughts, hoping it would make it easier to leave him behind when the time came. But now working together again the way they used to made her heart twist with the anticipation of future regret.

The shutters unlocked with a soft click. Crux smiled and pulled them open. The window had no glass, only heavy curtains to keep out the night air.

"Your turn again," Crux said.

Story crawled onto the window sill, drawing her knife. She teased open the curtains with the edge of the blade and peered into the room beyond. Blackness. Story eased the curtains open to let the dim red light of Hunter shine through.

The attic room was stuffed with old furniture and wooden crates. Paintings in heavy silver frames lay stacked against one wall. Faint slits of candlelight shone through the floorboards from below. She tested the floor with one soft boot.

"Come on," she whispered. "Be careful. The boards might creak."

They eased through the shadows, looking for easy pickings. Story recited Galon's mantra in her head to calm herself.

How does a thief steal?
She moves without sound. She walks unseen.
What does a thief take?
No more than she can carry.
What does she leave behind?
Silence and shadows.

Crux unlocked coffers and jewelry boxes, deftly picking each lock and moving to the next. Story followed behind, sifting through the jewelry and taking the most valuable, avoiding pieces that couldn't easily be discarded if they ended up in trouble. Soon, her pockets swelled with loot.

As she sifted through the third coffer, her fingers found an elaborate metal brooch with a family crest. She turned it over in the dim light of Hunter, running her thumb over its shape. Her heart froze when she recognized it.

House of Odarin. A name on Galon's red list. They were in the house of someone Galon had explicitly forbidden stealing from.

She punched Crux in the shoulder, hard. He recoiled.

"What?" he whispered. She shoved the crest into his face.

"We have to get out of here!"

He gazed at the crest for a moment, then met her gaze. His expression filled her with dread.

"Story—" he began.

"You knew? Crux, are you insane?" She struggled to keep her voice to a whisper.

"Story, calm down. He's not on the red list anymore. They had a falling-out. This isn't—"

"You're *lying*!" she hissed. "I'm getting out of here."

She turned to leave — knowing that she didn't dare try to put everything back at this point — and Crux grabbed her arm. The motion knocked her off-balance and she careened into the stack of paintings, sending them crashing to the floor. Her foot punched through the uppermost canvas and she went down with a thud.

Shouts from below. The candlelight flickered wildly.

"*Merathu—*" Crux swore and grabbed Story by the hand. He stomped on the painting to untangle her foot, pulling her to her feet. They dashed for the balcony. Behind them, the attic trap door banged open. More shouting.

Story grabbed the beam and swung herself onto the roof. She took only a few steps across the roof before she realized it had begun to rain after all.

So much for the dragon's favor.

She moved as quickly as she dared, putting one foot directly in front of the other. Crux followed behind, breathing heavily.

Halfway across, Crux slipped. He tumbled forward, sprawling into Story. He slid down the roof, quickly picking up speed.

"Story!" he shouted, reaching for her as he spun down the sloped roof. But she was in just as much trouble. She scrambled at the tiles to find some purchase, but her slide was inexorable.

Crux vanished off the roof with a yelp. Bracing herself, Story slid after him involuntarily.

In the fleeting second she fell from the roof, Story saw Crux drop hard and land in a thin pile of dirty straw. She twisted in the air, landing on her feet, slowing just enough to drop onto a short stack of hay bales. It stung, but it was better than hitting the ground.

"Crux!" She scrambled to roll him over. He coughed spasmodically into her face.

"Can you run?" she asked. "Anything broken? Let me see." She hauled him to his feet. He swayed, but remained standing.

The front door flew open and a guard waddled towards them, shouting an alarm.

"Go!" she cried, pushing Crux ahead of her. He swore in pain with every step, but they outdistanced the guard and ran full-tilt toward the Star, where they could get lost in the crowd.

So much for silence and shadows, Story thought. *We're more the screams and chaos sort.*

Without realizing it, she began to laugh as they fled into the night, warm rain pounding against their faces.

"So what did *you* do?" Dunnac asked as they surfaced from the Lowbridge tunnel into the Quay.

Wrynn fought the urge to keep examining his own hands. Power flowed into them like blood rushing to deadened limbs. He was tempted to try something to ensure everything still worked, but he pushed the thought away. Even if all went well, he'd be pushing the limits of his magic soon enough.

They walked into the Quay market, a rough crescent of shopfronts and carts stretching from Lowbridge on the east end to Role Point on the west. Jhal had returned Dunnac's sword to him — a broad, two-handed blade he wore slung across his back — and Shoneg gave them a purse of talons each. Enough to feed themselves, stay out of the rain, and get a change of clothes, but not enough to get out of the city.

Jhal, reluctant but mollified, had stopped following Wrynn everywhere. That alone was enough to boost Wrynn's mood significantly.

"Do about what?"

"To attract the gaze of the House of Serpents," Dunnac said. "And get those strands."

Before Wrynn answered, Dunnac stopped at a cart for a loaf of black bread, which he then tore into with his teeth. Lacking a change of clothes, they were both still grubby with the stench of the prison, which meant they fit right in with the stink of the wharf.

"I burned some documents," Wrynn said at last.

Dunnac nodded, chewing. "What kind of documents?"

Wrynn shrugged. "The Praxis school takes a measure of blood from each student when they join, in order to scry out the student's future: their capabilities, their moral compass, their proclivities toward particular magical disciplines."

"They get all that from a drop of blood?" Dunnac asked, cramming the last crust into his mouth.

"They weave what's called a skein — a map of the student's future with the school. Then they tailor all their guidance towards a specific end."

"What's wrong with that?" Dunnac asked.

They turned north down an alley strewn with garbage. Dunnac now trailed a step behind Wrynn.

"The students aren't aware it takes place," Wrynn said. "They're molded into a magical discipline, into a way of thinking, simply because the magisters think that's where they belong."

"So?"

"So, a man should be able to choose his own fate."

Dunnac snorted. "That's not Ladrish thinking. You think Imperial slaves choose their fate?"

"I don't own any slaves."

"Plenty of Ladrish do."

"You see why I was kicked out, then," Wrynn said peevishly.

Dunnac pieced things together. "So you burned these skeins to set the students free of their fates."

"The knowledge of their fates. Maybe that's the same thing."

"Did it work?"

"Probably not," Wrynn said. "The magisters likely just took everyone's blood again and the students went along so they wouldn't be expelled."

Dunnac grunted. "At least your conscience is clear."

It sounded like a taunt. Wrynn let it pass.

They emerged into the ring of clustered tenements and broken-down row houses that surrounded the Star. Wrynn started looking for a taverner's, someplace he could get a drink and a bath.

"A tragic story," Dunnac said at last. "But it doesn't answer my question."

76

Wrynn faced the warrior. "Which was?"

"Some old wizards might throw you out of their school for burning their papers, but they wouldn't send assassins. Or cripple your magic." Dunnac's laid-back expression twisted into a scowl. "Just because I don't practice sorcery doesn't mean I don't know how they act."

Wrynn swallowed, his eyes flicking to the heavy blade on the warrior's back. "I wasn't—"

"No. But you're not telling me the truth, either." Dunnac took a step closer to Wrynn, his voice soft. "Despite what you said in the prison, mage, we're not friends. Not yet. If we're going to work together, give me a reason to trust you."

Wrynn balled his fists stiffly at his sides. "How do I know I can trust *you*?"

"Because we're still talking."

Wrynn scowled. "I didn't burn the skeins to save the other students. I did it because I was angry. Because I saw my skein and what they'd planned for me."

Dunnac lifted his eyebrows. "And what was that?"

"They wanted me for the Seventh House. They thought I'd make a good assassin."

"And you didn't agree?"

Wrynn looked away. "I didn't say that."

Dunnac shrugged. "Good enough."

They started walking again.

Shoneg had given them a letter of credit with a clothing shop in the Star - "so you can represent me respectably," the merchant had said. Wrynn bought a gray shirt, black pants and a long charcoal coat with polished black iron buttons. His own clothes were so caked with filth that the clothier was convinced he was a beggar.

Dunnac bought a new cloak, but nothing else. Before changing, they found a hostel with private baths. For a half-talon Wrynn got a tub of hot water, some soap, and what looked like a re-purposed horse brush. He scrubbed until his skin was bright red. Unable to restrain himself, he reheated the water twice with his magic, soaking in the pleasing hum of mild confluence. It still hurt when he cast the spells, but it was not the blinding pain he'd experienced with the strands.

When he returned to the common room, it was evening. He'd almost forgotten how good it was to wear clean clothes and not feel greasy and itchy. Between that and losing the strands, he felt like a real person again.

All he needed now was a drink.

Dunnac waited for him at a table near the back, with two cold mugs of beer. As Wrynn sat, Dunnac pushed one across the table.

"Never had a Halak buy me a drink before," Wrynn said.

"We'll settle up with our fists later," Dunnac answered. "One punch for beer, two for wine. Whiskey or rum, a kick in the grapes. An open-handed slap for mead."

Wrynn sucked foam off the mug. "I never know if you're joking."

Dunnac nodded expressionlessly.

Wrynn drank and set his mug back on the table. "We need to talk about this job."

"I imagine so," Dunnac said.

According to Shoneg, their man was a pilgrim named Credo, ostensibly on a holy journey from the Eiler dragon temples to the Shattered Citadel in north Ladris. Apparently, he was more of a traveling confidence man than a priest, scoping opportunities for his employer.

One such opportunity was the orison, uncovered by a mining excavation in the Nirrenwall and pilfered by a pair of light-fingered miners. How it had gotten into Credo's hands didn't matter, said Shoneg. Credo was in the city and ready to pass it along.

Wrynn and Dunnac would meet him at a gambling house in Lowbridge called the Silver Wheel. Credo would give them the orison, whereupon they would return to the Prestigious Bastard and give it to Jhal. Jhal would pay them off and report their deaths to the Seventh House and the kingdom of Rull Halak, respectively.

It sounded easy enough — which was the whole problem.

"Nothing this straightforward ever goes off well," Wrynn said.

"Finally, some pessimistic Ladrish thinking," Dunnac said.

"Shoneg said he told us about the orison because he needed people who knew the stakes. Do you really think he'll let us go when this is over? He'll have a dozen men waiting to cut our throats."

Dunnac shook his head. "How would our deaths benefit him?"

"We're the classic loose end. Shoneg will have an item of tremendous value and, more importantly, power. If it were just worth a lot of money, that would be one thing. But in the right hands, an artifact like that could topple kingdoms."

"He said it kills those it finds unworthy. Wouldn't that discourage most people?"

Wrynn shook his head. "Men would readily gamble their lives for that kind of power."

"But not you," Dunnac said.

"No. Not me."

Dunnac began drawing invisible lines on the table with his forefinger, mapping the plot of their doom. "So because we know what it is, he will try to kill us?"

"I'm more worried about the next person in the chain. Shoneg will sell that thing to somebody, at a very high price. And the person who purchases it will either be dead or powerful beyond measure. It's that last one that worries me. We're pieces in someone else's game and we can't see the whole board yet."

They sat in silence for a while. The barmaid refilled their mugs and they drank.

Dunnac said at last, "How does Shoneg know we won't try to sell it ourselves?"

"We have no one to sell it to. It could empty a royal treasury. Would you try to sell ancient draconic magic to someone like the Queen of Storms and hope she'd let you trot merrily on your way afterward?"

Dunnac considered it. "No. But I wouldn't trust men like us to make such an important delivery, either."

"Can't say I disagree."

Dunnac drank. "You think it's a trap."

Wrynn nodded. "But maybe not for us. We were already trapped."

"So what do you suggest?" Dunnac asked.

Wrynn sighed and lifted his mug. "We blunder through, my new friend. We blunder through."

The Halak considered, then shrugged. "I'll drink to that."

CHAPTER SIX

AFTER THE JOB AT THE ODARIN HOUSE, Story went home, refusing to speak to Crux further. He made a show of being contrite, as he always did, and insisted that Odarin was no longer on the red list and that they'd done nothing wrong. She ignored him. Maybe he was telling the truth and maybe he wasn't. Either way, she would settle it up with Galon later. Maybe.

She returned to the Doorstop and slept through the morning and afternoon, staying out of the heat. As the sun crawled into the afternoon, she decided to go back to work.

Encountering the raizhi demon in Harrows left her cautious about going back there. She decided to hit something, like one of the cheaper merchant residences along Redwell. It wouldn't net much, but it felt safer than Harrows.

Wrynn's room was still empty. On her way downstairs, she stopped by his crate, hoping to buy more lochweed. He wasn't there either. Story left in disappointment.

Once in Redwell, she scoped out the upstairs storeroom to a spice merchant's shop, cracked the lock on the window, and stole a sack full of expensive herbs and powders, including an entire jar of nightclaw tobacco imported from Sethwas. She took the high road back to Fiver's Quay and was back at the Doorstop well before sunset. Not bad for a night's work – uneventful and productive, just how she liked it.

On her way into the alley, she checked Wrynn's crate again. Still empty. She left the jar of tobacco in the crate for him. It was worth a decent bit of coin, but it made her happier to think of him enjoying the mildly hallucinogenic smoke. She hoped he was all right.

Story climbed the side of the building in silence and slid through the window to her room. She began sorting the goods in her sack, trying to decide whether to put anything in the stash. Spices were a bit more dangerous. The smell could tip off someone with a sharp nose. Methodically, she began to uncork the jars and sniff them, one by one.

Something shifted in the darkness. She realized she hadn't checked the room thoroughly.

"Hallo, girlie."

Story drew her knife in a reverse grip, rose, and spun on one foot.

Nibs leaned against the locked door, grinning. He raised beefy hands to show they were empty. "Easy now, girl."

"What the hell are you doing here?" He didn't consider her a threat. That was fine. He could go on thinking it right up until she put the knife in his groin.

He chuckled. "You're like to maim some poor soul with that."

"Any second now, unless you explain why you're in my room."

"I'm to present a formal invitation from the man Galon himself." Nibs was still utterly at ease.

"Galon ordered you to ambush me?"

"Wouldn't really call it an ambush, would you? I could have dropped you easy while you were sniffing your weed there."

"I guess we'll never know," Story said, hoping the bravado covered the shame of her carelessness. "What does Galon want?"

"Nothing serious," Nibs said. "A bit of a post-Counting Day bequest for his top earners."

Story lowered the knife. "Is that sarcasm?"

Nibs shrugged. "Couldn't rightly tell you. He didn't *say* it was sarcasm."

Reluctantly, Story sheathed her blade. "Since when am I a top earner?"

"I guess last night put you over the top," Nibs said. "Galon wants to dispense some special recompense and avoid cultivating jealousy amongst the unwashed rank and file, so he's doing it quiet-like."

"You could have just left a note," Story said.

"I rather doubt that, my literacy being what it is."

"Anyone ever say you use a lot of fancy words for a man who can't read?"

"Thank you."

Story felt uneasy. Maybe Crux had asked Galon for some kind of special favor, to earn her forgiveness for the disaster at the Odarin house. Or maybe she was being paranoid and it was on the level. Either way, she couldn't decline without raising undue suspicion.

"So when is this surprise… bequeathment… thing?" she asked.

Nibs grinned. "Soon as you're ready, dear. I promise to keep my hands to myself."

"You *are* smart."

She followed Nibs back to a mostly-empty Bladesbarrow. Galon, Crux, and perhaps a half-dozen of his personal guard stood in the main chamber. There was no music this time. Galon was drinking heavily from a goblet so ornate as to be vulgar. The great round table in the room's center lay empty, sacked of its riches from the previous Counting Day.

"Story, my darling," Galon said as they entered. "Thank you, Nibs."

Nibs stepped aside to join those sitting in shadow along the walls. Story realized she stood alone in the center of the chamber. The soft bells of suspicion that had sounded on finding Nibs in her room now pealed loudly in the back of her skull.

"A drink?" Galon gestured at the jug beside his chair. "Plenty to go around."

"No thank you, sir."

"I must thank you for coming," Galon said contentedly. "I trust Nibs mentioned your new-found status among us?"

Story looked at Crux. He stood stock-still, his expression blank.

"He hinted at it," Story said.

"I like to show my gratitude to those who exceed my expectations. So I'd like to offer you this gift, in recognition of your service."

Crux stepped forward with a large sack. Walking past her to the round table, he poured out the entire contents of Story's hidden stash.

Suddenly she couldn't breathe. She stared at Crux, wide-eyed, hoping for some signal from him. He looked down at his boots, not meeting her gaze.

Galon lounged in his chair. "I hope it's enough to satisfy your ambition."

Story licked her lips. "Galon—"

"I'd hate to think I've shortchanged you in some way," Galon said.

"No," Story said, not daring to look for other exits from the room. "About that. Listen, I have a story..."

"So do I!" Galon said. The shadows in the room chuckled.

Story's gaze lifted to the row of heads in jars watching her above Galon's chair. "Galon, I was going to give you that loot. I was just building up a nice sum, to surprise you."

"Oh!" Galon said. "I didn't know that. A surprise around my birthday, perhaps? When is that? Does anybody know?"

He made a show of looking around the room. More snickers.

Galon looked back to Story. "Do *you* know?"

Story clamped her mouth shut on the pointless lie. She couldn't think through the cloud of panic.

Galon set down his cup. "I'm disappointed, Story. I took you off the streets. I made you a part of our crew, at your brother's urging. I gave you the clothes on your back, a good knife. I even let you stay in Bront's quaint little cesspit."

The crime lord's face turned red, his voice rising. Spittle flew from his lips. "All I asked was a little appreciation. A little recompense for the time and money I lost. *And you couldn't give me that much!*"

Story stood motionless, her hands bunched into fists at her sides. Galon sat back, the fury disappearing like a candle blowing out. He rubbed his nose with one forefinger.

"Your problem, Story, is that you don't understand loyalty. Your brother does. He understands gratitude. So when I asked him to start following you, to see what you stole and what you brought back, he did so without question. And what you brought back, Story, was less than expected."

Galon stood and held out a hand. Crux drew his sword and placed it in Galon's palm. Galon sauntered down the dais.

Story tried to wish herself smaller, but she stood her ground. If she was going to die here, over a handful of semi-valuable junk, she wouldn't cower. Galon stepped so close she could smell him: a sour, powdery stench masked with too much perfume.

"Crux is one of my teachers, Story," he said. "And this is the lesson: Galon does not tolerate snakes in his nest. Little snakes do not take bread from the mouths of his people to serve their own greed."

Galon's face twisted in rage and he pushed her, hard. As she sprawled to the floor, Galon thrust the blade's tip an inch from her stomach.

"Don't kill me," Story said quickly. "You won't get the rest of your money."

"Your brother found your stash already, little one."

"Not all of it. You don't think I stashed it all in one place, do you?"

Galon's face froze. Then he laughed softly. Without warning, he pushed the blade into Story's side. The tip bit through her clothes, then her flesh. He twisted it. The pain was nauseating. Story clenched her teeth to keep herself from screaming.

Galon withdrew the blade, revealing a half-inch of bright blood. A shallow cut, just enough to hurt. A lot.

"Whatever else you've holed up, I'd wager watching you die would be worth it." Galon asked, standing over her. The tip of the blade touched her throat, and he gently tilted her chin up. "Or do you lie in the hopes I'll spare you?"

"There's more," she lied. "I made a mistake. Give me a chance to pay it back."

"Oh, you'll repay it, girl. Until I'm satisfied, every talon, every Imperial eagle's claw you steal, belongs to me. You'll pay for the time and effort I've spent teaching a stupid young thief who doesn't understand this city belongs to me."

The point of the blade left her throat. She breathed again.

"Are we clear?" Galon tilted his head.

Story didn't dare move as a trickle of blood ran down her belly. "We're clear."

As Story cradled her cut stomach, soft laughter echoed from all around her.

"Glad to hear that, girl," Galon said, turning back to his chair. He tossed the sword to Crux, who placed it, still bloody, back in the scabbard.

"Now," Galon said, picking up his wine glass again, "Let's talk about how you can start working off your debt. Crux, how much was Story's little cache worth?"

"Three hundred and twelve talons," Crux said.

"Three hundred and twelve. I really have to admire you, girl. Here's my offer: make it an even six hundred by the end of the week and you can keep working for me as a thief. Any less, and you join my pretty row of heads."

Story's heart froze. Her stash had taken months to accumulate. There was no way to get so much money in a matter of days. This was no kind of deal at all and they both knew it.

Galon studied her carefully. "Or do you not like that bargain?"

"I like it fine," she said, trying not to let her voice crack. "You'll get your money."

His leer curdled a little and she knew he'd been expecting her to beg. Story suspected that tiny scrap of satisfaction was the last she'd be getting for awhile.

After dismissing Story, Galon called an end to the evening's entertainment. The men in the shadows dispersed. Crux followed Galon into the corridor behind the throne, fists clenched.

"You promised you'd treat her fairly," he said to Galon's back.

Galon turned. "You don't feel that was fair?"

Crux knew by the man's soft tone that he trod dangerous ground, but he didn't back down. "You know there's no way she can raise that kind of money in a week. You're asking the impossible."

"Story's a resourceful young woman. I'm sure she'll come up with something clever."

"I won't let you hurt my sister," Crux said.

"Won't let me," Galon repeated carefully. He took a step toward Crux. "Won't *let* me."

"You know what I mean," Crux said. "Sir."

"It sounds like you're confused about who gives the orders in Bladesbarrow."

Crux licked his lips. "You promised me—"

"I promised I'd spare her life. And I will, as long as she fulfills the bargain she agreed to. Is that not fair?" Galon jabbed his forefinger into Crux's chest, hard enough to hurt. "If I let every petty thief in my employ walk all over me, how long do you imagine I'd be in charge? Your sister made herself into a lesson. That was her choice. Just as betraying her secret was yours."

Crux hung his head. "I only did what I thought was best."

"Crux." Galon's tone softened. He put a hand on the boy's shoulder. "Of course you did. We take care of each other."

"I suppose," Crux whispered.

"Good," Galon said. "I'm glad we settled that. I've already lost a good left hand, Crux. I'd hate to lose my right, too."

He tapped Crux on the cheek and went into his room.

Ashen plunged into the confluence, allowing its currents to carry him near the shoals of oblivion. He willed the arcane tides to take shape, trying to rebuild the ghostly twin of Calushain where he'd met Penumbra. His constructions were unruly, warping into elastic mockeries of architecture, the streets collapsing into muddy darkness. He could not encompass the details his vision demanded. His city was a child's scrawl etched in misused magic.

Frustrated, he let the illusion collapse and returned to the cradling warmth of formlessness to ponder his next action. Should he craft Penumbra herself from the arcane clay? Would simulacrum call to semblance? Even to him, that smacked of blasphemy, and he abandoned the thought immediately.

The beating heart of his dilemma remained, the orison itself. If it was concentrated magic, perhaps he could hunt it in this endless sea. He shaped the confluence into a compact sphere, painstakingly recalling every gleam of light on the red orb, every crawling black blemish, the illusory copper smell of ancient magic.

Ashen gave himself hands so he could hold it as he'd seen Penumbra hold it, gingerly as an egg. He focused his will into a single point of incandescent crimson, willing the illusion to life.

Fiery shards of confluence bloomed, trailing smudges of flame as they spun out in all directions. The flames became streets, the shadows rising into angular shapes. Ashen saw Calushain beneath him, its streets arteries of flame, the architecture its bones, the orison its beating heart, pumping sorcery through the city with every pulse.

He released his orison doppelganger into the flowing tide of magic and followed it down, diving like a fish into the luminous orange waters. If his divination had assumed a life of its own, as he hoped, it would lead him to revelation.

The currents carried him through the city, past a population of phantoms. He followed the bright sphere as it bobbed along the stream, throwing off streamers of light. The fiery river churned into rapids, bouncing him wildly until he was thrown free to land in a jumble of shadows.

Ashen stretched out with his senses, not seeing but feeling his surroundings, his consciousness melding to the shapes of the buildings, seeping into the cracks in the streets, into every door and window sill.

He knew this place. He was in Highbridge. A decaying town-house stood before him with a granite fountain, lined with overgrown hedges. As he watched, the orison's burning flare rocketed past him into the house, lighting the windows with orange fire. The vision quivered, then shattered like glass.

On his cot, Ashen opened his eyes. The room stank of the acrid smell of magic, the air humming with confluence. His clay tea bowls chattered on their plates.

He had overtaxed his power. It would take time to bleed off. But if his vision was correct and not just some fever dream, he knew where to find the orison — or, at least, where to begin looking. He rose, pulled on his cloak and took up his sword. He had a house to find.

Ashen took his horse from the stable and rode to Highbridge, crossing the canal just as the sun dipped below the horizon. Once there, he systematically searched each street for the house he'd seen in his vision. Even if he were a natural diviner — even if he were sure the house really existed — he couldn't ride the confluence and a horse at the same time.

But after only five trips searching the well-trimmed hedges of Highbridge, he found it. The same anemic ferns, the same decaying fountain: there was no doubt this was the place.

Ashen dismounted and stalked toward the house. The door was locked, but gave way with a simple twist of sorcery — a trick he'd learned studying the ways of the Iron School. He stepped into a foyer of fraying carpet and peeling paint. The hall was lined with cheap Merrekani statuary from the Lowbridge markets and ornate wall lamps that looked expensive, but were made of cheap pounded tin. They weren't meant to be lit. He smelled perfume, and beneath that, an under-tang of mildew and stale air — and beneath that, something else he couldn't place yet.

This house, like his vision, was artifice. It was meant to look as though people lived here.

He drew his sword. The air shimmered as he summoned a protective aegis spell around him. He crossed into the unoccupied parlor, empty wine bottles and glasses the only sign of habitation. An ornate wooden box sat on the table, its lid closed. Ashen caught a sharp whiff of sorcery.

He touched the lid with the point of his blade and flipped it back. Inside, a round red orb decorated with black fire. Ashen caught his breath — then sniffed. Its scent was wrong. This was not the aura of draconic power.

Ashen tapped the orb with the point of his sword. It cracked. The sorcery unraveled. It was plaster and illusion.

A figure stepped into the room: short, fat, dressed in bronze-colored silks. He spotted Ashen and stopped short. Ashen's senses sharpened, his ears picking up every whisper. He could smell the man's sweat, the dirt on his shoes, the days-old perfume lingering on his skin.

"Oh," the fat man said. "I thought I heard the door."

"Where is it?" Ashen walked around the table.

"I'm sorry, have we met? My name is Shoneg. I'm—"

"Tell me where it is, and I may let you live."

The man seemed unimpressed. "I don't think I understand."

Ashen grabbed the broken orb from its box and tossed it at the man. It bounced off Shoneg's belly to the floor.

"The orison," Ashen said.

"That thing? It's a replica. A showpiece. I'm afraid the real thing would be a little out of my—"

"Now," Ashen said, and the man backed up a step.

"I think you have the wrong idea about me," Shoneg said.

An instant too late, Ashen understood how strong the man's illusion was.

Sorcery bloomed in a blue nova. Something hit him, hard. He flew over the table and into the wall. His aegis spell shattered into glittering shards and was gone. Ashen grunted as a bookshelf toppled onto him.

By the time he'd crawled out from under it, the man had fled. A tracking spell revealed a trail of dim blue radiance winding out the back door and into the garden.

Iron School. The man was a sorcerer, battle-trained. He was fast. Ashen was faster.

The warborn sprang into a barely-controlled run and almost reached the end of the garden before something caught his nostrils — or a lack of something. The man's perfume. The magical trail was just another illusion, designed to throw him off.

Clever.

He slid to a halt, doubled back toward the house. A sniff revealed the true path the man had followed. Up the front stairs, probably to come down the other end and out the back door.

Ashen gambled and bolted back through the hallway, sword in hand.

He'd guessed correctly. When he rounded the parlor corner, the man was almost to the door. Ashen threw a force spell and the door slammed, catching the fugitive in its swing and knocking him into the wall.

Ashen rested his blade against the portly man's throat. The man propped himself up on his elbows and opened his hands in formal surrender. The nimbus of sorcery around him faded into the background noise of confluence. The room swam with it now.

"You move fast for a fat man," Ashen said.

"Not fast enough, it seems. You're the Queen of Storm's hound, aren't you? And Iron School."

"Not exactly." Ashen narrowed his eyes. "But neither are you. The Iron School does not teach illusion."

"I picked up a few things from all over," Shoneg said.

Ashen tired of the banter. He twisted the point of the blade in the man's neck until Shoneg hissed with pain.

"The orison," Ashen said. "You know where it is. Stop wasting time. Tell me, and I promise you mercy."

Shoneg grinned. "We'll both soon be dead. I assure you it's not personal." The man's shroud spell buckled and seeped open like hot tar. Beneath it, Ashen saw the confluence blazing like a white-hot star in the center of the man's chest.

"*What are you doing?*" he bellowed, but his voice was lost in the shriek of sorcerous backlash. Ashen channeled what little he had left into an aegis before Shoneg exploded into fire and light. As Ashen flew through the door, it shattered to splinters.

Ashen's world quivered, and the world faded to darkness.

CHAPTER SEVEN

AFTER THEIR DRINK, DUNNAC AND Wrynn walked back toward the Star. Even with the approach of sunset, the market bristled with activity, traders and customers crowding the stalls.

The time for their meeting with Credo approached. As the hours went by, Wrynn found himself growing anxious. He didn't yet feel comfortable using his sorcery, but now that the strands were gone, he felt curiously vulnerable in a way he hadn't before.

Reluctantly, he admitted to himself that Jhal's words at the alchemist's shop had bothered him. If Dunnac really was some sort of exiled noble, trouble would rarely be far behind. There was also the question of why Shoneg would dangle the orison in front of a man like Dunnac. Shoneg was right about Wrynn — he had no more desire to partake of dragon's blood than drink from the Calushain canals. But the Halakin cultural biases against magic notwithstanding, the lure of such power might tempt even a man like Dunnac. With so many elements in play, things would get complicated soon enough.

It turned out to be sooner than he expected.

As they left the hostel, Wrynn caught sight of four Fireborn in battle leathers and dark gray tunics. As Wrynn and Dunnac shouldered their way through the crowd, the men casually fell into step a few paces behind.

Wrynn glanced back, scratching his head to cover the motion. The men turned and pretended to be interested in a row of clay jugs. *Subtle.*

Their leader had a bald head livid with scars. These were the same men from the statue of Silandra, the men who would've beaten Wrynn to death if Dunnac hadn't stepped in.

"Do you see them?" Wrynn asked quietly as they walked through the market square. Dunnac had paused to admire some daggers at a weaponsmith's stall, picking up each blade and examining it. "Your friends from the other night."

"I see them," Dunnac said calmly, not looking up from the knife he was inspecting. "It seems they weren't properly discouraged."

"What do you think they want?"

"Capture me. Kill me. Take my head back to Rull Halak. I didn't actually ask last time."

The knife merchant gave them a nervous look. Gingerly, Wrynn removed the blade from Dunnac's hands and put it back with the others. "Sorry, we're not buying today," he said with a smile, and tugged at Dunnac's sleeve. The Halak looked nonplussed, but allowed himself to be pulled away.

"What are we going to do?" he asked Dunnac in a half-whisper as they waded into the thinning crowd again. The evening grew dim, and some merchants had begun to close up shop.

Dunnac sighed through his nose. "We'll have to deal with them. Permanently this time." The tall man straightened his shoulders and picked up the pace, apparently looking for something. He offered no explanation.

Wrynn struggled to keep up as the tall man shouldered his way through the crowd. He occasionally glanced back to see if the Fireborn were following. He didn't see them, for all that meant.

"Are we running?" he managed to say as they reached the edge of the Star, where the crowds thinned a little.

"Not exactly," Dunnac said. "We need someplace out of sight, where the Scarlets won't see."

Wrynn didn't like the sound of that. He felt the need to explain about his magic, but he didn't exactly have Dunnac's full attention. "Don't we want the opposite? I could do with some Scarlets around."

"The Scarlets won't help us," Dunnac said.

"That's encouraging," Wrynn mumbled. He touched Dunnac's shoulder and pointed. "You'll want to turn southwest, then, into Harrows. The city guard doesn't give a toss what happens in there."

"Perfect," Dunnac said with his omnipresent scowl.

They left the crowds behind at a brisk walk. Soon the ragged brown rooftops of Harrows rose to greet them. The sunlight faded fast now, but the broken gaslights of Harrows didn't ignite as they did in better neighborhoods. Blanket-wrapped beggars lined the curbs, huddled in crowded box shanties.

Wrynn shuddered. A day ago, this had been his home, for all practical purposes. Now he might die here. Unexpectedly, he found himself thinking of Story, hoping she was all right.

Dunnac pointed toward a wide alley between two tenements. "There."

As they left the street, the armed figures stalked from the square toward them, moving faster now.

"They're following us," Wrynn said, trying to keep his voice from cracking. Fear clutched at his heart. He felt more vulnerable than ever. He shook his fingers, trying to work up some confidence.

"I know." Dunnac came to a halt and kicked a lone beggar curled up in a doorway.

The man mumbled sleepily. "Clear off."

"Get out of here unless you want to be killed," Dunnac said. Something in his voice got the beggar to his feet. The man scampered away.

Dunnac looked around the alley, then nodded, satisfied. He made no move to draw his sword. "This will do."

Wrynn shot a nervous glance toward the alley mouth. The other men hadn't shown up yet. Wrynn briefly hoped they'd rethought their lives and gone home, but he doubted that. More likely they were drawing up a plan for their quarry's organized murder.

"What exactly is our plan?" he asked Dunnac.

"We reason with them."

Wrynn gaped. Dunnac's expression was unreadable. The Halak stood with his hands on his belt, apparently relaxed. "Do you think that's going to work?"

"Not really. But every man deserves a chance at redemption. Have you killed anyone before?"

Wrynn's eyes bulged. "What?"

"Yes or no."

Wrynn swallowed hard and decided there was little reason to start keeping secrets now. "Yes. Once."

"You may have to do so again."

"If I must," Wrynn said, not feeling particularly confident. His pulse quickened with sudden terror. He needed to explain his magic to Dunnac *now*. "Listen, there's another—"

"Mar Dunnac!"

The four men stood in a line at the mouth of the alley, hands on their swords. The leader — the one with the scars — stepped forward.

"You should have stayed in prison," he said. The others followed a step behind, cautiously.

"I had unfinished business," Dunnac said, cracking his knuckles idly. "As, it seems, do we."

The leader sneered. "We do."

Dunnac spread his hands. "May I ask what? It seems rude for me to kill you without even knowing why."

The Fireborn soldiers bristled, reaching for their swords. Glaring, the leader held up a hand to stay them.

Wrynn flexed his fingers, triggered a faint flow of sorcery through them. It felt uncomfortable, like putting his hand in water that was just slightly too hot. He didn't like these odds, or where the conversation was headed. He amplified his senses as much as he dared, feeling a low ache course through him, as if every muscle in his body tensed.

"Why are we deliberately antagonizing them?" he asked in a fierce whisper.

"Be quiet," Dunnac said calmly.

The leader's venomous gaze turned in Wrynn's direction. "You make friends with this *magician*, Mar Dunnac? You have truly betrayed your people."

"I am not the traitor here," Dunnac said. "I am here in the king's name. You break Maag's edict by following me."

"Maag is dead," the Fireborn said. "His edict is broken. The Fireborn come to collect your head for Silandra."

Wrynn saw Dunnac's cheek twitch, saw his muscles tense slightly. Wrynn's hands and wrists grew hot. When things went badly — and he no longer doubted that they would — he would probably be little help.

Merathu, don't let us die here—

"I care nothing for Fireborn lies," Dunnac said at last, shifting his footing slightly. The Fireborn fanned out in the alley. None of them had yet drawn their weapons.

"I offer you this choice," the leader said. "Return with us to Rull Halak. Denounce Maag and the apostate kingdom, and give your life to Silandra. She will draw you into her arms and forgive you."

With his augmented senses, Wrynn saw Dunnac's demeanor subtly shift, saw his fingers loosen at his side. Whatever the Fireborn had just said, it was too great an insult for Dunnac to bear.

"You do not have to die," the leader said.

The Halak smiled, almost sadly. "You do."

The man with the scars reached for his sword.

Wrynn never saw Dunnac draw. He saw only a flash of metal arcing downwards. Suddenly the man with the scars was cut nearly in half, a jet of blood spraying from a yard-long wound. The leader's blade never cleared its sheath. He fumbled for it, gurgling, then collapsed to his knees with a look of confusion.

Wrynn's eyes widened in shock. The other men jumped back, drawing their swords with whispers of leather on steel. Dunnac held his sword low, feet in a defensive stance.

"You seek a dragon?" Dunnac said in a low voice. "One stands before you. Here is its claw. Come and die as men."

The Fireborn soldiers hesitated, then charged, swords upraised. Two went for Dunnac, the other for Wrynn.

Without thinking, Wrynn jabbed two fingers at the Fireborn running toward him. He reached into the man's mind with his sorcery, twisting his sense of balance. The Fireborn lurched to the right, knocking over the soldier next to him. They stumbled, then sprawled to the oily ground.

Wrynn's arm pulsed with discomfort, as if he'd wrapped a tourniquet around it.

The Fireborn left standing swung his blade at Dunnac with a cry. Dunnac parried and turned the sword aside. They exchanged a rapid series of blows, almost too fast for Wrynn to follow, the flat ring of steel on steel echoing in the narrow alley.

One of the Fireborn's swings grazed Dunnac's leg, drawing a dark line of blood. Dunnac grimaced with pain and limped back a step. Over-eager, the Fireborn stepped into Dunnac's reach. Dunnac batted aside the man's blade and ran him through. The man spit up a mouthful of blood and slid off Dunnac's blade, twitching.

Once they scrambled back to their feet, the other two Fireborn advanced, more cautious than their fallen brethren. Wrynn could see the fear in their eyes, the beads of sweat on their foreheads. Dunnac, calm as still waters, dropped back into guard and waited. Both soldiers focused on Dunnac now, clearly seeing him as the more dangerous opponent.

They're not wrong.

The Fireborn nearest Wrynn moved first, jabbing with his weapon. It was a feint. As Dunnac moved to counter, the other soldier swung into Dunnac's guard. Reflexively, Wrynn threw an aegis spell. A glassy, translucent oblong two feet across glimmered into view by Dunnac's left arm, then shattered into multicolored fragments when the Fireborn's weapon struck it. The force of the backlash opened the Fireborn's guard, and Dunnac slashed him open with an underhand swing. Blood sprayed the alley wall as the man pitched backward, screaming.

Wrynn turned his attention to the last remaining Fireborn. The man took a few scuttling steps backward, his sword at the ready, then his will broke. He turned to run.

"Stop him!" Dunnac said hoarsely.

Wrynn's head already pounded with confluence. Something definitely wasn't right. Desperately, he tried to reach out and disrupt the man's balance again, then hissed with pain as the spell turned in on itself and failed. "I can't—"

Something flashed between Wrynn and Dunnac with a whistle. A barbed arrow buried itself in the fleeing Fireborn's back. The man cried out and fell down hard, cracking his head on the street. He didn't move again.

Wrynn and Dunnac whirled to see the source of the arrow. A tall, muscular man swaggered out of the shadows at the far end of the alley, crossbow in hand. His skin was dark like chestnut, a bristly black half-moon of beard around his chin and jowls, black hair combed back from his forehead.

"Mar Dunnac," he said with a toothy grin. "You're a difficult man to find."

"Orain," Dunnac said. Dunnac knelt, and for one moment Wrynn thought he was about to pay obeisance to the other man. But Dunnac used the dead Fireborn's cloak to wipe the blood from his sword. "These men found me easily enough. What took you so long?"

"Bastard Scarlets wouldn't take my bribes," the other man said in a jovial tone. He slung his crossbow. "Apparently whomever paid your bond wanted it kept quiet. But I saw those Fireborn staking out our tavern—"

"*Your* tavern?" Wrynn asked, throwing a glare in Dunnac's direction.

"The tavern where we agreed to meet." Dunnac tied a scrap of cloth around the cut on his leg, unconcerned.

"—and figured they probably knew something I didn't," Orain finished. "I was already late. So I followed them and circled back around the alley." He nodded at Wrynn with a half-smile. "Who's your sorcerer friend here?"

"A fellow exile," Dunnac said, rising and sheathing his sword. "Met him in the gaol. Shoneg paid his bond, too."

"Shoneg!" Orain snapped his fingers. "I knew it!"

"All right," Wrynn said peevishly, trying not to look as suspicious as he felt. "Obviously you two know each other, as well as a great deal more than me about what's going on. How about sharing?"

"We will," Dunnac said. "But not here."

"Don't worry, friend," the other man said, extending a hand to Wrynn. "There's a place we can talk. I'm Lios Orain of Rull Halak."

Wrynn hesitantly offered his hand in return. "Wrynn Sendir. Recently of the gaol."

The man shook it enthusiastically. "Well met. Magician or not, any friend of Dunnac's—"

"That's enough," Dunnac said curtly. "Let's go."

Wrynn followed the two men as they walked south. The sun dipped lower, painting red streaks above the spindled skyline of Calushain. As they traveled, Wrynn rubbed his wrists, trying to massage away the ache of using his magic too early. *A day, maybe more*, the alchemist at the shop had said. It had only been a few hours, and already he'd broken the rules. He hadn't planned on people trying to kill him so soon.

They crossed into Lowbridge, stopping at a dank-looking hovel with boarded-up windows. Orain produced a key and opened the sturdy lock. He gestured for Wrynn and Dunnac to enter. The inside held only a single room that reeked of mildew. Wrynn squinted in the dark until Orain lit a candle, revealing a low table spotted with wax and four wooden chairs.

"Drink?" Orain asked, placing a heavy jug on the table. It made a thick sloshing sound as Orain produced some clay cups.

"No," Wrynn said. "All right, yes."

Orain paused in mid-pour, eyeing Wrynn dubiously. "You sure?"

"Yes. Sorry, it's been an eventful day." Wrynn sat and took a cup.

Orain poured, and they all drank. The wine was dry and astringent, but good. Wrynn felt his headache recede almost immediately.

"Now," he said cautiously, painfully aware that he was no match for either of the other men. "Would someone mind telling me what's going on?"

Orain looked at Wrynn, his smile tight, his eyes probing. "That depends. How much do you know now?"

Fine, if that's how you want it. Wrynn nodded reluctantly and gestured at Dunnac with his cup. "Jhal told me that you're nobility. You tried to overthrow King Maag, and he exiled you."

Dunnac drained his cup and laughed. "Jhal is a liar."

"I knew that much already," Wrynn said.

"I am of a noble house, it's true," Dunnac said. "But I sought no coup. I was exiled for discovering the Fireborn had infiltrated the court of Maag."

Orain hissed in irritation and poured fresh wine for them.

"I don't understand," Wrynn said, looking back and forth between them. "I thought the Fireborn were respected in Rull Halak."

"Things have changed," Orain said. "They've grown more radical, more violent."

"They seek to wake Silandra," Orain said, all trace of good humor gone from his face.

Wrynn had heard the legends of the Semblance of Dreams slumbering in her draconic form, somewhere beneath the desert sands of Rull Halak. He wasn't sure he believed it. "So Maag exiled you because you might reveal the truth?"

Dunnac shook his head. "The exile was for show. Maag made a show of casting me out so the Fireborn wouldn't consider me a threat and continue to think Maag weak. That would give us time."

"Time to do what?" Wrynn asked.

Dunnac drank more wine. "Carry out royal business," he said tersely.

Orain's fierce, toothy grin returned. "But they've made a fatal mistake. They broke the King's edict. Now we can go home and prove their treason. Maag will dispense *justice*." He banged his fist on the table, making Wrynn jump.

"Orain," Dunnac said softly. "Maag is dead."

Slowly, Orain's face fell into disbelief. "What?"

"The Fireborn told me. The edict is lifted. They have taken Rull Halak."

"It's a lie," Orain said, standing up in anger. "It has to be!"

Dunnac put his wine cup down. "I do not think so."

Orain gripped the surface of the table as if he planned to flip it over. Wrynn leaned back hastily, cradling his cup to his chest.

Then Orain relaxed, pounding both fists on the table's surface. "Then we go back. We take back the throne and exterminate the Fireborn once and for all."

Dunnac shook his head. "Not yet. We have unfinished business here."

Orain sputtered with rising fury. "*Dunnac—*"

Dunnac ignored him and turned to Wrynn. "I'd like you to finish your wine outside while we talk," he said in a tone that did not sound like a request.

Wrynn looked nervously between the other two men. "You do know we're supposed to meet Shoneg's contact soon."

"I know." Dunnac gestured toward the door. "This will only take a moment."

Wrynn refilled his wine cup and stepped outside, unhappy about standing around in Lowbridge after dark, annoyed at yet another turn of events, but relieved at being away from the angry conversation. The sun had gone down, a cool but rank breeze from the river wafting in the direction of the hovel. In a little while, what few Scarlets patrolled this area would call it a night, and the roving gangs would be out in force.

Putting his back to the door, he swirled the wine around in his cup for awhile, then decided he didn't want it and tossed it into the street.

He didn't like any of this. He had made a nice, terrible life for himself in Calushain. He swindled or gambled just enough to get by. He harmed no one. The Seventh House wanted him back in Ladris, which was terrifying and still unexplained, and the deal with Shoneg was too pat for him to place any faith in it. He was being swept up in matters bigger than him, and Dunnac's involvement with a coup in Rull Halak — or whatever it was — only further complicated the situation.

His life had been small, predictable, measured in drink and sleep. He had made his peace with exile. But now, he was in the dark, spiraling out of control, as forces manipulated him to their own ends.

The dragon's principle has me again.

Voices rose inside the hovel, speaking Halakin. The men were arguing. Wrynn doubted they knew he spoke Halakin. On impulse, he amplified his hearing, turning an ear toward the door. Discomfort swelled in his neck and wrists, but the spell worked.

"—need to leave," Orain's voice said, strained with anger. "Forget your contract with Shoneg. We have a ship waiting at the harbor and enough gold to get back in comfort. We can be back in Rull Halak in a matter of weeks."

Enough gold? Wrynn hadn't considered that a Halakin noble would have money, and Dunnac certainly hadn't brought it up.

"I said, not yet," Dunnac's soft, implacable growl. "I want to complete this job. I found out what Shoneg Vulker is looking for."

A pause. "The weapon?"

"An orison," Dunnac said.

Orain hissed. "The vessel of dragon's blood? Dunnac, have you gone mad?"

"Maag's seers gave me what was supposed to be an impossible task," Dunnac said, his voice strangely reverent now. "They said the edict would be lifted when I found a weapon in the west to defeat the enemies of the king."

"Dunnac, that prophecy came straight from Maag's lips. The edict was a sham! You told the foreigner yourself!" Wrynn imagined Orain gesturing wildly in the direction of the door.

"I believe the seers knew what we would find. They sent us here for a reason. The orison could change the fate of Rull Halak. We could use it to destroy the Fireborn."

"Who?" Orain asked incredulously. "*You?*"

"Perhaps," Dunnac answered, almost inaudibly.

Orain, quieter now: "What about your sorcerer friend out there?"

"I saved him from the Fireborn once, then met him again in the gaol. I do not know what purpose he serves in all this, but it is not coincidence."

"Of course it is," Orain said, his voice tight with frustration. "You both made this bargain with Shoneg. Do you think either of them will just let you take the orison for Rull Halak?"

103

"No, I don't," Dunnac said, his voice low and dangerous. "Let me deal with that."

Wrynn backed away from the door, his heart pounding. The headache that had slowly been building grew to alarming proportions, and he broke the spell. The voices faded to unintelligible mutters again.

A few moments later, the door opened, and Dunnac emerged, now wearing a chain shirt under an unadorned black tabard.

"Time to go," Dunnac said. "Are you ready?"

"Just waiting for you," Wrynn said, trying hard to be casual. He smiled uncomfortably. Dunnac studied his face for a moment, his expression unreadable. Then he brushed past Wrynn and stalked down the street, heading west for the river.

Wondering if prayer to the semblances would help or harm him at this point, Wrynn followed, feeling more than ever like an instrument of someone else's will.

CHAPTER EIGHT

STORY LEFT BLADESBARROW AND TOOK to the high road again, walking the rooftops and heading south. She allowed impulse to carry her toward the Star as she thought about the choices that lay open to her now.

She found few.

Crux's betrayal had sealed her fate. Galon owned her now. Without her small hoard of money, there was no way to get passage out of Calushain — not without becoming a slave or a stowaway. If she tried to strike out on her own, Galon would blacklist her, and she would end up with a price on her head. All the good fences were in Galon's pocket. Sooner or later, she would end up in the line of jars, a warning for others.

To be free, Story needed the biggest score she could pull off. Something far beyond what she'd attempted before. Something miraculous.

But miracles were few in Calushain, and she didn't know how to make any of her own.

After climbing up four rooftops, the pain in her side slowed her down. She crouched on a ledge, looking down at the amber glow of the street lamps near the Star. She briefly considered going to the docks and watching the ships, but the thought only filled her with pain now. That dream had been pulled from her reach.

"You should come back, sister."

For a moment, she thought it was Crux's phantom voice in her head again, questioning her, doubting her. But he was there in the flesh, six steps behind.

She rose painfully to her feet. "Go away, Crux."

"We have to talk."

Reluctantly, she turned to face him. He stood near the edge of the roof, hands at his side, looking hangdog and forlorn. For a moment, she wanted very much to push him off.

"You have nothing to say that I want to hear," she said.

"I'm sorry," he whispered.

She scoffed. "The most worthless words of all. You're sorry? You just made me Galon's slave. You realize that, don't you?"

"No," Crux said, raising his hands. "He promised that wouldn't happen."

"Galon's the only person in this city whose promises mean less to me than yours." She turned away and started looking for a path down to the street. With her brother here, the high road no longer felt like a refuge. It was just another reminder that this entire city was her prison.

He scrambled in front of her.

"I won't let it happen," he said, earnest determination written all over on his face. It was the face he made when he lied to himself, when he made a useless vow or a promise he couldn't keep.

"You won't let it happen? You *made* it happen, Crux!"

Her fury spiked, making her hands shake. She stepped toward him, thinking again of the long drop to the street. Sensing her anger, Crux quietly sidestepped from the edge of the roof.

"I was only looking out for you," Crux said. "Calushain is the only home we've ever known, Story. How could you leave it? Here we have work, a home. We have family."

Story laughed bitterly. "Feed yourself that lie if it makes you feel better, Crux, but don't feed it to me. You couldn't stand the thought of me getting away from here, so you turned me in to get a scrap from Galon's table. It's as simple as that."

Crux's face reddened. "What makes you so high and mighty? You went behind my back and then lied to my face. You were going to leave me behind. Were you even planning to tell me?"

The truth of the accusation stung. She'd never thought through that last bit of her plan, fearing the moment when she had to leave her brother behind. She'd agonized over whether she dared tell him her desire to leave the city; whether to stash enough wealth to take him too, or just leave him behind.

But Story had never truly faced that moment. Not until now. "No," she said, folding her arms. "Because I didn't trust you. And I was right."

Crux flinched as if she'd slapped him.

"You've always liked this hole, Crux. Stealing to live, taking their leftovers like they're gifts. You want that life? Fine. But I don't. And you've never listened when I told you that."

"You never told—" Crux switched tactics. "I can find us a big score, appease Galon."

Story rolled her eyes. "I pay my own debts, Crux. I don't want your help. Just stay out of my way."

As she turned to go, Crux sprang forward and grabbed her elbow. "Story. Don't do this. We're family."

Story batted his hand away. "No. We *were* family. Now we're nothing."

She leaped across the gap between rooftops and vanished into the night.

Story ran east until the pain in her side grew unbearable again, then collapsed on the balcony of an abandoned Redwell house. She lay there panting, gazing at the fog-clouded stars and let herself weep a little for the bond she'd severed.

A whisper of regret flickered by, asking if she hadn't been too hard on Crux. She pushed it away. It didn't matter anymore. Crux was nothing to her now. She hadn't seen Wrynn in what already felt like forever. She had no friends to help her now. She was on her own.

The thought emptied her of grief. Wiping away her tears, she rolled to her feet and began moving along the rooftops toward Shadowcourt. A plan had begun to unfurl in her mind, quietly, as if fearing to make its presence known.

Here in Shadowcourt, the rooftops leveled off, red shingles giving way to old gray brick and stone. Story ran recklessly along the top ledges, passing through the shadows of the dragons' wings. Each sunrise, Shadowcourt swam with perfunctory throngs eager to toss coin at their consciences. At this time of night, the great dragon temples stood empty, the statues gazing down on abandoned streets. The people of Calushain worshiped their gods only self-consciously, their shadowy monuments built in the hopes of avoiding divine attention altogether.

Story stopped below one of the statues and sat cross-legged at its feet. The street below lay quiet, and she heard only the hiss of the gaslights and the distant rumble of the ocean.

Story had never felt much interest in the dragons. She'd heard the tales everyone knew: Silandra, whose dreams wrote the thoughts of men; Penumbra, temptress and kingmaker; Lond slaying the dragon Lehemoth at the Shattered Citadel. These were just myths, disconnected from everyday life. She'd rarely found much reason to pray to a semblance for favors. Any faith she had in the kindness of dragons faded with every story she heard. Even the most benevolent among them were deadly and fickle. The semblances cared nothing for their creations. They were best left alone. To Galon and his people, Calushain's god was named gold, and it favored those who held it in their praying hands.

So why was she here, atop this somber temple, if not to pray that some semblance would hear her?

The plan finished unfurling in her mind. She would do what she did best: burglary. She would rob a dragon temple.

She could already hear Crux's phantom voice crying out in dismay. While the temples were not technically on Galon's red list, no one stole from the semblances, out of fear that it would bring terrible luck to the entire crew. Even the dragon-priests, who often dressed in finery and sported silver rings and jewelry, were considered off-limits.

But Story had seen the crowds that passed through the temples at sunrise. Somewhere inside each of these buildings were lockboxes brimming with coin.

This is reckless, Story.

The cautioning voice was not Crux's, but her own. Robbing a dragon temple was not something to rush into. Most of the temples were well-guarded by the queen's Scarlets, and though Shadowcourt was not as well-patrolled by night as the upscale neighborhoods, getting in and out would still be a challenge.

Galon would have her killed if she showed up bearing temple loot, of course, but she no longer cared about that. She wasn't going back to Bladesbarrow. With one night's work, she would gather enough coin to buy herself passage out of Calushain.

The more she thought about it, the more she realized how much her caution and half-measures had held her back. Slowly scraping together coins and trinkets had only given Crux more time to sniff out her plans. His betrayal had wiped out months of hard work. Now, with one quick job, she could take it all back. With a little luck, she could be gone from Calushain before sunrise. She would leave without goodbyes, without any trace of her passage.

What does she leave behind? Shadows and silence.

Story stood and looked up at the statue looming over her. The figure was female, dressed in long robes, with a long head of streaming hair and a ruthless expression, hands upraised as if cradling something invisible and precious. Above the human statue loomed the semblance's other form, a serpentine shape spiked with barbs.

Story had no idea who she was supposed to be. She didn't know her dragons well enough. The semblance's human face seemed to stare past at her in disapproval.

"So?" she asked the statue quietly, fists held at her sides in defiance. "If you don't like it, why don't you stop me? Better yet, why don't you do something useful and help me?"

The semblance did not reply.

"I'm not afraid of you," Story said, wondering why she felt the need to point that out to an inanimate object. The statue's gaze remained unbroken.

Finally, Story sighed. "Fine. How about this deal: keep the guards out of my way for a little while, and you'll never hear from me again. And to show my gratitude, I'll even steal from one of your rivals."

Holding out one arm, she turned slowly in place, pointing toward each of the temples in turn, waiting for a sign or portent to guide her way. When none came, she chose one of the smaller temples, slightly more run-down and darker than the rest. No guardian statue loomed over its roof.

"That one." She smiled up at the statue and patted it on the foot. "Hope you two aren't friends."

Story hopped down to a third-floor balcony, vaulted across a ledge to a sturdy trellis, then climbed down. Flipping up her hood, she moved across the street to the temple shrine.

She didn't notice as a second figure, waiting in the dark, slipped out of the shadows and followed her.

Ashen woke to darkness and silence. He sat up from where he laid sprawled on the grass. A fog had settled around him, chilling his bones.

His ears flicked forward. The street was curiously quiet, devoid of people. He looked around quickly and spied no one. He sniffed the air and smelled nothing.

Slow realization dawned. He wasn't truly awake. The buildings were shadows, the street a sluggish flow of sorcery, iced over with blue-black shards. His body still lay unconscious, beyond the reach of his mind.

Ashen willed himself to wakefulness, but nothing happened. He was locked in sleep, but aware, a lucid dream in the slumber of confluence.

He stood and looked around. As before, the shadowy double of Calushain surrounded him, drawn in radiant smears of magic. The house blazed with orange magelight, the remnants of his battle with the one called Shoneg.

As he watched, a fragment broke off from the inferno and blazed across the sky like a comet into Lowbridge.

A sign. Without hesitation, he threw himself into the featureless sky, following.

The fiery trail arced toward the canals and into the roof of a gambling house, burning through the illusory building like a cinder through paper. Ashen tore through the shadow and followed it down. The orange fragment rounded, deepened in color, orange fading to blood crimson. The orison.

He knew this place. He knew the room. He'd been there before, breaking up a gang smuggling pirated goods from Karsh.

The simplicity of it disturbed him. He walked through empty corridors out to the shadow-cast street. He was alone.

"Penumbra!" he called.

The name stung his lips. The warborn did not swear by any dragon gods, nor name them if they could help it. To do so risked being caught up in their cosmic mischief — but he was already in that trap. His choices had slowly narrowed, the paths he could take quietly blocked until all that remained was to walk into the maw.

His first vision had left him elated at the prospect of drinking knowledge straight from the well of the universe. But now he understood that well belonged to the semblances, and every taste was poison.

"*I know you are here!*" he called. Silence answered.

Ashen growled in frustration. He could either follow the path of this divination, knowing it was set for him by Penumbra, or turn away and try to find the orison on his own. But he would have no idea where to begin and time was short.

Now he understood the uselessness of prophecy, the malice of foreknowledge. He could not disappoint his queen.

"So be it," he hissed to the darkness. Something in the darkness seemed to accept his capitulation. The vision faded, and Ashen woke.

He lay on dry grass, smelling smoke and feeling the ringing shudder of confluence. He sat up. The front of the house had blown into kindling, the edges of the walls glowing with arcane burn-off. There was no fire, nor a crowd. The hedges in front of the house had shielded his unceremonious exit from view.

A small mercy. There would be no gawkers or Scarlets or questions.

Ashen rolled to his feet and stalked back into the house. The man's corpse was a smoking husk, the fine silks turned to ash. He had turned his sorcery in on himself, stoking the fire until it burned him from within — and had cased it in illusion. That took formidable skill.

This man knew about the orison and had burned himself alive to protect that knowledge — but Ashen's vision had shown him where to go, rendering Shoneg's sacrifice worthless. A pointless death was no doubt pleasing to Penumbra, but this made no sense.

Was he being herded toward some unavoidable fate?

It didn't matter. He had a job and there was a clear path to completing it.

He retrieved his fallen sword, mounted his horse, and made for Lowbridge at a gallop.

Story crossed the empty street into an alley and found an unlocked basement window on the temple's west face. She slid through the narrow window onto the floor, fumbling around in near-complete darkness.

Slowly, her eyes adjusted and the blackness became a jumble of shadows. From the dust and silence, it was clear no one had been down here in a long time. Battered furniture, old tapestries and crates of candles lay in piles along the walls. Story looked around quickly, looking for anything she could pilfer easily.

There wasn't much. No trinkets for her tonight. She wouldn't be going back for Counting Day. Tonight, she needed coin.

In the darkness, she spied a dusty staircase leading up to a trap door. She crept up the stairs and put her ear to the hatch. She heard nothing.

Story pushed it open an inch at a time, holding her breath involuntarily. The door didn't creak. A quick glimpse revealed that it opened out onto the temple nave. There was no one in sight. She slipped through and quietly pushed the door shut without latching it.

A faint voice reached her ears: someone chanting. Story crouched behind a weathered wooden pew and peeked over the top.

A man stood in the frescoed apse of the temple, flanked by burning candles before the altar, dressed in silk robes of dark gray.

His shaved head and bronze skin hinted at Karsh heritage, perhaps, or Merrekan. Even from here, she could see his fingers glittered with rings. He was alone, unarmed.

Story fleetingly wished that Crux were with her. By now, he likely would have already clubbed the man on the back of the neck, giving them enough time to scoop up some riches and run into the night—

She pushed the absurd fantasy away. Crux would never have agreed to this.

The man bowed his head, chanting in a language Story had never heard before. His voice, deep and resonant, echoed in the emptiness of the chamber. The hairs on the back of Story's neck stood up.

Then she realized the frescoes above the altar were lit with a crimson radiance, too deep and vivid to come from the candles. Something glowed on that altar.

Sudden fear gripped her. Her instincts told her to retreat. She turned on her heel and braced herself, glancing at the closed front doors. If she ran now, she could be on the street before he even knew she was here —

She took half a step before realizing the doors were barred. From the inside.

"You don't have to hide back there, child."

Story hissed between her teeth and almost ran anyway. But something tranquil in the man's tone held her back.

She turned back to face the apse. The man turned to face her, his hands slipping into the pockets of his robes. The red glow was gone, if it had ever been there in the first place.

"All are welcome in the shrine of Penumbra," the man said. "These walls have been silent too long. Let them hear voices again."

Story stood, rubbing clammy hands on her trousers. He had to know she hadn't come in through the front door. Yet he'd greeted her like a friend. Why wasn't he sounding an alarm right now?

"I don't know much about Penumbra, actually." She said cautiously. He seemed harmless enough. Maybe she could case him out a bit after all. Whatever the glowing thing was, she wanted to get another look at it.

"She is the creator of the etheric Drog Ungru." He pointed to one of the frescoes, where a stone-skinned drokai wearing golden armor lay in the mouth of a great black serpent. "God to the drokai and scourge of the Lotus Throne."

Story squinted at the fresco. "Is she eating that guy?"

"The opposite," the man said. "She's bringing him to life again after his death."

"Looks messy."

"Life always is. Don't you know your history?"

"A little."

"Drog Ungru conquered Snowcastle and nearly toppled the entire Ladris Empire."

"Until Amaraxis ate him."

The man chuckled. "So you do know a little history. She owed a debt. That was her payment."

"Dragons can owe people?"

"Oh yes," the man said and sat on the stairs leading to the altar. "You can come closer. I don't bite."

Story chose the aisle side of a pew and perched on the edge. "So, what? Amaraxis ate him because he was too powerful?"

"Sometimes power must be checked. That is the way of Amaraxis. She corrects the imbalances of power created by the other dragons."

Story pointed to a painting on the left side of the apse: two women standing beside one another, one raven-haired and all in black, the other red-haired and dressed in crimson. "Who are those two?"

The man craned his neck. "The first is Amaraxis, Semblance of Power, in her human form. The other is her sister, Penumbra, Semblance of Shadow."

"Why shadow?"

The man shrugged. "She exists where the light cannot reach. Like Amaraxis, she bestows power, but only to sow discord and upheaval."

"Oh," she said. "So I take it the sisters don't get along."

"Siblings often don't."

She laughed humorlessly.

The priest pointed at the woman in black. "History casts Penumbra as a temptress, whore and kingdom-breaker. And she has brought kingdoms to ruin. But greater ones have risen in their place."

"So without evil, there is no good," she said. She'd heard this one before, from the rantings of some loudmouth priest in Harrows, until someone had thrown a stone at him and broken his arm.

The man shrugged. "I believe good and evil are leaky ships that will not hold the weight we place in them."

"But a man will climb aboard either ship if he's drowning," Story said.

The man laughed again, louder this time. "I like you. What's your name?"

"Story," she blurted before she could think twice.

"A pleasure to meet you, Story. I'm Credo."

Story nodded, not quite ready to shake hands. She looked at the scarlet dragon hopefully. "So is there a semblance that looks after people who have nothing?"

"Everyone has something, child."

The answer disappointed her. "You must be joking."

The man laughed, an easy, good-natured laugh made Story smile a little. His teeth gleamed white in the gloom.

"Not all power is the same," he said. "Some rule over others, some over only themselves. Amaraxis gives us the choice to pursue what we will rule, large or small."

"For a priest of Penumbra, you know an awful lot about Amaraxis."

Credo glanced at her sharply. "There are no priests of Penumbra."

Story looked around the temple: the dust-free pews, the jeweled statue of the semblance herself on the glossy marble altar. "Oh. I just assumed..."

"The temple is looked after so she will not feel offended," Credo said, a look of disdain in his eye. "As if the Semblance of Shadow has an ego to wound."

"Doesn't she? If the dragons created us, wouldn't they have personalities like us?" She tried to imagine a god as amoral and greedy as Galon, as stubborn and patronizing as Crux. It wasn't difficult.

Credo gazed at the statue. "She is nothing like us. Nothing like the other semblances. Her temples lay empty. The songs written in her name are no longer sung. There are only those she calls to her service. Those whose hearts she knows and understands."

She didn't particularly like the sound of that. "Like whom?"

He turned to face her. "You came here tonight to rob the temple," he said.

Story leaped off the pew and took a few steps back. "How would you know that?" she said before it even occurred to her to deny it.

He laughed softly, still perfectly at ease. "Do not fret, Story. There are no guards here. No one will raise an alarm. I have seen to it."

Something in his voice chilled her blood. She put her hand on her knife. "What's that supposed to mean?"

"We are all called in some way, Story. We are all shaped by the divine in this world, whether we accept that or not." He stood, and Story caught sight of the glowing red shape in the folds of his robe. "I was called, and now I must answer, though it means my life. Can you understand the beauty of that?"

"No," Story said, edging back. "Stay away from me."

"I'm not going to hurt you, Story. I must leave."

"Fine." She stepped between the pews, moving out from between Credo and the door. The profound badness of this entire idea suddenly crashed in on her. "Then do it."

Credo walked past her, that placid expression still on his face. Story watched him carefully, not moving. The priest unbarred the door, then paused and spoke.

"You asked me if there was a semblance that looked out for those who have nothing. You stand in her presence. She favors those who have the courage to take what they wish from life. Ask yourself what you are willing to do, in the dark, when no one watches. No one but Penumbra."

He set the bar aside and opened the door. As he stepped through, he looked back and smiled. "Have a good life, Story. Watch for leaky ships."

Then he was gone. Story was alone in the darkened temple. Slowly, she turned her gaze to the jeweled statue of Penumbra that stood on the altar.

"Is this really the place?" Wrynn asked.

"Good question," Dunnac said, frowning at the ruined edifice of the Silver Wheel. If it had once been a gambling house, it was long since abandoned. The windows gaped dark mouthfuls of broken glass, the front awning sagging and torn. Paint and boards peeled back from the building on all sides. The remains of a sign tilted against the front steps: a broken silver circle rendered in faded paint.

"I guess business hasn't been going too well," Wrynn said. He adjusted the cuffs of his coat, his nervous habit when he expected to be slinging magic.

"At least we won't have to worry about eavesdroppers." Dunnac gestured at the door. "After you."

"Thanks." After overhearing the conversation at the hovel, he didn't like the idea of showing Dunnac his back, but there wasn't much to be done about it. Wrynn ascended the creaking steps and tested the door. Though it was falling off its hinges, it was unlocked. He stepped inside.

In the darkness, wreckage and neglect. A handful of tables, stacked with chairs, collected dust along with the empty bar. The floor was strewn with glass, garbage and the telltale detritus of frequent squatters. A broken staircase led up to the second level.

"Smells like a latrine in here," Dunnac said, hand on his blade.

"So does the job. Guess we must be in the right place."

"Imagine you feel right at home." Dunnac cracked a dry smile. His apparent relaxation put Wrynn ill at ease.

"Very. I'm going to retire here when we're all through."

"Can you give us a little light?"

Wrynn lit off a lux spell, forming a marble-sized ball of light and sending it to hover behind his right shoulder. The light scattered shadows across the room. His wrists ached again.

"Not much of a welcome," Wrynn said. "Perhaps he's waiting in the back."

"Hope so. I wouldn't want to brave those stairs." Dunnac pointed to a hallway leading into darkness behind the bar and led the way.

Wrynn's uneasiness grew as they approached the rear of the building. Something was amiss — and not just in the sense that he was in far over his head with a stranger he couldn't trust. Something felt off in the arcane flows, something he couldn't quite place. Perhaps it was the presence of the orison itself. That would make sense, although it was hardly comforting. If he could sense the unusual fluctuations, it was damn certain others in the city could as well.

Or maybe it was just nerves. He certainly had enough to feel nervous about. Wrynn fidgeted with his cuffs again.

Dunnac pushed open a door at the end of the hall. The corridor flooded with dim ruby light. Wrynn snuffed his spell. This was a room for cards and drinking; like the front room, it was now scattered with junk and furniture. A lean man in dark robes sat cross-legged on the floor, a glowing red orb cradled in his lap.

The two men approached cautiously.

"You're Credo?" Dunnac asked, moving to the man's left. Instinctively, Wrynn moved to flank.

"I am," the man said. "You are the ones sent by Shoneg."

Dunnac's eyes wandered to the ruby light of the orison. "We're here to take the delivery."

"Of course," Credo said. He held up the radiant red orb, its surface crawling with black patterns. "I was just taking a last moment to admire it. Lovely, isn't it?"

"Yes, it's adorable," Wrynn said. "Would you put a cover over it or something, please?"

For some reason the man found this funny. "Of course," he said as he produced a heavy leather drawstring bag and dropped the orb inside, leaving the strings loose. "Will that suffice?"

118

Wrynn held out his hand for the bag. The man made no move to hand it over.

Dunnac shifted his weight. "Is there a problem?" he asked at last.

"Yes," Credo said. "There is one more thing."

Dunnac scowled. "If you're expecting some sort of payment, Shoneg didn't say anything about it."

"No, no payment," Credo said, smiling wider.

Wrynn thought he saw something sad in the man's expression. He felt the surge of confluence, too late. Then the front door of the Silver Wheel blew inward off its hinges.

The blur moved too fast in the dark for Wrynn to identify it. It wore an aegis spell and wielded a blade that hummed with sorcery. Then it burst upon them like a gale, and Wrynn saw a blur of fangs and pointed, furry ears.

A warborn. Wielding sorcery.

As the creature barreled down the corridor, Wrynn threw a polarizing spell, violently redirecting the warborn's direction. The other sorcerer's aegis partially deflected the spell, blowing the hallway doors open in a column of dust and dirt. The warborn spun sideways into the room, careened into the wall and landed hard on his back.

Wrynn screamed as both his arms burst into searing agony. He felt a sensation of something arcane breaking inside him. Through a blur of tears, he saw angry orange strands of light sear down his forearms, forming an intricate braid of shapes—

The strands were still there. The alchemist had only masked them, suppressed their effect, fooling him into thinking they were gone. Now the masking spell shattered, and pain paralyzed both his arms. He gagged with pain.

Dunnac drew his blade the moment the front door blew open. The Halak moved to head off the stunned warborn. Credo rose up, dark tendrils of sorcery blooming around him. The man's eyes turned black.

This is bad.

Wrynn's hands and arms burned with agony. In desperation, he slapped at the orison in Credo's hand, knocking it out of his grip. It came loose from the bag and rolled across the floor. Wrynn dove for it, winced as his hand closed around its smooth surface for a moment. He felt the warm, greasy touch of its power, like acid against his burned flesh, reaching for him, assessing him with an inhuman intelligence. Then Credo grabbed him by the collar of his coat and yanked him up.

"Unworthy," Credo growled, snatching the jewel away, and threw Wrynn to the floor.

Credo turned and darted for the rear door of the Silver Wheel. Dunnac spun on his heel and whirled his sword in a downward arc, chopping through Credo's collarbone from behind. Blood sprayed in a dark jet. Credo stumbled, then crashed through the back door. Wrynn heard him tumble down the rear steps.

The warborn had regained his feet and now stepped forward, sword ready.

"*Get him!*" Dunnac pointed to the door Credo fell through, then moved to intercept the warborn.

"Got it—" Wrynn groaned and turned to pursue. Then a shimmering fist of sorcery from the warborn backhanded him, hard as brick. He sailed through the air to hit the far wall head-first. His head filled with a ringing gray fog as he slid to the floor again.

Wrynn blinked through the pain as Dunnac and the warborn engaged in the tight confines of the room. The warborn's reflexes were accelerated, his sword moving in a blur of silver light. Dunnac sidestepped some swings, parrying others, as if he knew where the blows were coming from. But his teeth clenched, his left sleeve already dripping with blood where the warborn had landed a hit.

Wrynn couldn't figure why the warborn hadn't simply tossed Dunnac through a window. Then he measured the arcane force in the room and realized the warborn's confluence, like his reflexes, was cranked so high he couldn't use any more magic without risking death.

It wasn't much of a disadvantage. As Wrynn struggled to his feet, he watched the warborn toss a heavy table aside with one sweep of his arm, his muscles knotted like the trunk of a pine. If he landed a hit, he'd cut Dunnac in half.

Wrynn almost put a bolt of sorcery in the warborn's back before he remembered the strands. He looked down at his arms, now a snarl of burst blood vessels and discolored flesh. Even throwing an aegis on Dunnac could cripple Wrynn for life.

So let them kill each other, a voice in Wrynn's mind whispered. He glanced at the open door that Credo had crashed through. *Get out of here and save yourself.*

No. He could never live with himself.

Dunnac and the warborn closed on each other again. The warborn swung in a downward slash; the Halak deflected it with his own blade. In a blink, the warborn smashed his elbow into Dunnac's face. Dunnac flew back into a stack of crates, his sword flipping out of his hands. The warborn stalked toward the stunned Dunnac, blade upraised.

Wrynn held out his hand. Long ago, in another lifetime, a Praxis instructor had shown him how to seize another sorcerer's confluence and amplify it. He called it the *metis praxa*. Wrynn's instructor had been clear: at no time should anyone use it on someone whose confluence was already leveraged to its maximum.

Which was exactly what Wrynn did now.

As such spells went, it was relatively minor — nothing compared to unleashing raw offensive power. It felt like both hands were being slowly crushed in a white-hot flywheel. Wrynn screamed himself raw, his world graying out into a blur of agony.

But it worked.

The room shuddered with magical energy. For a moment Wrynn couldn't breathe. Then the warborn and the room around him burst into flames. The warborn howled — a terrible keening sound that froze Wrynn's blood — and turned to charge him. Wrynn braced for death. Even without magic, the warrior could still take him apart. He had nothing left. Another spell thrown in this place could kill them all.

Then Dunnac clubbed the warborn in the back of the head with the pommel of his sword. Bellowing, the warborn swung, blind with pain and fury. Dunnac landed a front kick to his chest, sending him flying into the hall, trailing fire.

"*Come on!*" Dunnac shouted and grabbed Wrynn's sleeve, hauling him out the back door into the night.

Behind them, the Silver Wheel burned.

CHAPTER NINE

This is stupid, Story. Stop hesitating and just do it.

Story stood before the statue of Penumbra, knife in hand. The jeweled eyes of the dragon stared back impassively. Yet she couldn't seem to bring herself to prise them from the dragon's skull.

Her first impulse had been to run the moment Credo left the temple. But after a quick look around, she determined that she was, for whatever reason, alone here. The priest had been right: no guards, no witnesses. She could take what she wanted, including the statue's eyes, rubies fat as fingers. No lock-boxes to pry open, no heavy coin to lug around.

So she locked the temple doors, replaced the bar, drew her knife, and approached the idol of Penumbra with confidence. A few quick motions and freedom could be hers.

But now she couldn't do it. She had taken time to check the temple thoroughly for guards or squatters, finding no one. Even so, she had lost her nerve and almost left the temple empty-handed. Now she was back in front of the statue again, staring at it endlessly, *knowing* she was wasting time but unable to commit herself to the act of theft.

Penumbra's graven image stared at her with mute challenge. *She favors those who have the courage to take what they wish from life.*

Credo's words seemed to imply that Penumbra would want Story to take the jewels. But something about that bothered her. Credo also seemed to know why Story was here. He might have just figured it out on his own, but on the other hand —

"You're being stupid," she whispered to herself. "The gods aren't watching. They don't care what you do."

So take the jewels, the statue seemed to answer. *Take my eyes so I cannot see.*

Story hissed with annoyance at her overactive imagination. "I'll do it," she said. "But not because you're telling me to."

Grimacing at her own absurdity, she leaned forward and touched the dragon's head, working the point of her knife under its gleaming ruby eye.

A loud crash sounded behind her. The room shuddered, air pushing at her back. Story yelped and leaped away from the altar, knife at the ready. Suddenly, inexplicably, the temple smelled of smoke and blood, a curious ringing echoing through the nave.

A crumpled figure lay in the center aisle. As Story watched, blood began to seep out from under its gray robes. Credo.

Heart drumming in her ears, she approached him. He didn't move. She turned him onto his back. Her hand came away black with blood. Something had cut through the junction of his neck and shoulder, leaving a gaping, ragged wound.

Credo smiled, showing a mouthful of reddened teeth.

"Story," he said. "I hoped you'd still be here."

"Are you—" she began, then realized how stupid the question was; he wasn't all right and never would be again.

"How did you get back in here?" she asked instead, bewildered.

"It doesn't matter," Credo said, wheezing laughter.

Something fell out of his grasp onto the floor: an oily leather bag, strings tied tight. The source of that mysterious red glow.

Her fingers twitched. For a moment, she considered grabbing it and running. But desperate or not, she wouldn't leave this man to die alone like this. Not that there was much she could do.

Credo's eyes met hers. To her astonishment, he nodded slowly.

"Take it," he whispered.

"No. You need help."

His face contorted in agony. "It's far too late for that. Take it and run. Remember what I told you."

She drew back, feeling a pang of guilt.

With his one working hand, the man pushed the bag toward her. She realized the curious ringing in her ears was coming from the orb inside — discordant and yet somehow soothing, like a chorus of whispers.

"Hurry," Credo groaned, baring his teeth. His breath rattled in his lungs. He made an alarming coughing noise and spit up red.

"Why would you give me this?" she asked and then realized she was talking to a corpse, its lips still locked in that lunatic grin.

In the distance, she heard alarm bells and shouts. She had wasted too much time after all. It was time to go.

Hesitantly, Story knelt and took the bag. "I'm sorry," she said to the dead man.

As she made for the hatch in the floor, Story looked back at the statue of Penumbra. The dragon seemed to smile at her.

Dunnac dragged Wrynn away from the conflagration at Lowbridge. Flames roared into the sky behind them, the air ringing with confluence. They stumbled into the dark, away from the smoke and the alarm bells.

Wrynn coughed, trying to catch his breath. His hands and arms still throbbed with agony. He was afraid to look at them again after that last spell. He looked around. There was no sign of Credo.

"Can you stand?" Dunnac asked.

Wrynn nodded. Dunnac set him on his feet. They cut down a side street, away from the gathering crowd.

Dunnac grimaced as he caught sight of Wrynn's hands. "You're injured."

Self-consciously, Wrynn shoved his hands in his pockets. "In a sense. The strands are still on."

"How is that possible?"

"Shoneg's alchemist used a masking spell. Damned good one, too. It removed the tattoos and diminished the pain, but their fundamental effect was still in place. The masking spell broke when I hit that warborn. If I'd tried casting anything more powerful than I did, I'd probably have blown both my hands off."

"Shoneg betrayed you."

"Or Jhal. Or both."

Dunnac scratched his head, weighing this new information. "We need to get out of Lowbridge. The whole place will be crawling with Scarlets soon."

Wrynn set his jaw. "Not without the orison. I'm not going through all this for nothing."

Dunnac nodded. "He couldn't have gotten far. I scored a good hit on him."

Wrynn looked up and down the street where they'd emerged from the conflagration. "He didn't go this way. A man bleeding that much would leave a trail of blood and curiosity. We'll check the alleys first."

They moved, scouring the alleys and side streets as quickly as they could. The night sky was already orange with flame by the time they stopped searching. There was no sign of Credo — no blood, no trail, nothing left behind. The man was simply gone.

"Of course," Wrynn said with a sigh.

Dunnac spat on the ground. "He shouldn't have been able to run after that blow."

Wrynn leaned against the alley wall, his arms crossed tight, hands buried in coat sleeves. "He knew sorcery. Hidden spells all over him. I felt him drop the obfuscations when everything went to hell. It probably held his body together long enough for him to get a little distance."

"Why didn't he stay and fight, then?"

Wrynn pondered. "Wasn't that warborn there to fight for him?"

Dunnac shook his head with a scowl. "I don't think they were working together. He wore a brooch with the three blades of Calushain on it. Military elite. He works for the Queen of Storms."

Realization dawned on Wrynn. "That's why you didn't kill him."

"Figured we had enough trouble," Dunnac said.

"You aren't wrong. If the Queen of Storms knows about the orison, this was their only chance to keep it quiet. She'll have the gates and ports sealed now. No one's getting out until it's in her hands."

"That's unfortunate."

"Isn't it just?"

Dunnac rubbed his chin. "How did she come to know about it in the first place?"

"I don't know," Wrynn said, pushing away from the wall. "But I intend to find out."

By the time they reached the tunnel back to Harrows, an entire block was burning. The fire spread quickly, sending alarm bells clanging through the borough. Scarlets and citizens scrambled to form fire-chains along the canal in an attempt to contain the blaze. Wrynn felt a pang of guilt at causing so much destruction. That hadn't been his intention, but the *metis praxa* was unpredictable. His instructor would not be pleased.

They came to a halt in an abandoned park that looked down on Lowbridge, far from the crowds. Wrynn sat down and put his back against a tree, grimacing in pain.

"That went poorly," Dunnac said.

"Noticed that, did you?"

"You fought well."

Wrynn felt an inexplicable twist of pleasure at the compliment. He hadn't felt like he'd fought well — he'd felt like screaming with terror and curling into a ball until it all went away — but he hadn't panicked.

Then Wrynn remembered the conversation at the hovel, and the man's less complimentary words. *Let me deal with that.*

"Thanks," he said, clearing his throat. "I don't suppose you have a drink."

Dunnac produced a battered metal flask.

Wrynn pushed back his sleeves. It was about as bad as he'd imagined. Both arms were swollen from wrist to elbow, the strands once again visible: purple-black strands outlined in angry red.

He took the flask, gagged on a swallow. "Lond, what is this?"

"Halakin whiskey."

"It tastes like lamp oil." He drank again, then handed the flask back.

Dunnac put it away without drinking. "So you can't use your magic again until we get those strands off," he said after a long silence.

"That's right. And I can't exactly get a refund, can I? He's probably back in Galadrok for all I know."

The warrior frowned. "But if you had your magic, could you track the orison? Find out where it is?"

Wrynn nodded. "Yes, now that I've touched it. But—" He flexed his bruised fingers.

"Then we're going to need your abilities to find the thing," Dunnac said. "Unless you want to wait for the Queen of Storms to get her hands on it."

"No, thanks. I still have those Imperial assassins on my tail."

"And the Fireborn on mine."

Wrynn stood with a wince. "Doesn't sound like we have much of a choice, does it? We need to find our friend Shoneg and get the truth about what's going on."

Mercy Shoals lay west of the Quay, a broken-down old dock that no one ever used anymore, a graveyard of rotten pilings and dry-docked hulls. It was home to squatters, beggars and prostitutes, grimy castoffs from the bustle of the Quay itself.

Even by the standards of Calushain, it was a hellhole. There was no good reason to go there — so it was the first place Story headed after leaving Shadowcourt.

She ran, sticking to the shadows, holding the bag close to her chest. Occasionally, she caught a glimpse of the tower of flame and smoke billowing above Lowbridge. In a perverse way, she was thankful. The fire averted curious eyes from one lone girl moving through the Quay.

Story spotted her tail just as she reached the southern end of the Star: cloaked, probably male from his shape. Probably some cutthroat she'd picked up, waiting for a good time to strike.

Continuing west, she stuck to the back alleys of the Quay, staying on the north side, away from the open space of the docks. As she neared Mercy Shoals, the passers-by became less frequent, the architecture older and more dilapidated. She emerged into an old fisherman's row: a dozen long, empty stalls, still stinking of rancid sea life where the fishmongers once plied their trade.

She jinked right at the end of a narrow alley, with an eye toward finding a dark place somewhere in the line of stalls to hide.

He was waiting for her around the corner. The dark figure tripped her, sending her flying. She skidded, the bag still clutched to her chest. Reaching for her knife, she flipped over as the figure approached. Story felt a surge of terror, which shifted to anger when her attacker threw back his hood.

"Crux?"

"Gods, Story, but you run fast when you want to." He reached out a hand to help her up.

She slapped it away and stood up on her own. "How long have you been following me?"

"Since Shadowcourt."

"Why?"

"I told you, I'm looking after you. Keeping you safe."

She stomped on his boot, hard. He yowled, hopping on his good foot.

"I don't need you to keep me safe," she said. "I need you to leave me *alone.*"

He grimaced. "Story, I understand you're upset—"

"Furious, more like it. Get out of here, Crux. I don't want to see you again. Ever."

He gave her a hurt expression. "You don't mean that."

She lunged as if to stomp on his other foot, and he scrambled back. Desperate to change the subject, he nodded at the bag. "So what did you lift off that crazy old man in the temple?"

She didn't bother asking how he knew. "Why? Want to steal it from me like you did the rest of my things?"

"I did that for your own good, Story. Let me see what's in the bag."

"No."

"Come on." He swiped for it and she yanked it out of his reach. But he was fast. He stepped behind her and wrapped his arms around her, grabbing for the bag. She elbowed him hard in the ribs, but he fell back with the bag and wrenched it from her grasp.

She rounded on him. "Crux, give it back. I mean it."

"I just want to see. Don't be such a child."

Story advanced, ready to tax her brother a couple of teeth for that remark. She stopped when Crux pulled the luminous red orb out of the bag, flooding the wet street with crimson light.

"Sweet Lehemoth," Crux swore, turning the orb over in his hands. "What is it?"

"I don't know," Story said, momentarily hypnotized by the fluid motion of black motes inside the orb. "It's beautiful."

"Is it full of liquid or something?" Crux shook it. The motion in the orb didn't change. "I wonder if there's a way to open it."

"I doubt it. Give it back."

"Just a second. Remember, I'm the man who can open anything."

"You're the boy with delusions of grandeur. Give it to me or I'll break your other foot. For real this time."

Annoyed, Crux tossed the orb carelessly back to her. She scrambled to catch it. Something stirred deep inside the orb as she touched it, like an egg ready to hatch. She ran a thumb across its surface, noticing how warm and almost soft it felt, watching the black motes flow behind the path of her thumb like leaves in a river.

Her brother handed her the bag. "You're going to give that to Galon, right?"

"Maybe," she said, hurriedly putting the orb away.

"Maybe? Story, that thing could probably pay off your debt in one night. He'll be overjoyed."

"One, you don't know what this thing is and he probably doesn't either. Two, he'll never let me pay off the debt. You're an idiot if you think so."

Crux's jaw clenched and he broke into an angry scowl. "I won't let you abandon your family, Story."

Story fumed. She couldn't believe he had the audacity to try that line on her yet again. "We're not family, Crux. You're Galon's lackey, and I'm his slave."

He grabbed her arm, fingers digging into her flesh. "You take that back!"

Then he froze as he felt the cold steel of Story's knife at his throat.

"Take. Your hands. Off me," she said slowly.

"Or what — you're going to cut my throat?" The bravado in his tone quivered a little.

She pressed the blade a little harder against his flesh. "Try me."

He held very still, his eyes pleading with her. "Story, what happened to you?"

"Funny you should ask. My brother and only family betrayed me. Now let go or you'll be eating through a hole in your neck."

He let go. She backed up, still pointing the knife at his face.

"Do not follow me," she said. "Do not talk to me. From now on, you're Galon's toady and nothing else to me, do you understand?" She heard her voice breaking, felt a single hot tear escape down her cheek. She hated herself for it.

Crux hung his head, saying nothing. Story turned her back on him and ran north, back toward the Star, the bag clutched under one arm, knife in hand.

She managed not to weep again until he was out of her sight.

Ashen One-Howl rode north to Stormhelt, to report failure to his queen and accept his punishment.

Warborn did not damage easily. The flames conjured by the human sorcerer singed his fine cloak to bits of flaking ash, but the sting was not enough to stop him. Only the human's alteration of his confluence, transforming the controlled burn of his sorcery into a reckless inferno, had turned him aside. Against such a conflagration, even he had no defense. He chose to withdraw until the magic bled off enough for him to think clearly again.

By that time, it had been too late. Ashen doubled back to track his quarry, muscles ragged and raw in the aftermath of his augmentative spells, only to find the trail cold. The smoke from the burning hovel masked any scent the humans left behind and the bright streaks of runaway confluence hopelessly confounded the magical trail.

In his desperation, Ashen found a quiet corner away from the flames and sought another vision, but could not break through his keening frustration. Whatever favor the semblances granted him, he had squandered. There were no more visions for him now.

If he could have touched the orison, he could have tracked it to the ends of the earth. But now he had no choice but to return to Stormhelt and mount a search for the remaining humans.

Ashen stabled his horse at the Citadel and stalked inside, ignoring the salutes from the terrified subordinates. Sour defeat gnawed at his belly. He did not want to admit his failure before the queen, but neither could he hide it. Her every word would sear him with silent admonishment.

As he passed through the bronze-lined pillars of the Citadel, his footsteps echoed off the marble walls. Servants scuttled into the shadows at the sound.

"One-Howl."

A wizened shape emerged from the arched hallway that led to his quarters.

"I'd like a word," Ravano said.

"Now is not the time."

"It's important," the old man said. "I ask only a moment."

Ashen sighed through his nose. "Very well."

He followed Ravano to his chambers. The old scholar lived largely out of a single room, every surface piled with books and parchment cases, the carpet worn thin from endless pacing. Faint light streamed in through grubby windows, half-blocked with piled books.

After closing the heavy door behind them, Ravano sat, leaving Ashen to stand.

Ashen crossed furred arms across his chest. "I do not intend to stay long, Ravano. What do you want?"

Ravano excavated a carafe and two bronze cups from his desk, triggering a small avalanche of papers in the process. "Care for some wine?"

"No."

Ravano shrugged and poured himself a cup. "This is a matter of some delicacy, One-Howl. I hope I can count on—"

"My discretion," Ashen said through clenched teeth. The human instinct for circumlocution infuriated him. "We shall see. Get on with it."

Ravano sneered. "I know what you seek, One-Howl. I know there is an orison in Calushain. I suspect the Queen of Storms ordered you to find and deliver it to her."

"A reasonable suspicion, seer."

Ravano drummed his fingers on the desk. "You must not give it to her."

The reluctance of the seer's tone stoked Ashen's suspicions. "Why not?"

"Do you know what that thing is, One-Howl?"

Ashen shook his head. "The word itself means prayer. In my vision, Penumbra called it power. The Queen called it discord."

"All are correct. An orison is encapsulated gnosis, draconic communion — the blood of the semblances. Not literally, of course. If sorcery is an opening of the way to Kulraizhan, the orison is a fragment of true power. It has the power to reshape souls. It is said an orison created the first etheric."

Ashen shifted uncomfortably. "Say on."

Ravano poured himself another cup of wine, sipping nervous draughts between sentences. "It takes several semblances working in concert for centuries to make an orison. But the artifact assumes the aspects of one semblance maker in particular. If that semblance is Penumbra, then that orison resonates with her power and demeanor."

"And?" Ashen said. "If the queen is powerful enough to master it— "

"She isn't," Ravano said. "Even if it did not destroy her outright, she could not control it. The orison belongs to Penumbra, made in her image, to sow discord to feed upon. If she partakes of its power, all of Calushain will fly apart and the Red Cities will follow."

"You presume a great deal," Ashen said.

"Do I?" Ravano slammed open a book, rifled through the pages. "Have you read the histories? Have you researched the myths? I have. I know you don't care for me, warborn, but trust what I say. You must deny her this."

"You ask the impossible. What the queen commands, I fulfill. She is my Sworn."

"No." Ravano stood, jabbing two fingers at the warborn. "I know warborn culture too, One-Howl. You protect your Sworn. You don't obey them to their own detriment. If you do this for her, you will be killing her — and us in the bargain."

Ashen growled under his breath. "Suppose what you say is true. What do you suggest I do? Destroy it?"

Ravano shook his head. "No, to try would be a very bad idea. We must dispose of it some other way. If you were to bring it to me—"

Ashen barked laughter. "You must think I'm a fool, Ravano. You want me to give it to you instead of my queen."

"I don't mean it like that," Ravano said. "But I can keep it safe—"

"Where the queen could not," Ashen finished. "That's very noble. And the queen must be kept ignorant that I handed it over to you. For her own protection, naturally."

"One-Howl, be reasonable. I don't want that kind of power."

"Why would you?" Ashen bared his teeth. "I'm finished with you, Ravano. We will not speak of this again." He turned to leave.

"Ashen, please!" The old man's voice cracked with desperation. "Listen to me, I beg you! You'll be killing her!"

The warborn slammed the door on his cries.

Long past midnight, Dunnac and Wrynn returned to Shoneg's house near Role Point. The second moon, Hunter, rose orange and blotchy over the eastern horizon, adding an infernal tint to the narrow streets above High Canal.

"I smell smoke," Dunnac said as they trudged up the hill to the townhouse. Wrynn had been lagging further and further behind as the journey wore on.

Wrynn was too winded to pay him heed. "We should have bought horses," Wrynn gasped. "I'm an academic; I can't take all this exertion."

"I thought the Praxis were explorers." Dunnac sounded amused.

"They kicked me out. Also, I'd rather explore a nice dry book than streets designed by insane people."

"We don't have money for a horse. Shoneg made sure of that."

"We could rent one."

Dunnac looked back, aghast. "What sort of person rents a horse?"

Wrynn spat politely off to one side. "I forgot, you Halakin consider your horses family."

"A gross distortion of the truth," Dunnac growled.

"Maybe you can explain it sometime when I'm not about to pass out."

They rounded the corner to the street where they'd met with Shoneg. Now Wrynn smelled it too — the acrid tang of smoke and the aura of runaway confluence. Wrynn blinked to summon his magesight: he saw ragged red currents of energy bent inward toward the house, gathered like storm clouds.

"Something bad happened," he said. "Magically speaking," he added when Dunnac gave him a wry look.

They pushed through the thick hedges surrounding Shoneg's house. Wrynn groaned at the destruction: windows blown onto the lawn, the front door sundered into planks.

"I think the warborn was here," Wrynn said, hanging back as Dunnac advanced cautiously toward the door. "The energies look like his. Mixed with something else. Something powerful."

"You'd better come see this," Dunnac said from inside the doorway.

Wrynn caught the sweet stench just before he saw the blackened corpse crumpled in the foyer.

"Is it Shoneg?"

Dunnac drew his blade to prod at a charred swatch of golden silk. "Looks like. Your warborn must have gotten to him first."

Wrynn peered at the carnage with magesight, trying to unravel the snarl of magical energies. "I don't think the warborn did this. His magic had the signature of Iron School training. There's some of that here, but…" He shook his head.

"We'd best not linger." Dunnac took a quick look around the room. "If the Scarlets find us here, it'll be the gallows before sunup."

"I'm not leaving until I get some answers." Wrynn brushed past Dunnac into the wrecked parlor.

"We don't have time for this."

"You can leave if you want," Wrynn snapped. "Our little assignment is clearly a failure. You certainly don't owe me anything at this point."

Dunnac glared, but remained by the front door while Wrynn searched.

Wrynn rifled through drawers, bookshelves, piles of disorganized papers. He found the broken orison replica on the floor, dismantled the velvet backing and searched the box. He opened the door to Shoneg's study, went through the desk piled with ledgers, manifests, and bills of sale. Nothing that told him anything.

Wrynn's temper broke. He started hurling books against the walls. In his rage, he threw a spell to yank a tall bookshelf from the wall and sent it crashing across the desk. The strands flared. His yelp of pain brought Dunnac running.

"What are you doing?" Dunnac grabbed him by the shoulder. "You're going to get us noticed."

"There's nothing here," Wrynn seethed, throwing off Dunnac's hand. "There are people after us, we've been lied to at every turn, there's a bright ball of very bad magic loose in the city, and *I have no idea what's going on!*"

"Calm down." Dunnac sheathed his blade.

"We're being played, Dunnac. Herded like cattle into an abattoir and I don't like it."

"Neither do I. But panic will get us both killed. We have some options left."

Wrynn pressed his fingers to his temples to hold back the burgeoning headache forming there. "Like what?"

"We meet with Jhal as planned."

"Without the orison? For all we know, he's the one who killed Shoneg."

"That would answer one question, at least. Do you think that's what happened?"

Wrynn rubbed his burning wrist. "No. It doesn't make sense. What killed Shoneg wasn't Iron School magic. It seems familiar, but I can't place it."

"Then we meet with Jhal. Maybe he has some answers."

"If he finds out this deal's gone around the bend, Jhal will just try to take me back to Snowcastle."

"He does and he'll die," Dunnac said.

Wrynn gaped at him, stunned.

Dunnac nodded. "You said I didn't owe you anything. You're wrong. Those Fireborn back at the statue were after me, not you. You just happened to be in the way. The warborn had me back at the gambling house. You suffered to buy me time." He pointed at Wrynn's bruised, sorcery-mottled arms.

"That was nothing."

"Not to me."

Wrynn felt a twist of embarrassment in his gut. "I'm sorry. I didn't mean—"

"Forget it. We finish this together. Good enough?"

"Good enough. But I have somewhere I need to stop off after—"

Wrynn trailed off, staring wide-eyed at the floor by the shattered bookshelf. "I don't believe it," he said.

Wrynn bent to retrieve a scrap of paper on the floor next to an open book. He smoothed it out to show it to Dunnac: a dozen lines scrawled in some insectile cipher, and above it, a sigil of seven reptilian heads springing from a single round body.

Dunnac squinted. "I can't read this."

"Neither can I, but I know that sigil."

"Dragons?"

"Serpents," Wrynn said. "Shoneg was working for the Seventh House."

Story trudged back home, bone-weary, holding the orb safely under one arm. She felt frightened, sad, hollowed-out by the events of the day. Her brother's betrayal, Galon's ultimatum, the wound in her side that still hurt with every step, the frightening encounter with

Credo — it was all too much. She wanted to curl up and sleep for days.

But first, she wanted to see Wrynn. He would know what the orb was, if it was anything special. He would probably even know what it was worth — Story knew the street value of most jewels, but she'd never handled, or even seen, anything like this before.

More than that, she just wanted to see him. He always had a joke and a kind word. After today, she could use both. Surely he had to be back by now.

She picked up the pace as she neared the Doorstop, the chill of night settling into her bones. "Wake up, old filthy hobo," she said as she approached his crate. "Are you in there? I've got something to tickle your scholarly sensibilities."

She knelt next to the crate and peeked inside. Empty. Disappointment swept over her. She sighed and stood, feeling a hundred years old. Wherever he was, she hoped he was all right.

Listlessly, she scaled the Doorstop to her room and crawled in through the window. She rekindled her optimism just long enough to check the adjoining room, just in case he'd come into some luck at the gaming tables. He wasn't there either.

Story returned to her room, locked the door, and collapsed onto her cot, exhausted. Distantly, a temple bell tolled the early morning hour. The orange moonlight of Hunter threw dim coral radiance against the wooden floor. She caught a faint whiff of smoke through the open window — that fire near Lowbridge, not far from where she'd been. She was too tired to care anymore.

Rolling over, she coaxed the red orb from its bag and laid it on the cot next to her. Its surface crawled with black motes that seemed to float just under the orb's red surface. She touched it hesitantly, pressing down on its hardness. Nothing happened this time. She wasn't sure what she'd expected.

It wasn't coin, like she'd wanted. All the same, it was probably magic, and that meant it was valuable. Maybe this new plan wasn't so great after all. Maybe she could present it to Galon after all and —

The thought invoked fresh despair. There was no going back. Despite what Crux might say, Galon would never trust her again.

She could repay what she owed, but her debt would never be cleared. He would make an example out of her. It was only a matter of time.

Of course Crux believed that throwing money at Galon would solve everything. He thought he knew better than Story. Everyone did.

Briefly, she thought about taking the orb to the Quay, trading it for passage on a ship. But she didn't know anyone there. The first sailor she showed the jewel to was likely as not to take it right out of her hands. Story was fast and small, but she was good at taking things, not trading them. A woman like her had no leverage on the Quay.

So, just give it to Galon, then? Accept your fate and wait for the hammer to fall?

"No," she murmured to herself, covering her face with her hand. Weakness welled up inside her, urging her surrender. *Give the jewel to Galon. Beg for his mercy. Wait for Wrynn. He'll tell you what to do. Look to Crux. He can protect you—*

No. No more living on the mercy of others. One way or another, she would settle this on her own. Tomorrow.

Her eyes grew heavy, her thoughts fragmenting. She held the orb close and curled around it. It felt almost warm as she drifted off to sleep.

The deserted streets began to stir with life by the time Dunnac and Wrynn reached the Prestigious Bastard. Drunks staggered home and shopkeepers along the Star opened their stalls for the day's business.

Wrynn's head throbbed with fatigue. His feet hurt. His arms hurt worse.

"I want a drink," he said.

"They're not going to be open at this hour," Dunnac said.

"Jhal's expecting us. He damn well better be there. If he isn't, I'll tear the Star apart until I find him—" Wrynn undermined his grim oath with a jaw-cracking yawn. "Shut up," he said at Dunnac's wry expression.

When they reached the Bastard, the shutters were drawn and the door locked. Dunnac knocked by kicking the door several times with his boot.

"Closed!" a muffled voice yelled from within. Dunnac kicked harder.

Finally, there was the sound of the bolt being thrown back. The door opened slightly and a face peered through the crack.

"Don't you know the meaning of the word 'closed?'"

"Sorry," Dunnac said, stone-faced. "I'm a godless foreign barbarian. We're looking for a man named Jhal. He said he'd be here."

"Don't know no Jhal." The man attempted to close the door. Dunnac stuck his boot in the gap.

"Maybe you could try to remember," he said.

"You don't know how bribes work in this town, do you?"

"I'm too uncultured to understand unspoken rules."

The man sighed. "He said you might show up. Said he'd be in the wayhouse across the street."

"Most kind," Dunnac said and removed his foot from the door. It slammed shut.

Wrynn scratched his stubble as they started across to the wayhouse. "You really have a way with people."

"The Halakin find bribery offensive."

"Interesting. What do you do with all the money you save?"

"We drink."

"I like your culture."

The wayhouse was almost empty. Wrynn purchased two mugs of beer and headed into the common room.

Jhal dozed in a chair in the common room, next to the fireplace, arms laced over his stomach.

Wrynn set the drinks on the table and squeaked out a chair, startling the man awake. Dunnac leaned against the nearby wall, arms folded.

Jhal sat up straight. "Boys."

"You shouldn't fall asleep on the job like that, Jhal," Wrynn said. "You could get murdered in your sleep."

"My apologies for being discourteous. I was up all night waiting for a pair of feckless reprobates to finish a simple job, which for some reason seemed to take them forever."

"Your job turned out not quite so simple," Wrynn said.

Jhal's eyes narrowed. "What's that supposed to mean?"

"Shoneg's dead. His man Credo is dead. There's a Red Cities sorcerer hunting the orison, which means the Queen of Storms probably knows it's in the city. The artifact itself is missing." Wrynn struggled to keep his voice low as his anger rose.

Jhal nodded slowly, gnawing the inside of his cheek. He looked concerned, but not frightened, which irritated Wrynn further. "Anything else?"

"Actually, yes." Wrynn dropped the folded paper onto the table. "Shoneg worked for the House of Serpents."

If Jhal was surprised, he made no sign. He unfolded the paper and peered at it, then folded it back up. "I'm going to go get a drink."

Wrynn slid a mug across to him. "Got you one. So you don't have to get up."

Jhal gave Wrynn a suspicious look, but sat back and finished half the beer in one long pull.

"We want to know what you know," Wrynn said as the bounty hunter drank. "We're in a lot of trouble and if we don't get some answers, we intend to start making some trouble of our own."

"Bold talk for a man whose magic doesn't work," Jhal said.

Wrynn smiled coldly. "I didn't mention anything about my magic not working, Jhal."

Jhal stiffened, caught in his lie, then sneered with irritation. He said nothing, but now Wrynn knew Jhal had lied about the strand removal intentionally. Now he just had to find out why.

"Besides, my blade works just fine," Dunnac said. He tapped the hilt with a forefinger.

"I suppose it does," Jhal said reluctantly. "All right, we can talk. But it's too public here. I have a room upstairs."

Wrynn finished off his own beer. "No tricks."

"You don't trust me?"

"Not even a little."

Jhal stood. "You're learning, at least."

The bounty hunter's room was windowless and cramped, but the door was solid and the walls were thick. Dunnac leaned against the door jamb as Jhal sat in a rickety wooden chair.

Wrynn stood over him, arms folded. "Start talking."

"You're really not going to like it."

"That seems likely."

Jhal took a deep breath. "You put more of it together than I thought. Shoneg *was* Seventh House. He was a spy for the Empire. His assignment was to destabilize Calushain from the inside."

"Why?" Dunnac asked.

"Diplomatic relations between the Red Cities and the Lotus Throne have been deteriorating for months. Calushain is one of the biggest ports between Four Kingdoms and Esterlund. The Empire wants it. The Seventh House is setting the stage for an invasion."

"The Seventh House's job is to keep the other six houses in line," Wrynn said.

"Not anymore," Jhal said. "The Emperor has given them a new mandate."

Wrynn frowned. "Is that why Shoneg wanted the orison? To use its power against the Queen of Storms?"

"Not quite," Jhal said. "The orison was always intended for the Queen. But we couldn't just give it to her as a gift. That would raise too many suspicions. It had to look like a hard-won prize."

"Then why send us after it?" Dunnac asked.

The bounty hunter fidgeted in his seat. "That's the part you won't like."

"I haven't liked any of this so far," Wrynn said.

Jhal shrugged. "You two were intended to fail. So was Credo, for that matter. Ashen One-Howl — that's the warborn — was tipped off to the exchange. The idea was, he would kill or imprison you, then deliver the orison to the Queen. That way, it would look like One-Howl thwarted some nefarious plot or other."

"Tipped off how?" Wrynn asked, his voice quaking with a fury that implied losing a hand to kill Jhal would be worth it.

"We have a man inside the Queen's court. He's been guiding things along for us."

"I don't understand," Dunnac said. "How does giving the Queen of Storms powerful magic benefit the Empire?"

Jhal grinned. "That orison's not the only one we brought into the Red Cities. There's one in Irongate, and rumors of one in Scarl. In a few months, they'll all start fighting amongst themselves for a chance at being demigods."

"What if one of them *achieves* godhood?" Dunnac asked.

"They won't," Jhal said.

"You don't know that—" Wrynn said, and then his blood froze. He paced the room, running fingers through his unruly hair. "Wait. Yes you do."

They looked at him expectantly: Dunnac perplexed, Jhal delighted, as if waiting for a child to finish putting together a puzzle.

"The orisons don't choose to make someone etheric," Wrynn said. "The dragons do. The Lotus Throne cut a deal with the semblances."

Jhal touched his nose.

"Has the Empire gone insane?" Wrynn shouted. "You can't trust them! The semblances don't give a damn about humanity! Which one is it? Amaraxis? Silindel?"

Jhal folded his hands. "It's not really my place to say."

Wrynn sat on the sunken mattress. "But why would the dragons get involved? What's their end of the deal?"

"Who knows? They're dragons. They love moving humanity like pieces on a game board. That's probably all it is."

"And how exactly do you know all this?" Dunnac asked.

"Simple," Wrynn said. "He's Seventh House too."

Jhal nodded grudging assent. "You think a student of the Iron School just up and turns mercenary? Not too common."

"So we were never supposed to survive," Dunnac said.

"That's right," Jhal said. "If One-Howl didn't get you, then Shoneg would."

"Shoneg?" Wrynn asked. Then realization broke across his face. "He was a sorcerer too. Black School."

Dunnac furrowed his brow. "What's the Black School?"

Wrynn rubbed his eyes. Exhaustion was setting in. He felt like his sanity was bleeding away. "The Black School belongs to the

Seventh House. Subterfuge magic. Intelligence gathering. Illusion and obfuscation. That's what I felt at his house. The magical aura I couldn't identify."

"Look how clever you are," Jhal said.

"But someone killed him before he could get to us," Dunnac said.

"I noticed," Jhal said. "That is troubling. My guess is, our man inside the Queen's court decided to pursue his own agenda. He's already betraying his city-state, why not betray us into the bargain? Probably hoping to get the orison for himself. Which suits the plan just fine. Everybody betraying everybody."

"I have only one question left," Wrynn said. "Why would you reveal all this to us now? You've been awfully forthcoming about all this."

Jhal spread his arms casually. "Because Shoneg's offer is still on the table. Get the orison, put it in the hands of the Queen of Storms, the Seventh House pays you, clears your names, and ships you home."

"Except that was never the deal," Dunnac said. "Shoneg was going to kill us, if the Queen's guard didn't."

"Shoneg is dead, so you're dealing with me now."

"We'd have to be *idiots* to trust you after what you just told us!" Wrynn shouted.

Jhal mock-pouted. "I'm hurt, Wrynn. You just said I was very forthcoming. I've told you the whole story. Doesn't that make us friends?"

Wrynn winced and massaged his temples.

Dunnac pushed away from the wall and approached Jhal slowly. "What guarantee do we have that you still wouldn't have us killed?"

Jhal shrugged. "Obviously, you're more resourceful than we gave you credit for. The Seventh House is not without a sense of gratitude."

"Sure," Wrynn said. "All we have to do is start a war."

"Don't be dramatic. The war's already here. Open conflict is the next chapter in a book that's already written."

Wrynn stood up. "If I have to listen to any more Imperial double-talk, I'm going to choke. I'm getting out of here. I want you to undo these strands. For real this time."

"Of course," Jhal said. He handed Wrynn a small black stone in the shape of an ouroboros, its coils gleaming with gold flecks. "They're tied to this shaper charm. Break it and they'll vanish—"

The charm shattered as Wrynn hurled it to the floor.

"...within an hour," Jhal finished. "Can't have you burning me down in a fit."

Wrynn made an obscene gesture in Jhal's direction, then turned to Dunnac. "Are you coming?"

"Yes," Dunnac said, and followed as Wrynn opened the door and stormed into the hall.

Wrynn left the wayhouse and walked into the street, slamming the door on the way out. He closed his eyes and took three deep breaths of morning air, closing his eyes against the rising dawn, trying to clear the anger rising in him.

Slow, casual footsteps sounded behind him.

"So?" Dunnac asked. "What do you want to do now?"

Wrynn thought it over for a long time. "I want to live a life without Imperial entanglements," he said at last. "I want my exile to mean something. I want a hot meal and a warm bed."

"I meant about the orison," Dunnac said in a flat tone.

Wrynn turned on him. "I know what you meant, dammit." Then he saw Dunnac smiling softly. "You're deliberately winding me up now."

"Didn't seem difficult, after that conversation."

"That's the Seventh House for you," Wrynn said. "This is how they deal with people. They stab you in the back and then wrap the knife up as a gift."

"At least you know they don't want you dead," Dunnac said.

"Do I?"

Dunnac squinted toward the eastern horizon. "Perhaps this is what they wanted you for all along. A man with no political power, whom they could control when they needed it. Maybe they knew you would serve them better as an exile than a loyal subject."

The thought made Wrynn feel slightly ill. He dismissed it, and all its uncomfortable complications, until another time.

"We find the orison," Wrynn said. "Our only other choice is to run, and I've got nowhere to go." He glanced at Dunnac.

The other man only nodded, stone-faced. "You said you can track it now."

"Up to a point. It's somewhere just north of Mercy Shoals at the moment. Not far from where I live. In fact, I want to stop there before we move on."

"Why?" Dunnac asked. "Not for that warm bed, I hope."

Wrynn shook his head. "I want to check in on a friend. After today, I may never see her again."

CHAPTER TEN

STORY WOKE TO THE RED GLOW of mid-morning sunlight on her eyelids. She sat bolt upright.

She'd slept too long.

In the air, a thick smell of rotten flowers.

She was in her room, where she'd come the night before after leaving Crux behind. She'd fallen asleep with the jewel wrapped in a cloth, holding it to her chest for safekeeping —

Story fumbled for the cloth, unwrapped the round object inside. A heavy gray rock rolled to the floor.

"No," she whispered. "No, damn it, *damn it, Crux!*"

Her eyes stung with tears. She rose to her feet and hurled the stone through the bolted shutters. They splintered, the rock sailing into the alley and cracking against the street.

Her gaze landed on the tiny bag of nightburn on the floor next to her mattress. She plucked it from the floor, almost flung it through the window, too, then thought better of it. She drew the strings tight and shoved it in her pocket.

Stupid. He'd even told her about that trick, right to her face. And she'd fallen for it. She should have found some other hiding spot, someplace far from where she slept, but she'd been too bone-weary, too lazy, too foolish — and too trusting.

She'd never really thought her brother would sink this low, that he would apologize and beg her forgiveness, then drug her and steal from her. She'd trusted that he had cared for her at least a little.

She wouldn't make that mistake again.

At least her path ahead was clear. He had gone to Galon again. That much was obvious. Crux was too loyal to try to take the prize for himself. The only question was whether he would hand it over in her name or his.

Story fetched her cloak from the floor, double-checked her knives were secure, and drew up her hood.

Her chances of finding him before he gave the orb to Galon were remote, but she had to try.

Suddenly, she heard a thump and shudder. Someone was trying the front door to her room. She glanced at the bolt. Still locked. The knob rattled for a moment, then went still. Then the door blew off its hinges.

Story rolled to one side before the flying hunk of wood could hit her, then rolled to her feet, knife drawn. The door bounced off the far wall, pulverizing her ancient chest of drawers.

Two figures ran into the room. One, a tall Halak in a chain shirt, brandished a sword. The other, a shorter man in a gray coat with a high collar, both hands alight with the white flame of sorcery. Not a fight she could win. Halfway to the window, she almost leaped through it before she realized what she'd seen. She skidded to turn back.

She tried to blink away what was clearly a hallucination. "Wrynn?"

"Hello, Story." Wrynn flexed his wrists and curled his fingers closed. The white flames flickered to smoke and vanished. "Sorry about your door."

She gaped in bewilderment. "What are you doing?"

"I heard a crash," Wrynn said. "Thought you were in trouble."

The Halak rolled his eyes and sheathed his sword with a disgusted expression.

"But I mean—" Story pointed at Wrynn's hands, at a loss for words. "How are you a wizard?"

"Oh." Wrynn looked at his hands as though he were just discovering them. "That's actually a rather complicated question."

"One we don't have time to answer," the Halak said pointedly.

"Right," Wrynn said. "Story, meet Dunnac. Dunnac, Story. We're working together now, apparently."

"Working on what?"

"That's even more complicated, if you can believe it."

"All right," Story said. "Maybe you can answer a simpler question, like why you thought hitting me with my own front door was a good idea." As if to punctuate her sentence, the remains of her door slid off the chest of drawers and hit the floor with a bang.

"Ah." Wrynn looked at the door with regret. "I'm a little out of practice, I'm afraid."

"I'd like to leave before someone shows up asking what all the noise is about," Dunnac said.

"I wouldn't worry about it," Story said. "Bront doesn't exactly come running at every loud noise."

This seemed to satisfy Dunnac, who shrugged and leaned against the wall. Wrynn wandered around the room, seeming to scrutinize thin air.

Story tilted her head. "Wrynn, what are you doing?"

"It's here," Wrynn said.

"What's here?"

"Here or close by, I swear."

Wrynn followed a winding path around the room and came to a stop directly in front of Story. Without warning, he grabbed her hands and held them up to his face.

"Wrynn, what are you—"

"You touched it," he said.

She yanked her wrists out of his grasp. "I beg your pardon."

Hearing this, Dunnac snapped to attention again. "You're certain?"

"Very," Wrynn said. "It was here recently. I sense it."

Story's stomach curdled as she realized what they were talking about. She didn't even think about playing dumb. Wrynn was her friend — if she couldn't trust him, she truly couldn't trust anybody. She held out her hand palm-up, fingers flexed into a claw. "By 'it,' do you mean a red orb about this big? Glows red sometimes? Looks like it's full of something disgusting?"

"You've seen it," Dunnac said.

"Seen it? I *stole* it. Had it in my hands until a few hours ago. I think."

Wrynn ran his fingers through his hair, his expression pained. "You can't be serious. Where is it now?"

"Stolen." She hoped he would appreciate the irony.

"Story, this isn't a game," Wrynn said. He grabbed her gently by the shoulders. "This orb is important." Then, without warning he drew her into a tight hug. "By the way, it's good to see you."

She laughed. "It's good to see you too, Wrynn. I was worried about you."

He released her reluctantly. "I can't really explain now. But I'm serious. This situation is dangerous."

"You'll have to do better than that. My life's been in danger for days now."

"Not this kind of danger," Wrynn said. He stopped, his face rearranging into a puzzled expression. "How on earth did you end up with it?"

She grinned and drew herself up haughtily. "I'm afraid that's rather *long and complicated*, Wrynn."

He sighed. "All right, I earned that. Can you tell us where to find it? I can track it with sorcery, but it would be helpful to know what we'd be getting into. Do you know who has it now?"

"It's not that simple. I need it."

Dunnac scowled. "Why would *you* need it?"

Story shot him a look. "I owe someone money, all right? What business it is of yours?"

The scowl turned into a glare. "This isn't the sort of thing you pay someone off with."

"If my life depends on it, you're damn right I can."

"It's not yours to sell," Dunnac said, taking a step toward her. Story held her ground, but slipped her knife from its wrist sheath into her hand.

"Doesn't really sound like it's yours either," she said. She saw by his angry expression that she'd guessed right. "Why in Lond's name would I hand it over to you?"

"Back off, Dunnac," Wrynn said. "Right now."

Dunnac ignored Wrynn and took another step toward Story. "Tell us where it is," he growled.

Story tensed into a guard position, knife raised. They locked gazes. The Halak's finger twitched, as if he might go for his weapon, and Story let a tiny anticipatory smile curl the corner of her mouth. Silence stretched out the seconds.

Dunnac broke first, stepping back and glowering at Wrynn. Story lowered her knife.

"We don't have time for this," Dunnac said. "If that warborn gets to it ahead of us, we're dead."

"I know the risks," Wrynn said. "Story, we need—"

"No," she said, slipping the knife back in its sheath. "If you want my help, you'll tell me exactly what's going on. Including why you suddenly know magic."

"We don't—"

"*Don't have time, I know.* Well, me neither. I can help you. But I think I deserve the truth, Wrynn."

Wrynn sighed. "All right, Story. But it will have to be the short version."

Ashen did not have to wait long to see the queen. As he entered her chambers, he felt a twinge of shame at the hope she would be too occupied to receive him. It was anathema to his kind to shirk such duties — and yet he felt an aversion to her displeasure that he'd never experienced with another living being.

Camana received him in her sun terrace, a broad balcony that overlooked the Southwind Sea. The balcony was empty save for some chairs and a single elegant table. The awnings shrouded the terrace in shadow, making Calushain gleam all the brighter in the hard glint of the late morning sun. His queen stood at the rail, in a simple gown of slate blue trimmed with gold, her hair worn up, held with golden pins.

Ashen waited, hands behind his back. Sometimes, when he knew no one else was watching, he would look at his queen with magesight. He did so now. Men called her beautiful, but to him, the radiance of her aura eclipsed any physical beauty. Bright silver strands of starburst light radiated from the luminous core of her being, a brilliant aurora that turned in a languid stream around her.

When she turned to face him, her eyes bled trails of silver fire that painted the air.

Seeing her like this was a privilege beyond his worth. Power was the only god the warborn revered, and his queen was power personified.

She beckoned to him. Ashen blinked to dismiss his magesight. The thought of speaking to her in that form terrified him.

"Don't just stand there, Ashen. Come sit."

"I would prefer to stand. It's disrespectful to—"

"Are you telling me what to find disrespectful?" Her voice was stern, though her eyes twinkled with amusement.

Ashen sat. He cleared his throat. The queen stood over him, apparently enjoying his discomfiture. He was certain she flaunted tradition in his presence to unsettle him.

"I did not mean—"

"Please," Camana said and sat across from him. "What have you found? I know you found *something*. I can still see Highbridge glowing from here."

Ashen drew a deep breath. "I was close, Majesty. I nearly had the orison in my grasp, but I lost it."

The queen listened silently as he detailed the battle with Shoneg, his encounter with the mage and the soldier, and the fiery aftermath. When he was finished, she sat back with a pensive frown.

"I am sorry, my queen. I tried."

"I'm not angry with you, One-Howl. We didn't know there would be so many other interested parties."

"There is some greater scheme at work, Majesty. This cannot all be coincidence."

"I should say not." Camana rose to pace the balcony. "Perhaps I should speak to Ravano about this."

The mention of Ravano's name taunted Ashen. *You protect your Sworn. You don't obey them to their own detriment. If you do this for her, you will be killing her.*

Ashen clenched his jaw. Now the hydra of human politics reared its head. If he told her the whole truth, Ravano might hang. If he lied, he would betray his oath to his Sworn.

Were the seer's words treasonous, or did he merely seek to protect his Queen, as Ashen did? Ashen had no proof the seer wanted the orison for himself. It seemed a safe wager, but if he was wrong, he could lose his Sworn's trust forever.

The possibilities swirled in his gut. Ashen spoke to let out his words before they rose to choke him.

"Ravano already spoke to me," he said. "He knows the orison is in the city. He understands its power."

Camana turned slowly on her heel to face him. "Has he spoken to anyone else of this?" she asked in a soft voice.

"Not that I am aware." He tried desperately to read some signal from her body language, but the queen had gone as still as water.

"Curious that he mentioned this to you, and not me," she said.

"Perhaps because he knew I sought for it."

"And how did he know that?"

The question struck him into momentary silence. "I assumed he had seen it in his visions."

"Not a safe assumption, my Born."

"You believe Ravano to be disloyal?" he asked, perhaps too eagerly.

"Let us say I consider it a possibility."

"What do you wish me to do?"

Finally flowing into motion, Camana gnawed delicately on a fingernail. "About Ravano? For the moment, nothing. Continue your pursuit of the orison. I will speak to Ravano and try to find out just how much he knows and from whom. Most of all, Ashen, bring me that orb."

"I will do so or die, Majesty."

She laughed a bit and brushed back the fur on his cheek. "So loyal and dramatic. My lovely Ashen. Go now. I have things to do."

He rose and bowed, then left the room nearly at a run, his heart racing at her touch.

When sorcery failed, Ashen fell back on the basics. He hunted.

Warborn were natural trackers. They had been bred to hunt down prey over miles of ground. But the city was hostile to his training. The stone streets held no prints; the scent of prey melted into the stench of thousands.

But there were other ways to hunt down a quarry. Living in Calushain had taught him how.

He began with his own men, the Scarlets. In the few moments he'd dealt with the humans at the Silver Wheel, he'd committed every detail of their appearance to memory and recited it to Mathes, the guard captain, in the hope that they had turned up in the gaol.

They had. The tall Halak's name was Mar Dunnac, a soldier from Esterlund; the short red-haired man was Wrynn Sendir, an exiled Praxis mage. Of the Halak, Mathes knew next to nothing, but the mage was a drunkard who had been in and out of the gaol on numerous occasions.

Both had been bonded by a merchant wearing bronze silk by the name of Shoneg Vulker – whom Ashen knew was no merchant. The mage, Wrynn, was a vagrant who sometimes slept on the streets in Harrows and the Quay. But he had no property, no home. He could be anywhere. The thought of searching every wayhouse and hostel in the city made Ashen nauseous.

The path was a serpent, eating itself.

When he asked Mathes for anything else, the captain had given him one last meager scrap. The mage had been seen and apprehended at the Prestigious Bastard in Redwell.

The gambling house would open at sundown. Ashen intended to be there when it did.

Crux perched on a ledge high above Redwell, nestled beneath the wing of a brooding stone gargoyle. It was one of the few places he knew how to get to that Story didn't. He'd kept it a secret from her for years.

He held the orb in his hands, turning it over, feeling its weight. It felt liquid somehow, even though there was no sound when he shook it. He ran his fingers and thumbs along its surface, searching for some seam, some irregularity. Crux was no scholar, but he understood that such a perfect orb didn't occur naturally. If it had been crafted, then it probably had some kind of imperfection or catch that would reveal its secrets.

The man who could open anything, Galon called him. He planned to live up to that sobriquet. If there was a way to open the orb, he would find it.

He worked to distract himself from the guilt he felt at stealing from Story. Not just stealing, but drugging her to sleep so he could take the orb without her knowing.

It was for her own good, he told himself. He knew she wanted to get out of Calushain, but now was not the time, with Galon's ultimatum hanging over her head. If she humiliated Galon, he would never rest until she was dead or part of his harem. It didn't matter how far she ran, Galon would turn the world upside down looking for her.

Crux couldn't let that happen. She was his sister, his only blood. The only way to keep her safe was to settle Story's debt with Galon. If he had to steal from her to do that, then that was what he'd do. It was a small price to keep her safe.

But a small voice in the back of his mind insisted that she *wouldn't* be safe, no matter the state of her debt to Galon. He'd seen too many heads go up on the crime lord's gallery, seen too many throats cut over offenses real or imagined. The voice told him that Galon would never let her go, even if she delivered him a king's ransom.

He ignored that voice. All he could do was try to keep Story out of danger. Maybe it wasn't what she wanted, but it was what she needed.

But something about the orb enticed him. A burning curiosity set in, nagging at him until he found a place where he could examine it in private. There was something in there, something great and wonderful. He could feel it. If only he could get it open.

The world drifted away as his focus narrowed, as it always did when he was working on a tough lock. He couldn't explain how he knew that the smooth flawlessness of the orb was a ruse — but somehow he did.

As he worked, he felt as if some presence were watching him with approval, waiting for him to break through. His fingers moved as if guided by some invisible force — something that surrounded him and drew him close as it moved his hands for him.

It should have been terrifying, but Crux found it oddly comforting. It made sense, somehow, that this presence would be here, guiding him to a truth he already knew.

A voice spoke in his head — or was it his ear? It seemed so real. Soft, feminine, soothing.

You want to save your sister, it said.

"Yes." Crux barely realized he was speaking aloud.

I want that, too. Will you let me help you?

"Yes."

I will show you how to open this gift. But know it is a dangerous gift. Whosoever receives it will die, but will live again. Do you believe?

"I believe."

I offer the power to save your sister, the power to have whatever you want. Galon would be the least of your servants. Would you like that?

"Very much."

Then I will show you the way.

Soft hands guided his. His thumb found an invisible crease and the warming orb parted like flesh beneath a knife, crimson radiance spilling out. He gasped at the beauty of it.

Then realization slammed back into him. He snapped out of his trance, almost dropping the orb. The seam sealed and disappeared.

Crux understood. In the moment the orb opened, it showed him what it was and what it could do.

It wasn't power. It was death. It was a fiery poison that would unmake him from the inside, unless the semblance chose him — for it *had* been a semblance, surrounding him, touching him, offering him everything.

His stomach churned with terror. He had come so close to letting the poison touch him, destroy him. He wasn't worthy of its power. He knew that.

He rose and cocked his arm back to throw the thing into the river. Let it find the ocean and stay there forever. He couldn't keep it. He certainly couldn't give it to Galon now.

Or could he?

He had to do something. This power needed a home, someone with the cunning and the willingness to use it. That person was not Crux. His own sister hated him. He'd made a disaster of everything he'd ever done.

Galon didn't have the talent to crack open the orb. He couldn't unlock its true power. If Crux handed it over as ransom to Galon, then he might forgive Story. And she, in turn, might forgive him.

Or you could just use the power yourself, the feminine voice tickled in the back of his mind.

"No." Crux shoved the orb in his pocket and wiped his hands. The whispers ceased. He stood to look out over the city.

He would put the orb in Galon's hands to redeem his sister's debt. Then it wouldn't be his problem anymore, his sister would be out of Galon's eye, and they could wait for a chance to leave Calushain forever. Together.

"This is a good plan," he said to himself. For a moment, it felt as if the feminine voice whispered along with him. "This is what's best for everyone."

He listened for the whispers, but they were gone.

With fresh resolve in his heart, Crux began his descent toward future and fate.

After they gingerly leaned the shattered door against the jamb — it seemed unlikely it would ever work properly again — Wrynn sat Story down and told her everything. Wrynn did most of the talking. Dunnac remained silent, standing against one wall and scowling as Story and Wrynn faced each other on the worn-down mattress.

Wrynn spoke of his incarceration, the deal with Shoneg, the fight at the Silver Wheel, discovering Shoneg was an Imperial spy, and the interrogation of Jhal. When Wrynn finished, Story took up her end of the tale, telling him about her lost nest egg, her brother's first (and second) betrayal, Galon's ultimatum, her conversation with Credo.

"An odd coincidence," she said, "me running into him like that."

Wrynn bit his thumbnail. "I wouldn't bet on that, actually."

"That it's not odd?"

"That it's coincidence. The semblances have a way of nudging people into situations. If they want something to happen, they make it happen."

"So, what?" Story wrinkled her nose, thinking of her indecision at the temple. "The dragons are controlling our actions?"

Wrynn shook his head. "It's more that they quietly encourage people to go in certain directions — directions they likely already want to go. But the semblances see through time, and so they're very good at putting people in specific places at specific moments."

"How do you know all this?" Story asked.

"I have some personal experience. It's a long tale. I'll tell you someday."

Her eyes widened. "Why would they pick me to get involved? I've got nothing to do with it."

"You were in Shadowcourt," Dunnac cut in. "In a temple, asking about the dragons. You think they wouldn't take notice?"

"To be honest, not really." She thought about the glib conversation she'd had with the statue, and decided not to mention it.

"It doesn't matter," Wrynn said. "You know our tale, we know yours. It's time we got out of here. We need the orison, and your brother is already far ahead of us."

"He's probably with Galon already," Story said. "If I know him, he scampered right on over there to hand it over."

"So we'll take it up with Galon," Wrynn said an easy confidence that surprised Story. This was not the same man she'd given food to in his crate outside. She liked this man better.

"Okay," she said, impressed but skeptical. "But with what? A king's ransom in pocket lint?"

"That's easy." Wrynn pointed at Dunnac with a cunning expression. "This man has money and a ship waiting to leave Calushain."

Story perked up in surprise. "You have a ship?" She jumped to her feet.

Dunnac looked stunned – and none too pleased.

"Yes, and enough money to get us to Rull Halak in comfort," Wrynn said peevishly from the floor.

"Really?" Story asked, a little quieter this time. Something was going on here. She wasn't sure about this tall, moody-looking Halak, but if he had a ship—

Dunnac recovered from his brief astonishment and stared at the sorcerer with a look of concern. "You heard all that?"

"Every bit," Wrynn said, and some invisible tension between the men grew taut. Wrynn spoke again after a moment of silence. "Chances are good Galon doesn't know what the orison is really worth. You get some money from Orain. We walk in and buy it off him, pay Story's debt, and leave Calushain."

Story opened her mouth to speak, but Dunnac interrupted her.

"What makes you think I have enough money to buy off Galon?" the Halak said.

Wrynn rose to his feet and squared his shoulders. "Don't you?"

Dunnac, apparently surprised by Wrynn's refusal to back down, rubbed his whiskers. "Possibly. But since you know about the ship, it might be better if we just left the city, and the orison, behind."

"Oh," Story said, pointing at Dunnac. "I rather like this suggestion. We should do that."

"What about your seers' prophecy, Dunnac?" Wrynn said. "What about your weapon and your king's edict?"

Story looked between the two men, puzzled.

Dunnac frowned uncomfortably. "None of that matters now. I'll deal with the seer's dream in my own way. I'm making you an offer, Wrynn. We take my ship and go."

"No," Wrynn said. "I can't let the semblances start a war between the Empire and the Red Cities."

"Why not?" Dunnac stepped forward, angry. "The Empire betrayed you and you don't owe the Red Cities anything."

"It's not about loyalty. It's about the dragon's principle."

Story shook her head. "I don't know what that means."

Wrynn walked to the window, running his hands through his hair pensively. "A long time ago, someone... important told me everyone is an instrument of someone else. That the whole world is a chain of people exploiting one another. At the top of it are the etherics and the semblances, using everyone for their own ends. In the end, he said, the choices we make don't matter. They've all been decided for us by someone else."

"Sounds like a sensible fellow," Dunnac said.

Wrynn turned on him. "He was a monster. And I'm going to prove him wrong. The Seventh House thinks war is inevitable. They used us. They intended us to fail and set us up to be killed. So I say we go in and we take the orison for ourselves and we prove them wrong."

"That's insane," Dunnac said.

"I hate to say it, but I'm rather inclined to agree with your new friend here," Story said. "If what you told me is true, this thing is too powerful for us to handle. Half the world would come after us."

"I don't intend to wield it," Wrynn said. "I intend to destroy it."

Story frowned. "Can that even be done?"

"Anything in the world can be broken," Wrynn said. "It's just a question of the right leverage."

They stood in silence for a few awkward moments.

Finally, Story shrugged. "And here I just thought that thing was worth a lot of money."

"It is," Wrynn said, staring steadily at Dunnac. "But I think we can afford it."

Dunnac stood silent, arms crossed. He sighed. "You're committed to this?"

"I am."

At length, Dunnac nodded. "All right. Let's go talk to Orain."

"Not so fast," Story said, raising her hand. "With all this manly talk about choices and free will, you're forgetting one thing. You need me to get into Bladesbarrow."

Wrynn looked perplexed. "And?"

"And I'm not trading one debt for another. If you want to pay my debt to Galon, fine. But that's payment for my help. When we get on that ship, I don't owe *you* anything." She jabbed a finger at Dunnac. "Deal?"

"How much do you owe Galon?" Dunnac asked.

Story grimaced hesitantly. "Six hundred talons."

Dunnac groaned softly and pinched the bridge of his nose. "Fine," he said. "You'll owe me nothing. Can we go now?"

"I'm ready," Story said enthusiastically. "Don't even have to gather my things. I don't have any!"

As they filed out of the room, Wrynn nudged Dunnac. "Imagine how much easier it might have been if you'd just told me you had money?"

"Be quiet," Dunnac said.

CHAPTER ELEVEN

JHAL LOUNGED AT A TABLE in the back of the Prestigious Bastard, where he could watch the front door. The warborn would be showing up soon. He wasn't sure how he knew this. But it had begun with the dream.

After setting Wrynn and Dunnac back on their assignment, he had taken a well-earned nap. He was concerned over how much the mage and mercenary knew, but not concerned enough to put a knife in their backs just yet. So he opted to send them on and get in touch with his people in the House of Serpents. They would need reinforcements in the city, in case something went too wrong.

And he would need men to put down Wrynn and Dunnac when they'd ceased to be useful. They had been liabilities since the beginning, but now were even more so. Jhal sent out some messengers, and then slept.

And he dreamed.

In his dream, Jhal was in a gambling house, richer and more opulent than any he'd ever seen. Beautiful men and women in shimmering robes threw bone dice at the tables, their faces like polished bronze. Bar wenches with scarlet skin carried golden goblets of clear wine between tables, reptilian tails flicking behind them as they walked. A group of musicians played a sequence of high-pitched, keening chords: discordant and yet somehow heartbreaking.

This was like no place he'd ever been, but Jhal loved it already.

A woman sat next to him, in a silk gown the color of old blood, a waterfall of black hair flowing down her shoulders. Her eyes glowed cat-like in the candlelight, set in skin like glossy marble.

I need you, the woman said, and placed her hand on his. Her fingernails were sharp and black. Her lips never moved.

For what? Jhal answered. Like hers, his voice carried wordlessly.

I need you to help me. I can't do it without you. Her gaze was terrifying and entrancing simultaneously. Her presence stirred some primal impulse he couldn't identify. *Will you help me?*

Anything, he said.

Good, she said, and smiled. She leaned over to whisper in his ear and told him what he had to do.

Then the dream ended. Now he was here at the Prestigious Bastard, waiting for the warborn.

He didn't have to wait long. The warborn soldier walked in with the confidence of a trained warrior, scanning the crowd, his dog's ears snapping forward to listen. The woman in his dream had told him the warborn's name: Ashen One-Howl.

One-Howl homed in on some foppish Theoria mage and began questioning him. The mage shrugged, saying something flippant. Ashen grabbed him by the collar and slowly lifted him off the floor, fangs bared.

Jhal decided it was time to do his job. It was time to help the beautiful woman from his dreams.

He crossed the room to meet the warborn. As he moved, a faint voice in the back of his brain began to wail with disbelief and indignation. Then he thought of his dream again and his doubts melted away.

The warborn was shaking the hapless mage by the neck when Jhal reached him.

"Ashen One-Howl?"

One baleful yellow eye turned toward him. "What do you want?" The Theoria mage hung like a rag doll, grimacing in relief.

"I have some information you may want. About a certain item lost by my employer."

"And who is this employer?" One-Howl snarled.

"Shoneg Vulker."

Ashen dropped the mage onto a table, tipping it over. The mage hit the floor with a grunt amidst an avalanche of playing cards.

"Speak."

"Perhaps outside? This isn't very private."

Ashen nodded brusquely, hand on his sword. "After you."

Jhal wound through the crowd to the back door of the gambling house. The patrons, already unsettled by the warborn's presence, parted hastily to let them pass. They emerged into the wet darkness of the alley, lit by Pale's blue-white glow.

Ashen apparently did not feel patient. He grabbed Jhal by the shoulder, spun him around and pushed him hard against the wall.

"Start talking."

"Of course," Jhal said. The small voice inside him moaned in despair, warned him to say nothing. His hands ached to find his sword. But he didn't move. He began to fear that he couldn't move on his own, not anymore.

"My name is Jhal. My employer, Shoneg Vulker, had the artifact you seek. The orison. He brought it into the city via a third party. The men you intercepted at the Silver Wheel belonged to us."

"I see," Ashen said warily. "And do your men have the orison?"

"No. They lost it, but they're on their way to retrieve it now. If you move fast, you might catch them."

"On their way where?"

"A place called Bladesbarrow, in Harrows. It's in the hands of a crime lord named Galon Luster."

Ashen narrowed his eyes, ears pressed flat against his skull. "And who does *your* employer work for?"

Say nothing! the voice in his head babbled. *Say nothing say nothing say nothing —*

Jhal grinned broadly, baring his teeth. "We work for the Seventh House of the Ladris Empire. We're here to tear your city apart from the inside."

"What?" the warborn hissed, and grabbed a fistful of Jhal's shirt. "You make no sense. Why would you tell me this?"

Jhal's fingers twitched. The voice in his head rose to a single shriek of terror.

"Because I'm going to slit your throat, you swag-bellied dog," he rasped, and reached for his weapon. Before he could so much as touch it, the warborn drew his short blade and stabbed him three times in the chest.

Jhal's knees buckled. He slid to the floor. Warm wetness flowed down his shirt. He felt nothing — only a confused curiosity at how all of this had happened. Somewhere, in some neglected back corner of his mind, the tiny voice understood his pain and sobbed its indignation.

Ashen sheathed his blade and squatted down to grab Jhal by the hair. "Why are you telling me this? Who are you, really? Tell me!"

Then Jhal felt the comforting presence of the woman with the black hair, invisible arms embracing him, folding him into the warmth and the wet, a bloody womb for him to sleep in. He spoke and her voice came from his mouth.

"*You wouldn't do what we asked, One-Howl. So we found an instrument who would.*"

Ashen pushed Jhal away in revulsion, and he slumped to the cold stones. The warborn turned and ran down the alley, out into the street.

Then the comforting warmth faded and the confidence and clarity Jhal had felt since his dream snuffed out like a candle. Agony struck him a hammer blow. He opened his mouth to scream, but coughed up a mouthful of blood instead.

Himself again, he finally understood the woman with the black hair was Penumbra herself. But why turn on him? Hadn't he done her will? Hadn't the Empire honored its pact?

Silently, Jhal swore he would gather the Seventh House agents in Calushain. He would send everything they had to find Galon Luster and retrieve the orison. He would tell Snowcastle that the semblances betrayed them all.

He was still planning when he shuddered and died.

Ashen recoiled from the bloodied body of the Imperial agent, fear and disgust coursing through his veins.

The man's words had not been his own. Ashen knew that now. He had spoken his final words in a woman's voice: Penumbra's.

He remembered refusing the orb she offered in his vision. Now he saw further into the depth of Penumbra's game. Had he accepted the orison, he might have stopped the whole plan. His pride may have cost his queen, and Calushain, everything.

Or, if he had accepted, it might have been even worse. He had no way of knowing now. He only knew that by refusing to serve her ends, he had handed that power to another.

We're here to tear your city apart from the inside.

The Empire was working with the dragons. They had struck some ill bargain and were given the power to set Calushain alight. That power was now loose in the city. If the man spoke true and the orison was with Galon Luster, then Ashen had only one road now. The future of his city lay with a thief in Bladesbarrow.

The *Copper Omen* was a lateen-sailed caravel of black oak, an argent lion painted on its prow. Anchored in the waters of Fiver's Quay, it swayed gently in the salt breeze.

Story and Wrynn sat on a stack of crates on the dock, waiting for Dunnac to finish dealing with Orain. The Halak warrior had politely suggested they not come aboard, saying that Orain would take the news better without "foreigners lurking around." Story resented that a little, but neither she nor Wrynn wanted to argue the point.

She stared at the ship, wondering if this would be the vessel that finally took her away from Calushain. Now that the dream lay so close to reality, she could barely stand to think about it. It seemed like a good ship — Story didn't know much about sailing vessels, but she didn't spot any battle scars or gaping holes in the sails — but it wasn't quite what she'd imagined.

What did you imagine? Crux's mocking voice. That was exactly what he'd say. The thought saddened her. Every memory of her brother was like a stone in her heart. Knowing she might soon leave him behind forever filled her with an ache of regret, mingled with guilty relief.

She shrugged off thoughts of Crux and turned to Wrynn. Wrynn was much more interesting. Especially now. Story hadn't realized how much she missed him, and the revelation that his fate had been loosely wound up with hers all this time — and that he was a sorcerer, with a past she had no knowledge of — *that* was scary and exhilarating simultaneously.

"So, you know magic," she said, nudging him.

Wrynn started and looked at her with a soft grin. Story suspected he had been thinking similar thoughts about the ship. "I suppose you could say that."

"How long has that been the case?"

"Since I was a child. I went to Praxis at eighteen. Finished at twenty-two."

Story counted off the years quickly. That was a little over a decade ago now. "All this time, I never knew."

He sighed. "They threw me out for disobedience and hobbled my magic. I couldn't use even a little power without a lot of pain. So I rarely used it. Didn't seem to be much point in talking about it."

"I suppose not. Still, I thought we were friends." It came out sounding more petulant than she'd wanted.

Wrynn laughed bitterly. "Story, you're my only friend in this city. Maybe the only true friend I've had, ever."

Story felt her face get a little hot. To distract herself, she pointed a thumb at the ship. "What about your boy up there? With the big sword?"

"I met him in prison. Only days ago. It seems like longer. Oh, and he saved me from being murdered on the street."

"Do you trust him?"

A troubled expression flickered across his face. "I suppose I have to, don't I?"

They sat for awhile in silence. Story broke it first. "So, only friend, huh?" She chided herself for acting like a sap — but at the same time, she wanted to hear him say it again.

He nodded. "Sometimes I think seeing you every day is about the only thing that kept me from drinking myself to death."

Story ducked her head. "Come on, Wrynn."

"I'm being serious. I played cards, I won money, I drank it away. Hearing about your thieving was the only adventure I really got."

Embarrassed, she turned toward the ship again, watching the crew mill about on the deck. "How are you liking this adventure?"

"Damned awful."

She laughed. "Seriously, why didn't you ever tell me? Even if you couldn't use your power, I would have loved to hear about it. You know how fascinated I am with magic."

Wrynn gave that sort of slow shrug she knew well: the gesture that said he'd thought about it, but hadn't found an answer that satisfied. "I had a price on my head. I was ashamed. I was afraid you'd want me to teach you something and I'd have nothing to teach you. None of that was because I didn't trust you, Story."

"Okay. Well, I guess you're forgiven."

"I'm glad."

"Now that's settled, can you teach me some magic?"

Wrynn raised an eyebrow skeptically. "We might be a little short on time."

"Not now. I mean when it's all over. Assuming, you know, we're still alive." The thought sobered her. Suddenly she didn't feel like laughing anymore.

"I've often been tempted. I think you'd have a natural affinity for it."

She blinked in surprise. "Really?"

"Really. But it takes time. Learning sorcery isn't the problem. Controlling it is. That's why the schools keep such a tight rein on instruction. It's very easy to kill yourself with it."

"I could handle it," she said. "With you to teach me."

He caught her gaze again and held it for a long moment.

"I'd like that," he said.

"This is a bad plan, Dunnac," Orain said, dropping a heavy purse of coin onto the table.

The two of them sat in the cramped cabin of the *Copper Omen*, a flickering lamp the only illumination. Dunnac refilled his flask from a bottle of Halakin whiskey, taking quiet note of Orain's scowl.

"Admittedly," Dunnac said. "But it's the only plan we have."

"It doesn't have to be," Orain took the bottle from Dunnac and poured himself a cup. "We have a ship. We have money. I say we go back to Rull Halak with what we have and take back the crown."

Dunnac stared at him blankly. "With twenty men."

"We can get more. The people know who you are. They will follow you. We can raise an army."

"To raise an army, we need a symbol. We need power. I was sent away to find a weapon of prophecy. If I return without it, my first word is that of failure. Who will follow that?"

"I would," Orain said softly.

Dunnac nodded slowly. "I know you would. I appreciate that, old friend. But these are not the old days of the war. We need more."

"I dislike the idea of using draconic magic." Orain scowled into his cup. "To use the dragon's power is to risk waking the Semblance of Sleep. That's just what the Fireborn want."

"Or perhaps the Fireborn want us to fear magic so we will not use it," Dunnac said.

Orain looked up sharply at the casual heresy, displeased. "Is that something your sorcerer friend said?"

Dunnac pushed his own cup toward Orain, who poured more whiskey. "Something I observed. His empire sought to write the future of his life in magic. When he refused, they took his power away."

"I still don't like the idea of using a dragon's power."

"We may not have to use it," Dunnac said. "We only need people to believe that we can."

Orain grunted disapproval, but conceded the point with a nod. After a moment of silence, he spoke again. "You still haven't told the sorcerer about any of this, have you?"

"He wants out of Calushain. When the time is right, I will make my case. What he does then is up to him."

"He seems all right for a sorcerer," Orain said reluctantly. "I suppose."

"He is resourceful, even without his magic. I owe him my life."

"Do you think he can be trusted around the orison?"

Dunnac sat in quiet thought for a moment. "As much as anyone can be." He finished his drink and stood. "We're going to go make this deal now. We should be back before the day is out. If not—"

"I'll come get you out of trouble again," Orain said with a grin, a shadow of his good humor returning. "I'm looking forward to going home, Dunnac."

Dunnac nodded and took the purse. "I wish I could say the same."

CHAPTER TWELVE

THEY REACHED HARROWS JUST BEFORE DUSK. Wrynn was bone-tired. He hadn't slept since the day Shoneg rousted him out of the gaol and his thoughts were beginning to unravel. Dunnac seemed none the worse for wear, but it was impossible to tell.

As they crossed into Harrows, he threw a spell to sharpen his mind. His senses grew brittle and hard-edged, his scattered thoughts solidifying into a regimented series of analyses. He'd used such arcane tools while at Praxis, but found they decreased his empathy. Which, in this case, might not be a bad thing. At least he knew his magic was working again — for real this time.

Story led them to Bladesbarrow, an abandoned Castari temple. They bypassed the front door to a side entry — it was locked, but Story apparently had a key. They slipped into the temple.

Wrynn's eyes adjusted to the darkness as Story led them down a narrow set of spiral stone steps. Pale orange light bled from a rounded passage blocked by an iron gate. At the gate stood a burly man with brown hair and unruly sideburns.

"Evening, Nibs," Story said. "I need to see Galon."

Nibs eyed the two men suspiciously. "No outsiders, Story. You know better than that. And you're not exactly in Galon's good graces at the moment."

"It's important, Nibs. I'll take responsibility."

"Responsibility, my arse. Who do you think Galon will blame if they make trouble?"

Story handed over the small purse of coin Dunnac had given her. It was heavy with talons. "There are seven ways in and out of Bladesbarrow, Nibs. You never saw me."

Nibs hefted it. "As you wish. They make a problem, Story, it's your throat gets cut, not mine. See to it."

"I'll cut it myself," Story said. "Now will you get out of our way?"

Nibs let them through. They wound through a series of narrow, dimly-lit tunnels and emerged into a wide oval chamber filled with long rows of battered wooden tables lined up before a shabby wooden dais. Wrynn counted seven armed men, each guarding one of the exits. No doubt more could be summoned within seconds.

A gaunt man in a velvet-cushioned chair nursed a goblet of wine, a half-dressed young woman in his lap. A boy of about eighteen with brown skin and black hair stood behind his left shoulder, dressed in a dark cloak and hood.

When Galon Luster spied them, he shooed the girl away and rose.

"What's this? Story, you brought me guests!" He made a gesture and the guards surrounded them. The boy's hands disappeared inside his cloak.

"I hope your idea's a good one," Dunnac said quietly.

Story cleared her throat. "Galon, these are fr— associates of mine. They have a business proposition for you."

"Business," Galon said. "Why doesn't the big one hand over his weapon and we'll talk?"

"No," Dunnac said. The guards shifted uneasily.

Galon lifted an eyebrow. "No?"

"I keep the weapon." Dunnac cast a look around at the guards. "I don't draw mine. Your men don't draw theirs. We talk. We leave. Nobody dies."

Galon narrowed his eyes, but laughed. "I like your style, Halak. Fine. Let's talk. What's this proposition of yours?" He returned to his chair.

No one moved. Silence drew out.

Dunnac nudged Wrynn. "Your turn."

"I know." Wrynn stepped forward, summoning every bit of confidence he had. "We believe you have something of ours. A red stone orb, less than a palm's width across. Your man Crux took it. We want it back."

Galon looked bored. "Assuming I have what you claim, what do you offer in return?"

"Money." Wrynn held up the other, larger bag of coin. "Two thousand talons. One thousand for the object, the other to square Story's obligation. With interest."

Galon narrowed his eyes. "And for that, you want this bauble Crux brought in? Why?"

"It's of historical interest to me," Wrynn said. "I'm a sorcerer."

"It must be valuable."

"To the Circle of the Watch or the Praxa, perhaps. Outside academic circles, it's a paperweight." It was a calculated bluff. Wrynn managed to keep his gaze and voice steady, even as his sorcery-amplified brain began exploring every possible outcome. A man like Galon Luster dealt in petty theft, graft and murder, not ancient artifacts.

Moreover, Wrynn was finally close enough to the orison to feel its presence nearby. The tracking spell he'd set up when they entered Bladesbarrow had thrummed to life as soon as they entered the chamber.

The crime lord sipped his wine as he thought it over. "And what about my little second-story girl?"

"I'm clearing her debt as a personal courtesy."

"To whom?" Galon asked. "Let me explain something to you, sorcerer. Story's debt is a matter of honor. It's about more than money. You can't just toss some coin at me and expect me to forget about the trust she betrayed."

"I told you," Story muttered.

"I'm not really concerned whether you forget it or not," Wrynn said. "My offer stands. Do we have a deal?"

The boy at Galon's side spoke. "Sir, Story isn't telling you the whole truth."

"Crux!" Story balled her fists.

So that *was* Crux. Wrynn felt a knot of dread form at the back of his neck. Galon gestured for Crux to speak.

Crux gestured at Wrynn. "I recognize that man. He lives in a crate outside the Doorstop and gambles for drink. There's no way he would have two thousand talons to throw around. Either he's not who he says he is, or something else is going on."

Story glowered. Falling silent, Crux turned away from her furious gaze.

Galon seemed to enjoy the exchange. "I see. So this orb is a bit more important than just a paperweight." He finished his wine. "I'm afraid the price for your bauble has doubled. I'll take the money you have, but Story's debt remains."

"That's not acceptable," Wrynn said.

Galon narrowed his eyes. "What is acceptable in the house of Galon is up to me, not you. Now get out of here before—"

"No," Wrynn said, closing his eyes.

Galon scowled. "What?"

Wrynn clenched his teeth. "No, no, *no not again*—"

A thunderclap deafened them all as the tunnel to Galon's right exploded into fire and debris. Wrynn saw a guard fly through the air, limp as a doll, and strike the far wall. His body left a red smear as it slid to the floor. Dust and smoke bloomed into the chamber.

Wrynn opened his magesight and pulled back his cuffs to free his bruised hands. Dunnac drew his sword. Story scrambled for cover.

Through the billowing smoke, Ashen One-Howl stalked into the room, shining with confluence, his sword an orange yard of burning iron. All his power was focused on the blade: as long as the warborn could hold it, it would slice through anything it touched.

Galon screamed something at the guards, who moved to intercept Ashen. They charged, weapons drawn, to fall back in screaming pieces as the warborn retaliated.

Dunnac walked past Wrynn, eyes on Ashen.

"*No!*" Wrynn shouted, and grabbed Dunnac by the shoulder.

Dunnac whirled on him, face twisted in anger. Wrynn grasped the hilt of the Halak's sword. It pulsed with silver light as he put an aegis spell on it.

"What is this?"

"His sword's enchanted. He'd kill you with one stroke," Wrynn said. "We have to work together. Let me distract him."

Dunnac nodded and moved left to flank Ashen. To Wrynn's magesight, the warborn was a blur of scarlet light, his sword trailing arcs of radiance in its wake as it hacked down the hapless guards.

Wrynn took quick stock of the room. Galon and Crux had fled. Story too. Maybe he could buy the girl some time. He just hoped she'd be safe.

Story ran into a side tunnel, head down. Behind her, the chamber rang like a discordant temple bell, punctuated with detonations as sorcery met sorcery.

Never steal from a sorcerer. Crux's words had never felt truer.

Something shoved her from behind. She careened off the wall and rolled, coming to her feet and turning to see Galon's face, scarlet with rage. His hand closed around her neck, pinning her to the wall.

"You little bitch. You did this. You brought him here!"

Story opened her mouth to speak, but his hand squeezed her throat shut. One look in his eyes made clear he was beyond reasoning.

A step behind him, Crux stood frozen. She caught his wide-eyed gaze for a moment before the whisper of a blade drawn from its sheath pulled her attention away.

Galon clenched his knife in his free hand, drawn back for a killing blow.

Story stomped on Galon's instep as hard as she could. Galon screamed and his hand loosened enough for her to twist it from her throat. Another kick to Galon's midsection sent him into the wall.

He grunted with pain, but Galon had already recovered, knife at the ready again. The hall was too narrow to get past him. If she moved, he'd have her.

She slipped her knife into her hand — for all the good it would do. She'd never killed anyone, least of all a man twice her size.

"Crux," Galon ordered as he advanced. "Hold this little harlot whelp. I'm going to teach—"

Crux punched his dagger through Galon's throat. The crime lord's eyes bulged and he grappled with Crux for a moment, spitting red. Galon weakly swung his dagger, but Crux blocked it with his free hand, holding tight as the crime lord's lifeblood spurted from his neck.

"You—" Galon spit up a mouthful of blood and choked on his final words.

Crux's face showed no emotion as he watched Galon collapse to the floor. Turning to Story, he took her hand.

"Come on. Let's get out of here."

Seconds into the battle, Wrynn could already feel the world beginning to tear open.

Only the three of them — Dunnac, Wrynn, and Ashen — still stood. The warborn fought like a thing possessed, attacking with single-minded ferocity. Wrynn tried to keep Ashen's focus on him, deflecting blows with his aegis, each parry sparking whining silver fragments of magic.

Dunnac fought alongside, trying to sidestep into the warborn's blind spot, but Ashen's enhanced reflexes were too fast. The warborn pivoted to keep them both in his sight, blocking Dunnac's blows with the aegis on his left arm, striking with the blade in his right, throwing gauntlet spells to blow furniture and obstacles out of his way as they moved. Soon there was little left but wreckage.

The room blared with shrill notes of confluence, growing ever louder. Wrynn's magesight had become a blinding flare of smeared light. Ashen glowed like a wrathful angel at the room's center, the corners receding into shadow.

Wrynn didn't dare switch back to his normal eyesight at this point. Only the twists and eddies of the magical currents allowed him to keep pace with the warborn's frantic blows. His magic was no match — and he was already at his limit. If he unleashed much more power in the next few minutes without bleeding off, the confluence would start tearing him to pieces.

Ashen seemed to sense it too. He disengaged and leaped backward, out of reach. The three of them paused, Dunnac's blade at ready, Ashen guarding behind the shimmering curve of his raised aegis, Wrynn's hands to his sides in defensive stance.

"I only want the orison," Ashen said. "Give it to me and you may leave with your lives. It doesn't have to end this way."

"End what way?" Dunnac said, taking a sidestep. Ashen turned to compensate. "So far, we seem about even. Granted, it's taking two of us." Wrynn looked at Dunnac, aghast. The Halak was *smiling*.

"This is your last chance," Ashen warned.

"You talk too much." Dunnac lunged and swung. Ashen turned to block the blow, and Wrynn took the opportunity. His fist radiated with luminous silver spokes as he threw a gauntlet spell and moved to deliver a killing blow.

Too slow. The warborn shifted his stance and his blade parried Dunnac's. The aegis spell glimmered to the warborn's hand and he caught Wrynn's spiked fist in it.

Wrynn felt the warborn's magic twist as they touched, snaking in under his defenses. The assault changed shape, probing into his consciousness. Wrynn slammed down barriers in his mind, but the move was too unexpected. Ashen's sorcery crawled into the base of his brain and plucked his thoughts.

"You don't have it," Ashen growled, and Wrynn felt his confluence surge out of control. He fell back, his skin turning red and blistering, spells shattering to fiery motes. The warborn had used his own trick on him.

Wrynn felt Kulraizhan burning through his body, overwriting him like a palimpsest. His legs gave out and he stumbled to the floor, writhing in agony.

His magesight failed and the world dimmed to shadows and dust. He saw Ashen strike Dunnac with the back of his hand, sending the mercenary flying.

"I will be back for you," the warborn said, and ran from the room in a blur.

Bladesbarrow emptied within moments of the warborn's destructive arrival. The warborn might as well have been a squad of Scarlets sent by the queen. As sorcery poured hot light into every empty corner of Bladesbarrow, the temple resembled a sinking ship, cloaked rats deserting in all directions.

Story and Crux fled with them. Story ran ahead. She'd always been faster than her brother, the one who knew more hiding places and side streets. She heard him puffing and struggling to keep up as she turned north toward the center of town. She had a few boltholes in the Star. Since it was consistently the most crowded, it seemed the best place to get lost.

"Stop," Crux wheezed as they ran into a narrow alley flanked by windowless brick tenements. "I can't run anymore."

Story slid to a halt in the filth and turned back to look after her brother. He stood slumped against the alley wall, hand on his knees, hawking and spitting.

"Sorry," Crux said. "I'm not the runner you are."

"It's okay. I know a place we can hole up. It's not far. Catch your breath. I think we've got a lead on them."

Crux nodded breathlessly and straightened. Story approached hesitantly, then put her arms around him and hugged him close. She felt him jump a little in surprise, then return the embrace.

"Thank you for... what you did."

Crux patted her shoulder uncomfortably. "I just did what you could have done. I've seen you take on bigger men than Galon."

"Maybe," she said and pulled away from the hug. "But you killed him. I'm not sure I could have done that."

Crux shrugged. "Killing's not a thing you should wish for, little sister."

She grinned a little. "You haven't called me little sister in a while. I like that."

He dipped his head, embarrassed. "I'm sorry for what I did to you, Story. I had no right to try to run your life. I just thought maybe, if I bought Galon off, he'd leave you alone."

"It doesn't matter now," Story said. "He's dead and Bladesbarrow is probably finished."

"Still, I didn't mean to hurt you."

She nodded. "It's all right. You made up for it by covering our backs."

"For all the good it did. That warborn started tearing the place apart."

"I know. I just hope Wrynn will be okay." She looked back toward Harrows, as if somehow she could sense him across the city.

"You like him a lot, don't you?"

Story blinked. "What?"

"I've seen how you are when you're with him. Always giving him food and money, taking care of him, joking with him."

"Yeah, well." Story shrugged. "Maybe I do. I've never really thought about it." She looked back toward Harrows again.

"There's nothing you could have done," Crux said. "Besides, it's good we got out of there. We still have the orb."

Crux reached into his cloak, then went pale and began fishing through the pockets frantically.

"Looking for this?" Story held up the orb.

Crux stared at her in astonishment, then laughed. "You lifted it? You little *sneak*."

"Falling for the old friendly hug gag. You're slipping, big brother."

Crux held out a hand. "Give it back."

"No way. This is still my ticket out of the city, Crux. We could go together, if you wanted." For the first time, she dared hope he might say yes, now that Galon was gone. With each passing moment, she felt a little more of the crime lord's weight disappear from her soul.

"I'm serious. That thing is dangerous. Let me hang on to it."

Story narrowed her eyes. "Dangerous? How do you know?"

"You wouldn't believe me if I told you."

"Try me."

Crux looked as though he were about to speak, then shook his head. "You just have to trust me."

That was the wrong thing for him to say. "Forget it."

Crux grabbed for it and she danced out of his reach, just like she had when they were kids. For a moment, she felt inexplicably like giggling.

Something struck the end of the alley like a falling star, sending cobbles flying into shards. The warborn stood at the mouth of the street, glowing blade in hand.

As one, Crux and Story turned to flee. But in a red blur of motion, the warborn flew past them and stood to block their path. Story could see the creature vibrating, feel the waves of magic coming off it in hot, nauseating pulses.

"Give me the orison," the warborn said. "You don't have to die."

Story realized Crux had snatched it from her. She whirled, anger and terror mingling, and saw he had stepped back, the orb held high in one hand.

"Leave us alone," Crux said. His voice quivered.

"Give it to me and I will. You have my word."

Crux barked a laugh. "Not good enough. Leave now or I break this thing in half."

The warborn made a snorting sound that might have been a chuckle. "You cannot break an orison. You're no sorcerer."

"Maybe not," Crux said. "But I am the man who can open anything."

Story watched, transfixed, as Crux drew his thumbnail down the side of the orb, leaving a tiny crack in his wake. Red light flooded through it and a single trickle of luminous liquid trailed down Crux's arm. She saw his skin redden and swell in its wake, saw him clench his teeth in pain.

"Crux, no."

The warborn looked stunned, and actually took a step back. "This cannot be. It is impossible."

"Back off," Crux said. "Leave us alone."

"Listen to me, boy," the warborn said, his voice low and steady. "You have it on my honor, no harm will come to you. But you must give the orison to me. Now."

"No." Crux looked to his sister with a pleading expression. "Run, Story. Run as fast as you can right now."

"Crux, don't—"

"Please, *run*." His voice hitched on a sob.

Story glanced at the warborn. She could hear — no, *see* the magic around him, gathering like storm clouds, winding into a tightening coil that ached to burst. It was beautiful and terrifying and she knew instinctively the warborn was about to strike.

"Crux, look out!" she screamed. Then the warborn flashed into a blur, bounding toward Crux. She leaped to intercept without thinking and felt herself hit something hard. The alley exploded into light. A whine of magic rose to a peal of thunder. Crushing blackness enveloped her like a closing fist.

The power burned.

Crux felt it the moment the liquid etched a line of silver fire down his wrist. He felt it wriggle into his bloodstream, burrowing for his heart with ethereal teeth. The whispers that had tickled the back of his mind now became a scream of lust and victory.

For a moment, Crux felt powerful — potent beyond measure, godlike and glorious, wish and whim his to create. The world opened up, a book in which he would scrawl new reality. Raw energy, burning bright, coiled up both arms and Crux was distantly aware of the smell of his own smoking flesh. There was no pain.

The world slowed. He saw the warborn gliding toward him in midair, sword bared for Crux's throat. His sister, leaping to intercept. His mind raced ahead along time's path, saw her death, his own soon to follow as the power burned him to cinders.

Whatever he did, his life was measured in instants now.

Crux chose.

A sweep of his hand changed Story's direction mid-flight, his arm turning the air as if it were water. Already, the sorcery spiraled out of his control and his sister hit the wall, hard, but she was out of the sword's path.

The warborn's blade took him instead. He could have stopped it, but he didn't. There was pain now in his burning flesh, his flayed consciousness already unraveling.

He had turned his sister away from the warborn's blade. He hoped she would be smart enough to run. He wished he had more time, time enough to know she would be safe.

His omnipotence unfurled like a burning ribbon, slipping from his grasp even as it consumed him. He gathered the last of it with all that he was and unleashed it on the warborn.

For a moment, Crux burned like a star.

CHAPTER THIRTEEN

ASHEN ONE-HOWL BLINKED SMOKE from his eyes. The skin on the right side of his face felt icy with pain. He touched his cheek, felt fur burned to stubble.

He rose to his feet, sword in hand. Its blade had been buried in the remains of the young thief's body, now a charred husk the color of soot. When he pulled the weapon free, the boy's body unraveled into swirls of ash.

The alley thrummed with confluence. His head ached with it. He looked up and saw the sky shudder, the clouds elongating into spikes and whorls that no wind could shape, talons reaching down from heaven.

In the distance, Ashen heard screams, panicked footfalls. All of Calushain had seen and felt the disturbance. Reality itself was straining at the seams, an overheated pot about to crack.

Penumbra's voice echoed in his mind. *We're here to tear your city apart from the inside.*

Gathering his wits, he searched the ground for the orison. It had rolled away in the conflagration and now rested against the crumpled body of the girl. He reached for it warily. He had seen it crack, seen a fraction of its power unleashed.

It astonished him that a common thief had managed such a thing. But then Ashen remembered the dragon's principle. The youth had become Penumbra's instrument, just as Jhal had been. The boy opened the sky because Penumbra willed it. Even now, the semblance likely feasted on everything the boy had ever been, gorging on memories, dining on desires.

But now the orison laid inert, black as mica, its silvery liquid life stillborn. He touched it with his fingertips and felt only cool stone. Whatever seam the boy had broken was sealed again.

Ashen clenched his fist around the orb and shoved it into his shirt. He should have felt satisfaction, if not joy. Instead he felt nothing but cold despair and anger at the gods who played games with mortal lives.

He prodded the girl's body with his foot. She didn't move. A waste. What had she died for? A bauble to sell for a full stomach? A warrior's end on the battlefield was one thing, but to die as a pawn for a dragon's amusement — that was horror.

And what are you if not a pawn, Ashen One-Howl? A voice whispered in the back of his mind. *You, about to hand power to your ivory mistress, not knowing if it will kill—*

You waste your time, Penumbra. Even as he spoke to himself, he was no longer certain if it was a dragon's temptation at work or the whispers of his own fear. It was long past time to be rid of this power and hand it over to those who could do something meaningful with it.

Let killers kill and rulers rule.

Ashen? A fresh voice in his head. No memory this time. It was Camana. *I felt something in the confluence. Where are you?*

On my way back to you, Majesty, he thought. *I will be there soon. I hope you will be pleased.*

He turned away from the carnage of the alley and headed for Stormhelt.

Behind him, a trickle of silver flowed between the cobbles and pooled around Story's motionless hand.

Wrynn and Dunnac stumbled out of Bladesbarrow into chaos. The crowd surged around them as people fled, screaming of omens and angry gods. The air stank of sulfur and ash.

Above Harrows, the skies turned the color of blood. The clouds churned, barking thunder. Hot purple streaks of lightning flickered above the skyline of Calushain.

"What is that?" Dunnac stared at the sky, aghast. When he tore his eyes away from the spectacle, he saw Wrynn leaning against a wall, hands clutching his stomach.

Dunnac sheathed his sword. "What's wrong? Are you wounded?"

Wrynn shook his head, grimacing in pain. "Not wounded. Something bad's happened. I can feel it."

Dunnac sheathed his sword quickly and took Wrynn's arm to support him. "Because of what's up there?"

"Confluence," Wrynn grunted. "Someone's unleashed a terrible amount of power all at once. More than I've ever seen."

Dunnac nodded, his expression as close to fear as Wrynn had ever seen it. "The orison?"

"If not, then something much worse." Wrynn pushed himself to his feet. "We need to go. Now."

They shoved their way through the crowd, anonymous in the chaos. To their right, a handful of Scarlets vainly tried to restore order, shouting instructions no one heard.

Dunnac followed Wrynn into the nest of Harrows back streets, barely keeping pace as the sorcerer ran with renewed energy. As they reached a scorched alleyway directly beneath fraying storm clouds, Wrynn stopped cold. A strangled sound escaped his throat and he stumbled to his knees.

A moment later, Dunnac saw it: the crumpled body of the girl, Story.

"Story?" Wrynn grabbed the girl by the shoulders and shook her. Her head lolled back against the stones, her eyes closed. "Come on, Story, don't do this, wake up." Wrynn's voice cracked. His words ended in a sob.

Dunnac watched helplessly as Wrynn tried to wake the girl, to no avail. Finally, he put a hand on Wrynn's shoulder. "I'm sorry."

"The warborn did this," Wrynn said, his eyes burning with fury. "One-Howl."

"You don't know that."

"It couldn't have been anyone else." Wrynn cupped his hand under Story's head and lowered her gently to the street. His fingertips brushed her cold cheek. "I'm going to kill him."

187

"Wrynn, that won't—"

"Don't tell me it won't accomplish anything," Wrynn said. Dunnac heard death in his voice. He had heard it many times before. There was no arguing with death.

"If that's your choice," he said.

"You don't have to come with me," Wrynn said.

"But I will."

Wrynn didn't meet his gaze. "We have to get out of here."

"What do we do?"

Wrynn shrugged off his coat and wrapped it around Story's body. "I'm not going to leave her lying here on the street. We take her home."

Story woke to darkness. She flailed in the void, crying out into nothing.

Sensation returned slowly. Beneath her, she felt a floor of warm, slick stone. As she lay in the dark, straining her eyes to see in the absolute blackness, she thought she felt the floor shift, as if taking a titan breath.

"Hello?" she called. Her own voice felt unimaginably small. The darkness swallowed it without so much as an echo.

She peered into the darkness. She could see now, a little: an amber snarl of gargantuan curves above her head, like the walls of some massive cave, shaped and smoothed into glistening forms somehow fleshy and obscene.

The floor swelled again beneath her feet. With it, she felt hot, foul air pass over her.

She had been swallowed. She was inside some vast, living thing. Like a child in the fairy tales, she had been eaten up.

"Easy, Story," she said to herself, her voice seeming smaller than ever. She collected the memories of the last few moments: seeing the halo of magic around the warborn, anticipating his leap, rushing to her brother's aid, the glint of light off the blade of a sword, then a thunderclap and blackness.

Was she dead? Was this the afterworld? Gods, she hoped not. But it seemed the only explanation.

Story drew a quivering breath. She didn't want to be dead. Her brother needed her. She'd come so close to escaping the city, to finding a life she could call her own — and now it was over? It wasn't fair.

She pushed aside the swell of self-pity. She was breathing, and unless people breathed in the afterlife, then she wasn't truly dead. She forced herself to focus. Either she was dead and there was nothing she could do or she was alive, in which case she needed to find a way out of here.

Resolved, Story picked her way through the shadows, eyes aching as she sought direction in the gloom. She touched the wall once to steady herself, but it had a warm, wet, yielding feel to it she didn't like. She didn't touch it again.

She wound her way down the spiral tunnel, further into the depths. It seemed like she should be going up, but somehow down felt natural. Beneath her lay some answer, for good or evil. She could feel it.

Story traveled so long through the featureless dark that her mind began to wander. She almost didn't feel the ledge beneath her foot until it was too late. She leaned back, arms pinwheeling, and fell to the wet floor, one foot dangling over the side. She crept to the edge and looked out into the blackness. Unlike the tunnel, which had slowly revealed itself, this was pure pitch darkness, devoid of form.

The tunnel ended here. A dead end, so to speak.

Story was still considering whether to turn back when a great green eye opened in the blackness, so large she could have stood in its pupil. Pale green light held her in place, like a bug on a pin, and her heart seized with terror. She registered only the barest intimation of the head attached to that eye, wreathed in a mountain of scaly flesh like knots of volcanic rock.

The eye tilted toward her, inquisitive.

I know you, a female voice spoke in her head, making her insides quiver with nausea. It was like being addressed by an earthquake.

"I'm afraid it's not mutual," she said. Insouciance was hardly risky if she were already dead. And if not, this monstrosity could obliterate her with a shake of its head. She had no idea how to show deference to such a thing.

The opportunist. You took the orison from my herald.

"You mean Credo?"

Yes. He served me well. Unlike your brother.

"My brother?" Story felt a cold tingle of fear. "Why would he serve you?"

He wouldn't.

"Do you know where he is?"

He's dead.

It came as no surprise, yet the revelation squeezed her heart with grief. It had been the two of them, in over their heads: first against Galon, then the warborn. They'd never really had a chance. Not just against the warborn, but against Galon, the city, their own lives. She knew that now.

"You killed him?" She remembered the hot liquid silver streaming down her brother's arm.

He died defying my wishes. The warborn killed him.

Story blinked back tears, closing her eyes to let the darkness shelter her from the terrible gaze. "Who are you?" She feared she already knew the answer.

I am this city's dreaming bones. Its streets are cut from my scales, its canals flow with my blood. My breath is the cry of merchant and slave, my teeth the blades that men die upon.

She remembered the idol in the temple. "Penumbra."

Yes.

She swallowed her tears. "Am I dead, too?" Might as well follow one hard truth with another.

No.

Story felt the faint spark of hope and ignored it, lest it get spooked and disappear. "Then where am I?"

Deep within yourself.

"How is that possible? Do I have a dragon inside—"

The truth of it struck her, numbing in shock. The eye narrowed, as if in amusement, and she felt the shudder of its unearthly chuckle.

Story remembered what Wrynn told her of the orison, about the blood of dragons — literal or metaphorical — how it changed those who touched it. She peered at her hands in the darkness, saw in her palms a nest of veins, radiant with silver light.

"Oh, no," she whispered.

You should feel honored, tiny thing. Few are chosen to receive the gift of my blood. The dragon's voice was oily with smugness.

"But I wasn't chosen," she said, following her instincts. "This was an accident."

The voice didn't reply. She felt the great shadow shift with displeasure.

Realization broke inside her. "You didn't foresee this," Story ventured, rising to her feet, still bathed in pale green light, dimmer now that the dragon's eye squinted in contempt.

The power was meant for someone else, it is true. But it no longer matters. The pieces are in play. The game has begun and the feast must follow.

"But you didn't expect this piece," she said. "I don't think you expected either my brother or me."

She'd read the look in people's eyes before. Human or not, this ancient thing had a gaze a mile wide — all the easier to read.

Be careful, stupid girl. At my whim, this gift will burn you to ashes.

Penumbra was lying. Story had never felt more sure of anything in her life. She wasn't even sure *how* she knew. But she did.

Story bared her teeth in the dark, even as terror clawed at her. She could feel the power now, moving inside her, a quicksilver burn fraying the edges of her existence. She could feel the weight of it, the unholy potency she'd unwittingly ingested: the power of semblances. It was too great to fight, yet not meant for her.

But in her life, she'd taken plenty of things that didn't belong to her.

How does a thief steal? Galon's voice, speaking to her from another lifetime.

She moves without sound. She walks unseen.

What does she leave behind?

Silence and shadows.

Story unclenched her bunched fists, no longer trying to fight the rising darkness. Instead, she gave herself to it, let it envelop her, become a part of her. She became shadow. The dragon's eye flickered as it began to seek her in the dark.

Where are you, tiny thing?

In the house of dragons, Story thought to herself. *Robbing you blind.*

Ashen returned to find Stormhelt in chaos. The Scarlets stood on full alert, cordoning off the gates with gleaming steel shield-walls, the battlements bristling with pikes and crossbows. Ashen pushed his way through the mewling crowd, the teeming masses barely held back by the shouts and blows of the guard.

As he passed through the cordon, Ashen saw the Scarlets were barely less terrified than the mob. The sky had opened. The people wanted answers, wanted protection. The guards had neither to give.

Penumbra had her feast of fear. The depth of Ashen's failure yawned before him, an abyss without bottom.

Mathes, the captain of the guard, intercepted Ashen as the war-born reached the inner keep. The captain's fists clenched, red cloak flying behind him.

"One-Howl! What's going on out there?"

"Sorcery, captain. A great deal of it. Beyond that, I cannot say." Ashen did not break stride. Mathes scrambled to fall in step with him.

"Cannot or will not?" Mathes asked. "The seer has said nothing of this. Normally, you can't stop the man from talking."

"Then I imagine he must have his reasons."

"The mob is in a panic. What do I say to them?"

"Advise them to return to their homes."

"Damn it, One-Howl, what aren't you telling me?"

Ashen turned on his heel. Mathes flinched as he noticed Ashen's burned face for the first time.

"Trust you are better off without some forms of knowledge, captain. And do not be dismayed. Soon enough, all the world will know what happened here today."

192

He walked away, leaving Mathes in stunned silence.

Camana was in her chambers, with Ravano. Ashen could see the worry on her face as she turned to face him.

"One-Howl. What do you have for me?"

Ashen glanced at Ravano.

"Don't worry," Camana said. "I've told Ravano everything. Did you retrieve the orison?"

Over Camana's right shoulder, Ravano shook his head, almost imperceptibly, his expression desperate.

"I have, my queen."

Ravano grimaced in disgust.

"But," Ashen said reluctantly, "I fear I have done so too late."

He produced the blackened orb and offered it to Camana, who took it with cautious reverence. He explained the encounter with the two thieves and the resulting explosion of magic. Camana listened intently, even as she gazed into the orb, running her thumbs over its surface.

"This is ridiculous," Ravano said. "A common street rat unleashed this power? Have you looked in the skies, One-Howl? Such magic has not been loosed in the world since the War of Ascent."

"I know only what I saw," Ashen replied. "The boy commanded the orb, at least for a moment. Then it destroyed him. The girl too."

"How is that possible?" Ravano scoffed.

"The dragon's principle," Camana said softly.

Ravano blinked. "I beg your pardon, Majesty?"

Camana ignored him and paced the room, cradling the orison. Ashen twitched with anxiety as he awaited her verdict on its condition.

"Perhaps the boy commanded it because Penumbra willed it," Camana said at last.

"How does *that* aid the dragon's cause?" Ravano asked.

"If she seeks to sow discord in the city, she has done it," Ashen said. "The people are mad with fear."

Ravano sneered, "Is that all she wants? To upset the people of Calushain?"

"I doubt it," Camana said. "A dragon's game always runs deeper." She set the black orison on her desk.

Ashen could no longer contain himself. "My queen?"

"It's gone," Camana said. "What power it had is gone. Perhaps into the sky, returned to Kulraizhan. Perhaps in someone else's hands now. Either way, the orison is dead."

Ashen fell to one knee, bowing his head in supplication. "I have failed you, my queen."

He would have preferred fury to disappointment. She answered him only with silence. When he lifted his head, he saw she had turned away. Ravano looked down on him, grinning with bitter victory.

CHAPTER FOURTEEN

WRYNN CARRIED STORY ALL THE WAY back to the Doorstop.

Dunnac trailed behind, voicing occasional quiet objections Wrynn didn't hear. They bumped their way through the crowd, away from the roiling clouds hanging over the center of the city.

No one gave them a second glance. No one cared.

Wrynn's muscles failed on the stairs to her room. He threw a charm to augment his strength long enough to make it the rest of the way. They didn't meet anyone in the halls. People were either holed up in their rooms or trying to flee the city altogether.

The door to Story's room still rested askew against the door-jamb. Wrynn kicked it aside and lowered her to the bed, her limp form loosely wrapped in his gray coat. As he put her down, he caught a glimpse of her face, slack and expressionless. He could not suppress a groan as he stumbled away. He sat on the floor, his back to Story's body, and buried his head in his hands.

Dunnac followed behind and bent to draw the tattered sheet over Story's face. "I'm sorry," he said again.

"Thank you," Wrynn said in a flat voice.

Dunnac stood in the center of the room, hands at his sides, a worried look on his face.

Long silence unfolded.

"I used to think about tutoring her, you know," Wrynn said. "When I had the Imperial strands on and I would still dream of doing magic again. She really did have a natural affinity. I could see it; I scried out her aura once with magesight. Natural ability, but more than that. She had fire. We — she could have been glorious, with the right teacher."

"I'm sure you would have taught her well," Dunnac said.

Wrynn hung his head. "It was a dream. In the real world, she brought me books and I'd sell them for drink. She brought me rare herbs she'd found and I'd gamble them away. What could I teach her, except how to be a failure?"

"Your self-pity won't honor her memory."

Wrynn shot Dunnac a venomous look. "What would you know about it?"

"She was your friend. She helped you when you needed it, because she saw something in you. That you didn't properly repay her is your failing, but it doesn't make her judgment wrong."

"I should have protected her."

"From what I saw, she was not yours to protect," Dunnac said. "She made her own way in the world."

Wrynn hissed. "It doesn't matter now. They killed her. I'm going to make them pay."

"That's a fool's sentiment."

"Then I'll be a fool!" Wrynn said, rising to his feet. "Why should I change now?"

Dunnac shook his head. "You'll be throwing your life away. You think that's what she would want?"

"What would you propose?"

"We leave Calushain. Walk away."

"We just give up?" Wrynn said, raising his voice. "Do you think the Seventh House will let either of us live?"

"I never did to begin with. But out there, we have a chance. March into Stormhelt and you'll die. You're smart enough to know that."

Wrynn stood over Story's body. His shoulders sagged and the strength seemed to disappear from his legs. He sank to the floor.

"I can't just leave her." Wrynn's voice cracked. "She was my only friend. I have to do something."

"Think this through, Wrynn."

"I have."

Dunnac sighed. "I cannot go with you."

Wrynn looked at him numbly. "You're leaving."

"Without the orison, I have nothing left but to go home." Dunnac paused uncomfortably. "And I'd rather not be witness to your suicide."

Wrynn nodded slowly. "Believe me, Dunnac, I understand. This isn't your fight. It's not worth dying for. Not for you."

"You can still come with me."

"No," Wrynn said at length. "What life I have left is here. I've wasted it here. I'll finish it here."

"Wrynn—"

"Go on, then."

"I'm sorry," Dunnac said. Then he was gone.

Wrynn watched the swirling clouds through the window, listening to distant peals of unnatural thunder.

"I wish it could have been different, Story. I wish I'd been a better friend to you. I wish I'd done one good thing in this world. I hope that maybe I still can. And if you were here, maybe you'd call me a fool, but I don't care."

Wrynn found Story's cold hand and grasped it, weeping.

Story clawed her way up through the darkness. The fleshy loam crumbled beneath her fingers, sliming her arms with oily black. Every move threatened to send her tumbling back into the abyss. She climbed with slow determination, her eyes on the distant glimmer of amber light far above.

The light was life. The light was the world, waiting for her return.

As she climbed up from the cold dark, Story felt the radiant burn of the semblance's power, growing hotter every moment. She could feel it like a consciousness all its own, aching with indignation. It wanted to immolate her from within, to consume her as fuel and make her a part of its alien cosmos. It wanted to return to its home, Kulraizhan.

But she wouldn't let it.

That was the lie of the dragon's principle: that humans were weak and needed the semblances to guide them. But they were strong, stronger than the magic of Kulraizhan, maybe stronger than the dragons themselves.

All it took was control and the will to survive. If she had anything left in this world, it was that.

The power coursed through her now. Knowledge opened like a wellspring in the base of her skull, flooding her mind with understanding. The confusion and ignorance of her life faded away, replaced by a vast skein of circumstances and relationships. She could follow the bright strands back through time, to see the why and how of everything that had come before. She could follow the strands forever, lose herself in the ocean of their truth.

Back along the shining path that led to history, she saw Credo, guided by voices, kneeling in an abandoned mine in some forgotten kingdom, his bloody fingers digging the orison from the dirt.

Further back, she saw a man in Imperial silks writing two contracts on men's lives, signed with the sigil of a coiling serpent.

Looking forward to the unruly snarl of possible futures, she saw the Queen of Storms standing on the balcony of Stormhelt, the orison cradled in her hands, whispering her allegiance to Penumbra as a fleet of Imperial warships sailed on Calushain. She saw Camana, queen of all the Red Cities, her soul rewritten, pay homage to the Semblance of Shadows. She saw new demigods born in the fires of war, carving out fresh myths in blood and flesh.

Deep inside yourself, Penumbra had said. Story understood now. She was dead or close to it. Her consciousness was a flickering shadow, lost in the labyrinth of her body. But the orison had given her life again, and more than that, it had showed her the beating heart of Penumbra's desires, the vast field on which she arranged her strategems. The dragon's ambition was an abattoir of hate and death, a game that rewarded the cruel and punished the weak.

People like her brother, seared to ashes by Penumbra's favor because he'd stepped in her path. She hadn't trusted Crux. But she had loved him.

Story would avenge him, and in doing so, punish his killer and undo the skein of Penumbra's future, all in one stroke. She would slay the Queen of Storms while Ashen One-Howl watched, and when it was over, she would let Calushain burn, along with Penumbra's plans.

This isn't you, Story, a quiet voice cried in the back of her mind. *You don't want any of this. You can still let it go.*

She pushed the voice away. It was the mewling of a weakling, an artifact from another life.

Beneath her, Penumbra roared, thrashing in the coiled depths of the crawling dark. Penumbra's specter sought her, furious to retrieve her stolen gift. But the orison's power was a part of Story now, hers to do with what she pleased.

Above her, life — and beyond that, vengeance. For her dead brother. For herself. For every pawn in Penumbra's depraved game.

What does she leave behind?

Silence and shadows.

With one last push, Story thrust herself toward the fire and was reborn.

She sat up and opened her eyes. She heard a yelp and a crash as someone jumped away from her, terrified.

Story blinked in the unbearably bright light of her room. It wasn't just her climb out of darkness. Her senses were sharper, faster, so keen they walked the edge of pain. She could feel the dragon's fire now, raw and physical, burning through her veins. It ached to be released, gnashing inside the cage of her body.

She stood, marveling at how effortless movement seemed now, after the long crawl through the muck of her own death. She felt like running. She felt like *flying* — and she wasn't entirely sure she couldn't.

A soft voice spoke, thick with disbelief and sorrow. "Story?"

Wrynn stood near her, eyes wide. She read astonishment on his face and the receding phantom of grief.

"Wrynn." She looked around her room curiously. It seemed familiar, and yet as if it now belonged to someone else. "How did I get here?"

She took a step toward him. He dropped into a guard stance, arms forward, fingers extended. She froze in surprise. "What's wrong?"

Wrynn's fingertips quivered. His face was slack with fear. "Story, your eyes. They're black."

Story touched her cheek. Confused, she half-turned from Wrynn and drew her knife. She held up the blade to see her reflection. Her eyes were pure black. No irises, no whites. Without thinking about it, she willed them back to normal and they obeyed. A helpless grin broke across her face, cutting through the longing smolder of her power. She could do *anything*.

She turned back to Wrynn. "Better?"

He didn't seem to think so. "Story, you were dead."

"I know. It's all right, Wrynn. It's still me." Even her voice sounded different — deeper somehow, more resonant. Powerful. She liked it.

Wrynn lowered his hands, but still didn't look entirely convinced. "What happened?"

She saw no reason to lie to him. "The orison, Wrynn. Crux opened it. He unleashed its power. Just before the warborn killed him."

His jaw dropped. "How?"

"I don't know. But some of it got into me. I think everything that was left." She looked at her hands. "He died, Wrynn. Trying to save me. Look at what he *did*."

Wrynn seemed paralyzed, bewildered, horrified. She could read every twist of emotion in the motions of his body. "I'm sorry."

"Thank you." Grief and joy clashed inside her. Crux, her only brother, was dead — but in dying, he had given her more than he ever could have imagined possible. She would cut the strands and watch Penumbra's skein unravel, and before the end, all the Empire would remember her name. She would make it a curse of regret.

The anger uncoiled in her stomach like a serpent, breathing flame as it awakened. The power wanted out. "She used him, Wrynn. Penumbra. She used him and then tossed his life aside like it was nothing. She and the warborn. They killed him."

"I thought they killed *you,*" Wrynn said. She met his gaze and saw an emotion she couldn't identify this time, something raw and open and uncertain.

"I'm here." She stepped into his arms and hugged him close, the bodily contact as poignant as pain. Her senses had never been so acute. She felt his body stiffen in fear for a moment. She felt a flicker of annoyance as his hands froze in midair. Then he returned the embrace, reluctantly.

"I'm going to make her pay for what she's done, Wrynn. Can you understand that?"

Wrynn gently pushed her back. "Someday, I hope to explain to you the irony of what I'm about to say. Story, you can't. It's not worth it."

"He was my brother."

"Killing them won't bring him back."

The serpentine anger flared brighter. "I don't care. I won't let them just forget what they did."

"Story, listen—"

"*No.*" All her life, Story had been nothing to anyone, sleeping in abandoned dumps, eating scraps from the tables of the mighty. And above them all feasted the dragon semblances, devouring lives for a moment's amusement. Now, finally, she had the power to strike back, to draw a livid scar across the face of divinity.

Wrynn's questions tainted the glory of her vision, sullied it with guilt and caution. She pushed it down into her belly, let the serpentine anger burn those feelings to ashes.

This isn't you, a voice whispered in her mind again.

Yes it is, the serpentine anger answered. *This has always been me.*

Wrynn was still talking. She found herself annoyed with him. "Story, listen to me, please—"

"Don't try to stop me, Wrynn. I'm going to do this."

He grabbed her shoulders. "Story, this is what she wants. Do you understand? It's what—"

With a flick of her arm, she sent him flying. He toppled over her dresser and hit the wall with a thud. Only then did she realize she hadn't physically struck him.

"Stay out of my way, Wrynn," Story warned. "You can't stop me."

She felt the anger thrash, anxious for release. She breathed deep and let the bonds of her control loose. The room burst into orange light.

The serpent took wing.

Ashen sat alone in his chambers, cross-legged on the cold stone floor. Incense smoke curled from a pewter bowl, stinging his nostrils into numbness. His eyes were closed, his breath deep and slow, as he sought for some scrap of wisdom.

His failure stung like bile in his mouth. He had held the orison in his hands. A world-shaping power, offered once and rejected, then sought, unleashed, and lost. Returned to Kulraizhan, or worse, in the hands of some other agent, some dark new pawn in Penumbra's chaotic gambit.

In sorrow, he sought out the comfort of his phantom city, its ethereal streets and dark blanket of sky. In here, thought and form held the same weight. The stuff of dreams would not slip from his grasp, would not defy him with fortune. He no longer hoped for revelation, but perhaps he could find solace, undeserved as it might be.

But all he saw in the darkness was the face of his disappointed mistress, the incline of her head, the line of her mouth as she realized the magnitude of his incompetence. Her pale hands, seeking the power ensconced in the orison, slowing, stopping.

Ashen realized her nod of approval meant as much to him as delivering the dragon's chaotic boon. More, perhaps. The realization filled him with shame. What had he done to be worthy of her affection? He was a soldier, a thing bred for war, reaching beyond its grasp and yearning to be a man. What were men but soft and sentimental, slaves to their unthinking passions and their egos?

The warborn had wandered too far from the path of his people. He had sought to become more than he was and, in his hubris, had become nothing.

He wandered the phantom streets in silence, losing himself in the flows of confluence. But even here, the breaking of the orison was like a boulder dropped in a still pond. Waves of force radiated through his vision, the astral city rolling and cracking beneath the sorcerous tide.

Was this all that remained of the orison's power — a violent echo, bleeding away into thin air, never to be seen again?

As Ashen watched his vision sway like pines in a summer gale, another question rose to the front of his mind. Why had Penumbra offered him this power? What had made him worthy of her notice?

Help me understand, he asked the roiling world before him.

The nauseating sway of the city slowed, froze. The shadowy architecture crystallized, edges cold and sharp as ice.

Once again, Ashen felt a presence. But this was different.

The somber blues of the city shifted, radiant orange tinged with scarlet. The night sky brightened to a cloudless noon. Fog blossomed into steam. From it emerged a tall woman with scarlet hair and eyes that burned hot as cinders. Her robes shimmered with scales of polished gold, her lips and nails the color of fresh blood.

Ashen breathed in a scent of citrus and smoke, a sharp tang like ginger. He allowed himself a moment's amusement in the face of divinity. Ravano would have murdered for a vision such as this, let alone two.

Do you know who I am? she asked, lush lips motionless. Unlike Penumbra, her voice rang a single clear note. The moment she spoke, he knew the answer as if born with the knowledge.

"Amaraxis," he said. "Semblance of Power."

The head tilted in the briefest nod. *Sister of Penumbra.*

Ashen squinted at her radiance. Her warmth stung his burned face. "What do the semblances want with me now?"

We want what my sister wanted. Your acceptance of our favor.

Scorched by its power, Ashen no longer felt so flippant in the presence of divinity. "With respect, I refused her. Why would you be any different?"

You saw the consequences of your refusal.

"That is a meaningless answer. I accept no power without knowing its cost."

You lie to yourself. Your sorcery is our power, our will incarnate, imposed upon your world. Work in sorcery and you work our will.

"The dragon's principle. And yet I still refuse."

Why?

"A pawn wielding another's power is still a pawn. I was bred to fight and die for Empire. My queen gave me the choice to be something more. What do you offer?"

The power to defend your precious queen. Even now, the maw of the Lotus Throne opens to devour the Red Cities. Penumbra is its herald.

"And you its savior?"

Its defender. If you accept our gift.

"What does the Semblance of Power care for the Red Cities?"

Our sister's power grows, as does her lust for discord. She creates a feast for herself, to devour and grow mighty. We move to check her appetite.

"Why?"

We must all act according to our nature.

The warborn bared his teeth mirthlessly. "Not all."

The dragon's human face twisted in annoyance. For a moment, Ashen heard the thunder of shadowed wings, saw a hint of the semblance's true form, a serpentine leviathan etched in the ether.

The Storm Queen's dog imagines it is not a pawn? The dragon's voice turned petulant.

"The Storm Queen's dog chooses its master. That master is not you."

Then you will not accept our gift.

"A dragon's power is no gift. I've seen enough to know that. It's a chain. I wear only one chain — it binds me to my Sworn."

The corners of the dragon's lips curled up, almost imperceptibly. *When shadow's instrument arrives to destroy your precious queen, you will think on these words. You will drink deep of their bitterness.*

"My words to speak. My choice to make."

Then I offer you this gift, warborn. Freely given, with nothing asked in return. Let it bring you wisdom.

Before Ashen could draw back, the dragon reached out and touched his head with one delicate finger. Knowledge bloomed like a thunderclap in his mind. Orange light shattered to glistening shards, hurling Ashen back into the weight of his body.

He woke to the sound of alarm bells, the shouts of soldiers. The walls shuddered.

Stormhelt was under siege.

CHAPTER FIFTEEN

ONCE, STORY HAD BEEN A THIEF. Now she was a storm. Wrynn followed in her shadow.

Though he lost a few moments thanks to her throwing him into the wall, she was not difficult to follow. From the Doorstop, she walked straight into the Star, bearing northeast toward Stormhelt. Wrynn's magesight revealed a trail scorched with shadows. Even the mundane populace, who possessed no second sight, knew enough to avoid her as she passed.

Bleary with fatigue and pain, Wrynn didn't catch up to her until she approached Stormhelt itself. He had hoped to have some idea how to stop her by the time he arrived. None came. He'd had time to let his confluence bleed off, but that was no advantage. Story wielded Penumbra's power now, and not even the Queen of Storms would be able to stand against her.

He had never imagined things could go this poorly. But he imagined the Empire could. This was just what they wanted.

Above the keep, the sky darkened. The blazing red corona of the orison's demise had turned black and splayed like fingers across the sky. Wrynn smelled the ozone tang of impending rain. Story looked tiny as she approached the keep's storm-shrouded walls. The crowds had dispersed from the stone gatehouse, driven off by zealous Scarlets. Anxiety knotted in Wrynn's stomach. If he approached her, she would just toss him aside again — or worse. Even without the mute black gleam of dragon's eyes, he knew what dwelt inside her, and it might soon overwhelm her.

A hand grasped his shoulder. Wrynn started, his magesight breaking. He extended his hand reflexively, magic at the ready.

The man ducked gently to one side, holding up a staying hand. "It's me," Dunnac said.

Wrynn relaxed. "I thought you'd be on your ship by now."

"I didn't make it very far," Dunnac said. "I had a crisis of conscience."

"How did it turn out?"

"I'll let you know. I was distracted by the dead girl walking past me."

Wrynn nodded. "Something happened to her. The orison—"

Dunnac shook his head. "Don't bother explaining. I won't grasp it anyway. Just tell me what we're going to do."

"We?" Wrynn raised one eyebrow.

Dunnac shrugged. "I can't keep track of who owes whom anymore. But I'm here to help, in any way I can."

Wrynn felt a rush of weary gratitude so keen he almost verged on tears again. Then again, he could just be exhausted. "Thank you."

"So what's your plan?"

Wrynn looked toward the keep, where Story was having some sort of conversation with the Scarlets. "I'm not going to avenge her now, if that's what you're asking."

"The question is, what is she doing?"

"Getting some vengeance of her own, it would seem. For her brother."

"Against whom?"

"Anybody."

The warrior nodded. "Can you help her?"

Wrynn looked at him askance. "I thought you didn't want to be witness to my suicide."

"I'm coming around on the matter."

"We wait," Wrynn said. "Safely out of bowshot. We wait to see."

"Wait to see what?" Dunnac asked, looking uneasy.

Wrynn took a deep breath. "What she's capable of."

Story walked silently toward the heavy wooden gate. Rain plastered her unruly hair to her head, soaked through her clothes, yet she felt infused with heat. She saw more than the gate, more than the sky, more than the past and future: she saw the lines of force that ran through the world, the tensions upon which reality was pinned. She saw the points where she could apply leverage to bend reality into new forms. She saw where reality itself would break at her touch.

She saw magic.

Is this what Wrynn sees? she wondered. A memory flickered across her consciousness, of Wrynn's face, scared and hurt. It could have been the past or the future. She saw both now, her perception a river flowing in every direction from the fount of time.

She knew the Scarlets at the wall would attempt to turn her away. She knew they would fire on her. And she knew she could break the gate like a child's toy.

A pair of soldiers turned to watch her, pointing as she approached. One of them whistled.

"Open the gate," she called, already weary, seeing their future, knowing they would refuse. The present was pantomime. "I am here to see the Queen of Storms."

Angry faces peered down at her.

"Get out of here, girl," a soldier called. "The keep is off-limits."

"Open this gate or I'll break it down."

Jeers and laughter exploded around her. The soldier on the wall shook his head, bewildered and amused.

"Break it down? Did you bring an army, girl?"

"Yes, I did." Story grinned. "Would you like to see it?"

She clenched her fist. The ground quivered beneath her feet. A rain of pebbles trickled from the walls. The soldiers' grins disappeared. She lifted her hand, turned her wrist. The gatehouse groaned, shuddered, and then split down the middle. The soldiers scattered. Jeers turned to screams. The gate blew into splinters.

She gave the men enough time to run to the unbroken part of the wall. More than they had ever given her. These were the men who ran the gaols, who patrolled the streets, hunting her like an animal.

Don't kill them, the tiny voice inside her whimpered. *You're not—*

"Quiet," she commanded with a hiss, and the voice receded.

As she walked through the shattered remains of the gatehouse, she heard someone scream an order to open fire. A hail of arrows whickered down from above.

With a thought, she wreathed herself in green flame. Heat rose in a stifling wave. The arrows flared to ash.

Amidst the screams, Story made for the inner keep of Stormhelt.

"Oh," Wrynn said, sick with despair as he watched Story's power tear apart the gates of the castle. "Oh, sweet Merathu, this is so much worse than I imagined. I was hoping maybe—"

He had hoped that maybe Story hadn't absorbed that much power from the orison. That it had bled off. That her fury would abate, that another semblance would notice and somehow intervene. A handful of foolish wishes.

Dunnac's face was slack with shock. "What just happened?" he asked.

"What I was hoping wouldn't." He rolled his cuffs. "I have to stop her."

"How? Wrynn, she's not human anymore."

"Don't say that. She's still Story. I can talk to her."

Dunnac grasped his sleeve. "Were you watching just now? I don't think she'll listen."

Wrynn shrugged off the hand. "She's my friend, Dunnac. I have to do something."

"Like what?"

Wrynn sighed. "I don't know."

He set off toward the smoking remains of the gatehouse. After a moment, Dunnac muttered a curse, drew his sword and followed.

Ashen burst into the inner courtyard of Stormhelt, fully armored, blade drawn. The attacker had not yet breached the second wall.

Beyond it, he could hear shouts, the thunder of impacts, and the harmonious ring of confluence. Ashen recognized its tone, too smooth and crystalline to be human magic.

This was draconic power. The orison had come home after all.

One-Howl, a voice spoke in his head. No dragon this time. It was Camana, his Sworn and queen, touching her mind to his.

I am here, he answered.

I feel its power, Ashen. What is it?

He heard a note of worry. The intimacy of her fear dismayed him.

He did not answer. He had none to give. Throwing every defensive spell he had at his command — aegis, auro, sensat — he stalked toward the gatehouse that led to the outer bailey.

Before he could reach it, a diminutive figure flew in a high arc over the battlements. It landed in front of him. Hard earth cracked to a starburst beneath her feet.

Ashen gaped. The girl from the alleyway. Burning with green flame, eyes like polished obsidian, hair fluttering in a sorcerous wind.

"You?" Ashen whispered. "How is it possible?"

Ashen! Camana's voice.

A girl, my queen. One of the thieves. She bears the orison's power. Here for me?

"No," Ashen said with mind and mouth. "She is here for me."

The girl nodded as if she understood. She approached, drawing twin knives from her belt.

"You murdered my brother," she said, her voice a chorus of voices: draconic, human, demonic, angelic. Her knives ignited with green fire, crawling up both wrists.

"I did not wish to," Ashen said. He could feel the fury emanating from her. Her aura was black with hate — hate not entirely her own. Something had stoked the fires of her grief into a white-hot rage. *So Penumbra's will is served after all.*

"Is that your apology?" she asked. They circled one another, slowly.

"An apology would be meaningless. His death cannot be undone."

"But you will beg all the same, when I gut your queen in front of you."

So this was the semblance's revenge for his insolence. Ashen understood at last. "You are wrong. I will die to defend her. With my last breath, I will place myself between her and harm. But a warborn does not beg."

She leveled a blade at him. "You will. Now step aside."

Ashen ignored the ultimatum. He squinted, unraveling her aura with his magesight. The orison's power flowed through her, true — but she did not carry the aspect of an etheric. She was neither mage nor chosen. She was something new. But he knew already that he could not defeat her.

He stepped into guard, aegis glittering along his left arm. "No."

One-Howl — Camana's voice in his head, thick with despair.

He smiled sadly. *One last good thing, my queen.*

The girl charged, keening with energy. Their blades clashed.

The sky opened.

Wrynn and Dunnac stumbled through the carnage echoing in Story's wake. The outer gatehouse was pulverized, the inner gate torn wide open. The courtyard vibrated with energy. Dead and unconscious soldiers lay sprawled, bodies broken from the fall or crushed under stones.

Oh, Story, Wrynn thought. *If you become yourself again, you will carry this with you.*

The civilians had either hidden or fled. What few Scarlets remained had circled around Story and Ashen facing off in the center courtyard, keeping a wide berth.

Dunnac tapped Wrynn on the shoulder and gestured to the left. They eased along the wall, behind the stables, out of the Scarlets' line of sight. In the chaos, no one paid them any attention.

They found a vantage point to watch, crouched between two outbuildings. Story and Ashen were saying something to one another. Wrynn couldn't tell what.

"You know it's only a matter of time before the rest of the city guard arrives in force," Dunnac said.

"All too well."

"Then what—"

The courtyard exploded into light and sound as Story and the warborn surged at each other. The confluence was deafening. Wrynn threw a spell to dull his senses to the violent bloom of arcane light. Their confrontation shook the ground. The Scarlets broke ranks as they retreated through the gates.

"They're running," Dunnac said, shielding his eyes.

Wrynn grimaced wryly. "They're the smart ones."

In the courtyard, the thief and the soldier battled. Wrynn had never seen Story fight with such ferocity. She moved like a living whirlwind, battering Ashen's aegis with a storm of blades, moving faster than his eye could track her. Ashen moved nearly as fast, fighting defensively, keeping his guard up. Each time Story struck Ashen's aegis, she shattered it to glittering fragments. Each time, he threw another. The confluence rose higher, building until the entire courtyard shuddered with it.

"What's he doing?" Dunnac asked.

"Buying time," Wrynn said. "He knows he can't beat her. He's trying to hold her off."

"Long enough for what?"

"Maybe for the orison's power to bleed off. If it's finite."

"Is it?" Dunnac asked.

"How would I know?"

The battle was turning. Ashen had shifted into full guard, sliding back on his heels as Story smashed at his defenses. She was a blur of green flame now, hammer blows of magic shattering Ashen's shields over and over. The warborn was bleeding, teeth bared. Wrynn could see the confluence straining him, singing through the fibers of his body, devouring his body in an attempt to reconcile normality. His body could not absorb the magic he was using. Hers could. In a few moments, Story would kill him.

"I'm about to do something extremely foolish," Wrynn said.

Dunnac scowled. "What?"

"Get my back," Wrynn said and charged into the courtyard. He heard Dunnac yell something behind him. The plan was still unfolding in his mind. By the time he found any flaw in it, it would be far too late.

Story struck at Ashen, knocking his sword out of his hands. It was now or never.

Wrynn braced himself, extended both arms, and threw the *metis praxa* — not boosting the confluence this time, but redirecting it.

To himself.

The pain hit him like an ocean of fire, raw and immediate. He had hoped for a moment's stern resolve. Instead, he screamed as the sorcerous fire between the two combatants bent and surged, arcing into him in agonizing waves.

From the corner of his eye, he saw Dunnac start toward him.

"*Stay back!*" he screamed. Reluctantly, Dunnac froze in place.

Wrynn could feel himself starting to fly apart. His nerves flared bright with agony and then, to his terror, went dead as his nerves simply seemed to burn out. He was deaf, nearly blind, his body a numbing shell withering beneath Story and Ashen's combined backlash.

He hoped it would be enough.

Through the blinding conflagration, he saw Ashen recover. An aegis flickered to life on the warborn's left arm, a gauntlet on his right. Ashen pulled together the power for a counterattack and smashed the aegis across Story's body. It shattered anew, but Story flew back. Their energies unraveled, flying into burning strands.

Story slid across the courtyard, trailing flame. She saw Wrynn. Her black eyes shone with fury.

Faster than he could have imagined, she was upon him. He saw nothing but a bright emerald blur before she knocked him to the ground. His body was a ragdoll. Wrynn's spell flickered and broke. The pain came back, so fierce that black spots clawed at the edge of his vision.

Story drew back her knife. The blade sang with green fire.

"I thought you didn't want to get involved, Wrynn," she said in a slither of voices. It wasn't her.

But she's in there, Wrynn thought. He lay motionless, heart pounding with terror and pain. His vision was a blur of gray motion. *Just a little closer.*

"Thesis could have made you a god," the voice said. "Do you understand? Now you won't even die like a man."

The blur leaned closer. Gathering the last of his power, Wrynn focused it into a tight ball in his hand. Confluence shrieked in his ears, taking the last of his senses. In a few moments, his magic would probably kill him. But first, he would get Story back.

He clapped his hand against Story's face, reaching into her mind with his sorcery, calling to her with all he had left. The semblance answered. Black tendrils uncoiled to envelop him, and Penumbra pulled him into the dark.

Wrynn felt an echo of his senses return, violent and disorienting. Hot blackness surrounded him. A burning charnel stench assailed his nostrils. He flailed in the dark and felt slimy wetness, throbbing as it pushed in on every side.

He focused his will and pushed away the smothering walls until only the featureless dark remained. None of this was real. He was inside Story's mind now, and her thoughts were raveled with Penumbra's, the semblance guiding her will.

Wrynn threw himself into the dark, searching for a flicker of Story's light. He fell forever into fathomless depths, glimpsing unholy shapes writhing in the gloom. Then, far below, he found the barest gleam of radiance. He surged toward it, calling on the last reservoir of his power, feeling it bleed away into the cold dark of Penumbra's will. The light brightened, a fading pool of gray against the dark: a figure climbing a wall of endless blackness, clawing her way upward even as the light faded around her.

As Wrynn descended, the darkness squeezed in on him again, crushing away his breath. He called out for her.

Story, listen to me. This is still the dragon's game. But you can turn it.

No, Story said. *This is my game now. My power.*

Wrynn clenched with pain. His vision was fading again. *The power is never yours, Story. It belongs to the dragons. All of it. That's the orison's lie. But you can still turn it.*

Her dark eyes looked up at him — the eyes of the girl he knew, not the cold demigod she had become.

They took everything, Wrynn. I have nothing left.

Then don't become nothing too, Wrynn said, reaching down for her. *Come back with me.*

Her eyes grew hard with anger — so much anger, raging like a storm. *I don't need you to save me, Wrynn.*

Wrynn reached out. *I'm not saving you. I'm just giving you a hand.*

Through the closing dark, Wrynn held her gaze, pleading with everything he had left. He saw the storm break behind her eyes, saw a dim blur of motion, and felt her hand close around his.

Story felt Wrynn's warm hand in hers, felt the tempest of vengeance and rage that had consumed her break apart like waves on rock. For one blinding instant, the skein of past and present burned bright, and she thought she could follow Wrynn's path along the parchment of time: his confrontation with the dragon Thesis, his rejection of fate, his exile to Calushain, all leading him here, to take her hand and cut the threads that tied her to Penumbra.

No. To create a new strand, threading their lives together, illuminating a new path in the darkness.

Then the vision was gone, swift as a fading dream, the knowledge that had filled her mind flowing away. She was Story again, holding a knife on her best friend. Even as she watched, the green flame on the blade flickered and died. Wrynn lay motionless beneath her, eyes closed, face bone-white.

The weight of her body fell in on her again, and she crumpled to the ground. Dimly, she saw the warborn, Ashen, stalk toward her. He stooped to fetch his sword as he came.

So she would die here after all. Maybe that was for the best.

The warborn lifted his sword. Another blade met his swing, knocked the blow aside with a ring of steel. A gloved fist met

Ashen's face. Ashen stumbled, blinking in surprise, raising his guard.

Mar Dunnac stood between her and Ashen, sword at the ready. "Don't," the warrior advised.

"She has to die, you fool," Ashen said. "Don't you know what she is? She'll murder us all."

"Take one more step and she'll have to wait her turn," Dunnac said.

Story felt a distant pang of annoyance. She was tired of men always discussing her fate as if she wasn't even there.

Painfully, she rolled over and touched Wrynn's face. He was clammy, but warm. He still breathed.

"Wake up, stupid," she said quietly, shaking him. He coughed and opened his eyes.

"Story," he rasped. "I hurt all over."

"Me too," she said. "Can you stand?"

He groaned. "I doubt it."

"Come on, I'll help you."

Rising, she took his hand and hauled him to his feet. He swayed, still pale and shaking, but remained upright.

"We're still in trouble," Story said, nodding toward Ashen, still locked in a stalemate with Dunnac. Dunnac stood at guard, ready as stone.

"The sorcerer can't help you now," Ashen growled to her. "He has nothing left. Another spell will kill him."

"You're right about that," Wrynn said, looking around the courtyard. The Scarlets had regrouped and now arrived in force, dozens of them, weapons at the ready. "But then, the same is true of you."

"Not an easy fight to get clear of," Dunnac said.

"No," Story said, stepping forward. She edged gently past Dunnac, stepping in front of Ashen. "No more fighting. I surrender."

Ashen's ears flicked back. He looked at Story with surprise.

"Story, don't—" Wrynn began.

"My choice," Story said, holding Ashen's gaze. "Let the Queen of Storms decide what to do with me. I'll accept her justice. Or kill me. That's your choice. Either way, I surrender. Just spare my friends."

Ashen glared at her. "Lies. You still bear Penumbra's power."

Wrynn gaped with shock. "*What?*"

The warborn was right. Story closed her eyes for a moment, reaching inside herself. She could feel the serpent coiled in her belly, slumbering as it waited to be reborn. If she focused her will, she could still see the faintest outlines of fate and fortune, the last glow of the semblance's knowledge. But Penumbra's will no longer raged inside her, no longer stoked the flame of her anger. She felt nothing but sadness now — for Crux, for Wrynn and his pain, for her dead dream of freedom, for the men she'd slain in the name of empty vengeance.

"It's true," she said, opening her eyes again. "The power is still here. But I won't use it. You have my word."

"You must think me a fool," Ashen said.

"Story," Wrynn said, touching her shoulder. "You don't have to do this."

She turned to him. "There's nothing else to do, Wrynn." She took his hand. "Thank you for helping me. But this next thing is mine to do."

A new voice spoke. "One-Howl."

The warborn turned. A young girl, no more than thirteen, stood at the edge of the courtyard, wearing a dress of golden silk. She was brown-skinned and freckled, her long chestnut hair tied in a loose ponytail.

"Queen Camana summons the girl Story Khai Tann to the keep," the girl said. "Alone, without escort."

Ashen bared his teeth, uncertain. "But—"

"The queen has commanded," the girl said with cold confidence.

Reluctantly, Ashen lowered his sword, then sheathed it. Dunnac did the same. The Scarlets surrounding them relaxed visibly.

Story turned toward the girl. "My friends?"

"You have the queen's word they will not be harmed," the girl said. "Accompany me, please."

Story looked back at Wrynn. He gave her a perplexed shrug, and reached for her one more time. She took his hand briefly, squeezed it, and then followed the girl into the keep.

Chapter Sixteen

The freckled girl led her down a wide arched corridor hung with tapestries, into an airy arcade that held a single triangular table of polished honeywood. Some cups and a pitcher of water lay on the table, along with some fruit. There were no chairs, no place to sit.

Story saw no guards. That alone made her uncomfortable.

"Would you care for some water?" the girl asked.

Story nodded, realizing she was desperately thirsty. The girl poured a cup and handed it to her. It was so clear and delicious that Story wondered if it came from another world entirely.

The freckled girl stood attentively off to one side, hands folded before her. Awkward silence stretched between them. Story cast an eye toward the doors that led to the inner keep, expecting the queen to burst through in a rage, probably accompanied by armed soldiers.

Terror thudded in her heart. She drank nervously, draining the cup and holding it, unsure if she should put it down or not. Deep in her belly, the power stirred again, urging her to allow it to uncoil and sing its ringing hymn once more. It felt uncoupled from Penumbra's will now, though Story wasn't sure yet how that was possible, or even how she knew that. But she no longer felt the hot rage that had blinded her, the voice that urged her to kill and avenge. All she felt now was sadness and bewilderment.

Closing her eyes, she bid the power to be still — and it obeyed.

"Do you think we'll be waiting long?" she asked the freckled girl, more to silence the nervous chattering in her mind than anything.

"I could not say," the girl said. "The queen acts in her own due time."

Story nodded, finally putting the cup down next to the pitcher. "Did you see what happened? In the courtyard, I mean."

"I saw," the girl said in her small, soft voice. "You fought the warborn. The other sorcerer pulled you away with his magic."

"I wanted to kill him. The warborn, I mean." She chided herself to stop talking before she said something incriminating, but the truth was bubbling out of her, welling up until her choices were either to confess or scream. "Or hurt the queen, to get back at him."

"What did he do?"

"He killed my brother."

The girl nodded solemnly. "I suppose the desire for revenge is only natural."

"This wasn't." Story began pouring herself another cup of water, then stopped. "Am I allowed to do this myself?"

"Go ahead."

Story poured and gulped more water. "It wasn't me. I mean, I wanted to hurt him for what he'd done, but not really. I don't like hurting people. I threatened my own brother a dozen times. One of the last things I ever said to Crux was that I'd cut his—"

Sudden tears welled in her eyes, and she wiped them away brusquely. Whatever else happened, she wouldn't be blubbering like a fool when the queen arrived.

"But you didn't," the girl said.

"No. But I hurt those men out there. And I might have done worse, if—" she trailed off with a shrug. "None of it matters now." She put the cup down carelessly, tipping it on its side.

Carefully, the freckled girl reached over and righted it. "What do you plan to tell the queen?"

"I'll tell her I'm sorry. I'll ask her to spare my friends. I'll tell her I never asked for this power."

"Neither did the queen," the girl said. "But she was never given any choice. It is what we choose to do with that power that matters."

We?

Story looked up at the girl in sudden shock. An ineffable echo passed between them, and Story felt the magic slumbering inside her respond to the other woman's power: like calling to like.

"Your Majesty," Story said softly. Unsure what else to do, she bowed her head to the queen. Given what just happened, further supplication seemed like farce.

The queen looked her up and down. "Your audience is granted," Camana said.

"I thought you'd be taller," Story blurted.

Camana nodded. "I am, slightly. I use this guise when I want to blend in. No one notices a short freckled girl."

"Tell me about it," Story said, then cleared her throat. "Your Majesty, I mean."

The queen's eyes showed momentary amusement, then hardened again. "I wanted us to be alone so we could speak freely. You've made a great deal of trouble for me, Story Khai Tann, through no fault of your own."

"I know."

Wordlessly, the queen produced a round object, seemingly from thin air, and laid it on the table between them. The orison. It was gray and dead now, its black motes unmoving. They both looked at it for a while, the center of their recent misery.

"Do you know why you're still alive?" the queen asked at length.

"Yes," Story said softly. "Because you can't kill me."

Camana nodded. "So you understand the power you carry."

"I understand I never asked for it."

The queen's expression was guarded, but curious. "And what do you want now?"

"I want you to know why I surrendered to you."

"Go on," Camana said.

Story took a deep breath. "When I touched Penumbra's mind, I saw the world as the semblances see it. Just for a few moments. I can't remember much of it now, but I do know this. The Lotus Throne brought the orison to Calushain. They wanted you to have it."

"An odd gift for an enemy to bestow."

"Once word spread that you had this power, the other city-states would feel threatened. They'd seek power of their own. The Red Cities would fall into war with one another. Then the Empire would mop up the remains."

"Undermine power by granting power," Camana said, tilting her head in thought. "An unusual plan. But the Empire always did think around corners."

"It's not just the Empire, though," Story said. "It's Penumbra herself. She wants even more than that. But everything I knew... it's all fading away now."

The queen turned her head toward the view of the ocean afforded by the arcades. "Penumbra's scheme is plain enough. To create conflict and see who rises to the top. History is a graveyard of such schemes."

"I wanted to kill you," Story said.

The queen looked at her sharply.

Story winced. *That's right, girl, talk yourself right into the gallows.* But it was important that the queen know the truth. "I mean, Penumbra wanted that. But I wanted it a little, too. For my brother."

"You don't need to explain further," Camana said. "The semblances lead us toward that which we think we want. To accept or deny is the only choice we have."

"Yes," Story said, doubt gnawing at her. She searched herself for some buried, murderous impulse, some desire to hurt the queen, and found none. But another impulse had been gathering since her surrender.

"You could still try to kill me," the queen said, darkly amused. "I see the power gathered inside you."

"I could try. But that wouldn't change anything. I kill you, Ashen kills me, Calushain falls into ruin. The Empire gets what it wants. The semblances play their game, but we're the ones who lose."

"Yes," the queen said quietly.

"With respect, Majesty, I think I know a better way." Story gestured toward the dead orison. "May I?"

With a curious expression, the queen nodded. Story took the orison and wrapped her hands around it delicately. She closed her eyes. Green light spilled between her fingers. Quiet thunder echoed through the room. The green slowly turned to red, stirring the black motes to life, sending them swimming again.

"You said it's what we do with power that matters. This is what I can do." She opened her hands again. The orison glowed faint crimson. Story balanced it on her palm. "I can give it away."

She extended her hand to the queen.

Camana's eyes widened. "You do this freely?"

"I've tasted this kind of power. I didn't like what it did to me. I don't want to rule people. You do. And while I don't trust you, I trust the Empire far less."

The queen stared at the orison, entranced, eyes reflecting red light. Then she plucked it from Story's palm.

"Also," Story said, "this means you owe me one. Your Majesty."

"You trust that I won't just kill you now?"

"Are you going to?" Story asked.

The queen regarded her carefully. "No. As you say, it would change nothing."

Relief flooded her. "Thank you."

"There is, however, the matter of my men. And One-Howl."

Story cleared her throat. "I am sorry for your men. If I could undo it somehow... but I can't. Perhaps you'd settle for exiling my friends and I from the city, never to return. We have a ship waiting. All we require is your permission to leave."

Camana caressed the orison with her fingers, assessing Story coldly. "Granted," she said at last.

Story bowed. "Thank you, Majesty." She turned to leave, then paused and turned back. "Majesty, I have one other request. Not a demand. A personal favor, as one demigod to another."

Camana looked amused, though she did not quite crack a smile. "What is it?"

"There's a broken-down hostel in Harrows. The Doorstop. Do you know it?"

"Barely."

"I'd like it rebuilt. Made nice, funded with the royal coffers. And I'd like it renamed."

The queen raised one delicate eyebrow. "To what?"

Story took a deep breath. "The Crux."

Camana pondered for a moment, then nodded. "It shall be as you ask."

"Thank you, Majesty. I'd like to go now, if that's all right."

The queen nodded, still caressing the orb. "I will arrange for your transport to the Quay. You may go."

Story curtseyed awkwardly and headed for the door.

"Story Khai Tann," the queen called.

Story turned back.

"If you ever set foot in this city again, I will kill you."

The thief smiled. "If I ever return, Majesty, I will thank you for the favor."

"Well," Wrynn said, "here we are again."

He and Dunnac lay on cots in separate cells of the Stormhelt dungeons. At least the heat wasn't as bad in here.

"There is a certain symmetry to it," Dunnac said.

Wrynn folded his hands. "Overall, I'd say our plan went about as well as could be expected."

"Better, even."

"The good news is, the Queen of Storms will probably execute us quickly, and we won't have a long ship ride to deal with."

"The semblances are truly merciful."

Wrynn sighed and closed his eyes. He wondered what Story might possibly be saying to the queen. More than that, he hoped she was all right. His body still quivered at the venomous touch of Penumbra's mind, and Story had endured much worse than him. She was resilient, but the past hour had brought more violence and change to her life than anyone deserved to contend with.

He wondered if the queen's people had taken adequate precautions against their escape. The confluence had dulled to a low roaring in his ears, and they hadn't put manacles or any other restraints on him.

It didn't really matter. Wrynn no longer felt like running. And he wouldn't abandon Story. Not after everything they'd been through.

He hoped that Camana would be merciful. His hopes were not high. Story had laid siege to Stormhelt, killed the queen's soldiers, fought her bodyguard. There would be consequences, even if Story lived. If any of them did.

"I apologize for not telling you about the ship," Dunnac said suddenly from the next cell. "Or the whole story about why I was here."

Wrynn let the apology sit for a moment, enjoying it quietly. "I suppose you had your reasons."

"I would not have betrayed you. But I wanted to take the orison back with me. I would have, had the opportunity arisen. But we've fought together. That means something where I come from."

Wrynn smiled ruefully. "For what it's worth, I would have rather you took it than Story. Nothing's worked out the way I'd hoped."

"It still may."

"You Halakin are an awfully optimistic lot."

"Quite the opposite," Dunnac said, amused. "My countrymen kicked me out, remember?"

Wrynn laughed softly. He heard a key jangle in the dungeon lock, and the door opened, throwing light across the cells.

Ashen One-Howl approached, a guard in tow. He looked irate. Or he was gloating. Wrynn could never tell with the warborn.

"You are free to leave," Ashen said. The guard moved to unlock the cells.

Wrynn stepped out of the cell, Dunnac close behind.

"You are to depart Calushain immediately," The warborn handed them each a small sealed envelope.

Wrynn turned it over. It bore the seal of the queen's treasury. His eyes bulged. "A letter of credit? You're *paying* us to leave?"

"The queen appreciates your silence and discretion concerning matters of the artifact," Ashen said. "You will go to your ship and depart without further incident."

"What about Story?"

Ashen blew air through his nose, either annoyed or regretful. "The queen has pardoned her. She will accompany you."

Wrynn and Dunnac exchanged glances.

"We'll take that deal," Wrynn said, trying to seem casual.

The warborn escorted them up a set of stairs to the south court of Stormhelt. The courtyard bristled with soldiers in full battle gear, spears and bows at the ready. Wrynn looked up and saw the walls lined with archers.

I guess they took precautions after all.

Ashen led them to an enclosed carriage not that different from the one that had brought them into this adventure. Wrynn and Dunnac stepped up into the dark interior. Story waited for them inside, and Wrynn saw her aim a look of pure venom at Ashen. The warborn seemed to accept it as due and shut the door without a word. A moment later, the carriage rolled into motion.

Wrynn turned to Story. "What happened? How did we manage to avoid dying?"

Story smiled at him, an inexplicable look of sadness in her eyes. "I did the queen a favor. I'll tell you about it when we're far away from here."

"What's the matter?" Wrynn asked. He looked at her with his magesight and found his answer. The power of the orison was gone, bled away. Story was the same again—as much as she would ever possibly be. "Oh. I see."

"I miss it," Story said. "I don't know what I would have done with it, and I think maybe it would have killed me, but I miss it. And yet I hated it at the same time. Is that strange?"

Wrynn smiled and rubbed his wrists unconsciously. "No, Story. I don't think it's strange at all."

After the girl and her friends had gone, Ashen went to find Ravano. He made no appointment this time, no arrangement with the chamberlain. He stalked to Ravano's chambers and opened the door without knocking.

The seer sat behind his cluttered desk, quill in hand. He looked up and squinted with annoyance as Ashen entered.

"One-Howl," he said hesitantly. "This is unexpected."

"I imagine so," Ashen said, locking the door behind him.

Ravano put down his quill with a look of concern. "What can I do for you?" he asked.

Ashen turned to face the seer. His blood still hummed with confluence, running bright and hot through his veins. This casting would hurt, but it was necessary.

He triggered his sorcery. The air in the room grew thick, almost translucent, taking on a bluish cast, waves of magic radiating like the waters of a pond. A low tone of confluence sounded like a gong.

Ravano stood and backed up quickly, eyes wide. His wooden chair tipped over with a bang. "What are you doing?"

"I have learned some things, Ravano. You see, my kind know more than just the sword and the arrow. There is nothing but silence here now. No one will see or hear what happens in this room."

Ravano's back touched the window. In a panic, he turned to scrabble at the latch, as if he might throw himself into the courtyard below. Ashen leaped across the desk, sending books and papers flying. He grabbed the seer by the robes and threw him onto the desk, his hand around Ravano's throat.

"What are you doing?" Ravano shrieked. "Have you gone mad? Someone help me!"

The sound annoyed him. Ashen squeezed until the seer could no longer bleat. The man's eyes bulged with pain.

"An Imperial spy should have stronger nerves, Ravano. You break too easily. Amaraxis showed me the truth of you. Your lies, your manipulation — all in the service of Penumbra."

Ravano struggled to speak, but only agonized croaks came out. Ashen shoved the seer off the edge of the desk. Ravano hit the floor hard, coughing violently.

Ashen stalked around the desk to where Ravano huddled on his knees. He kicked the man onto his back and put a foot on his chest.

"Wait," Ravano rasped. "Hear me out."

"I will listen to no more lies," Ashen said, drawing his sword.

Ravano held up pleading hands. "You think a semblance speaks the truth? For what? Your benefit? They use us against each other, One-Howl. That is all they do!"

"And what are you?" Ashen poised the point of his blade inches from Ravano's face. "A victim of circumstance?"

"An instrument of gods," Ravano said. "Just as you are, if you kill me."

"You think the dragon's principle will save you?"

"I am no spy!" Ravano gurgled. "This is the dragon's game we're playing. Penumbra wants the Red Cities weak. She wants all of us fighting each other. What proof do you have that I betrayed anyone, save the word of a dragon?"

Ashen bristled in frustration. The seer was right. Though every instinct told him that Ravano lied, he had no proof. If he slayed the man now, Camana would never trust him again.

"Swear to me that you are loyal," he growled.

"I swear it," Ravano croaked. "I swear!"

With a snarl of disgust, Ashen stepped away, sheathing his blade. Ravano staggered painfully to his feet, coughing and clutching at his chest. "You mad animal. The queen should have—"

Ashen stepped close to Ravano, locking eyes with him. "The queen," he said, "is my Sworn. There is no one I will not defy to carry out her will. Not you. Not the gods themselves. And there is no one who will save you should you bring her to harm."

Ravano swallowed hard, quivering. "I am Camana's loyal servant, Ashen. I serve her above all."

"Pray I never find out otherwise, Ravano. Until the semblances themselves redeem you, you will live in fear of me."

As Ashen walked out of the seer's chambers, the queen's voice touched his mind. *Ashen.*

Yes, my queen.

Come back to the arcades. I wish to speak to you about Calushain's future. We have much planning to do.

Of course, Majesty, he responded. *Do you wish me to bring Ravano?*

Silence.

No, she answered at last. *I think we will keep this between us.*

Understood.

Ashen?

Yes, Majesty.

You have served me well today. I am most pleased with you.
Thank you, Majesty.

Ashen straightened his cloak and drew himself up as he returned to his queen's side.

CHAPTER SEVENTEEN

THE CARRIAGE DROVE THE THREE of them to Fiver's Quay, where the Scarlets ushered them out. The soldiers then physically escorted them up the ramp to the deck of the *Copper Omen*. Only when a very surprised Orain agreed to raise anchor and set sail for Rull Halak immediately did the soldiers release them from their custody. The Queen of Storms wasn't taking any chances.

Hours later, the *Copper Omen* sailed away from Calushain, heading east on a warm and favorable wind.

Wrynn found Story by the prow, leaning against the rail and looking out at the receding chaos of the harbor.

"Going to miss the place?" he asked as he stood beside her.

"Sweet Merathu, no." Her smile was melancholy. "I'm glad to be leaving. As a paying passenger, no less. And the ship doesn't leak."

Wrynn furrowed his brow, puzzle. "Doesn't leak?"

"Something someone told me to watch out for once."

They watched the waves in silence awhile. At the aft castle, Dunnac and Orain discussed something animatedly. Wrynn tried to find the strength to worry, but couldn't muster any. Very soon, he planned to find a hammock and sleep for the entire journey.

"I miss Crux," Story said at last. "I wish he could have come with us."

"He loved you," Wrynn said. He could think of nothing else to say.

She accepted it silently, staring at the waves for a while, then turned to him. She looked at him. "And what about you? You almost died trying to protect me."

The frankness of her gaze shook him, and he fidgeted. "Story, I don't think you've ever needed my protection."

"Maybe not." A lock of hair, painted by sunset, fell into her face. She brushed it behind her ear. "But I needed your friendship."

Wrynn watched the gulls swoop and quarrel. "You'll always have that." He reached to touch her forearm, and she took his hand and squeezed, her gaze turned curiously inward.

"Are you all right?" he asked.

"I will be, Wrynn. Nothing's changed." She pulled her hand away and turned to gaze at the rolling waves, her smile fading.

He circled so he was facing her again. "Story, everything's changed. Calushain is on the brink of war. The Empire is preparing an invasion. Dunnac and I are wanted by the Empire and you defied a dragon. You stole its power and then you gave it back to the Queen of Storms."

Story nodded, the sea wind blowing her hair back from her face.

"I know, Wrynn. I know Rull Halak won't be far enough to run. But I've spent my whole life one step ahead of trouble. Today is as good as forever; that's what Crux used to say. It took dying for me to figure out what that meant."

He sighed. "Just don't die to learn any more lessons, Story. Please. I'd like to keep you around."

She grinned at him. "You would, huh?"

Then she turned to walk away, leaving him alone on the foredeck.

Wrynn leaned on the railing and watched her go. "Impossible girl," he said, and smiled.

Below decks, Story nestled into the warmth of her cabin. The bed was soft, with a warm blanket. The rocking of the ship was a balm to her nerves, still raw from a hundred brushes with death and ruin.

It was cozy, even cramped, but it was all hers. In moments, she felt at peace, safer and more comfortable than she ever had in the city.

The sun dipped into the western sea, brushing bright fire across the waves before drowning into night. Darkness enfolded the cabin. Story wrapped herself in the blanket and listened to the creaking of the ship as it sailed east to Rull Halak, thousands of miles away.

An unfathomable distance. Terror and excitement each took a hand and pulled her toward an unknown future.

She had no idea what awaited them in Rull Halak. She had no stash of coin this time, no grand plan, nothing to her name but one old friend and one new. That alone was more than she'd expected.

When the thrill and terror of freedom faded, she would have to tell Wrynn what she'd kept from the queen. To keep the secret too long would drip poison into their friendship and sicken them from within. But she needed time. Time and quiet, to grieve for her brother and close the door on the life that had been.

Story wondered if she would have been better off keeping all that stolen power. Perhaps she could have taken the queen's throne, taken on the Empire, written her name on the sky. Story of Storms.

The thought of claiming a throne amused her. Rule Calushain? She couldn't even stand to live there.

But she had taken one thing with her.

In the deepening gloom, Story opened her eyes and clasped her hands together, lips pursed in concentration. Her fingers knitted tight, as if in whispered prayer to unseen gods. When she opened her hands again, a flicker of pale light bloomed between them, tinkling with the clear echo of confluence. Pale tendrils of silver bloomed beneath her flesh, coursing through her blood. It was a part of her now, an echo of what she had once been.

Every theft one-third honest. Every lie two-thirds truth.

What does a thief take?
No more than she can carry.

ABOUT THE AUTHOR

Born and raised in the hinterlands of Montana, Daniel Swensen has been a grocery clerk, sandwich artist, university student, pizza guy, web developer, and freelance writer — sometimes several at once. He lives with his wife and two cats in Missoula, where he cultivates his love for reading, movies, and storytelling in all its forms. He occasionally blogs at www.surlymuse.com and at www.danielswensen.com. *Orison* is his first full-length novel.

www.ingramcontent.com/pod-product-compliance
Lightning Source LLC
Chambersburg PA
CBHW060132130626
46556CB00006B/2315